Jade West

DIRTY
BAD
WRONG

Dirty Bad Wrong copyright © 2015 Jade West

The moral rights of the author have been asserted.

All rights reserved. No part of this publication may be reproduced, distributed, or transmitted in any form or by any means, including photocopying, recording, or other electronic or mechanical methods, without the prior written permission of the publisher, except in the case of brief quotations embodied in critical reviews and certain other non-commercial uses permitted by copyright law. For permission requests, write to the publisher, addressed "Attention: Permissions Coordinator," at the email address below.

Cover design by Letitia Hasser of RBA Designs http://designs.romantic-bookaffairs.com/
Edited by John Hudspith www.johnhudspith.co.uk
Interior formatting by Sammi Bee Designs.
All enquiries to jadewestauthor@gmail.com

First published 2015

WARNING

This book is exactly what it says on the tin. It's Dirty, it's Bad, and some readers may find it very, very Wrong.

It contains a lot of sex, a LOT, and a collection of sexual practices that some readers may well find offensive. The novel is entirely consensual, but please use your own discretion.

Most definitely 18+ only.

IF YOU DON'T LIKE READING ABOUT DIRTY BAD WRONG SEX THEN PLEASE WALK ON BY.

On the flip side if you DO enjoy Dirty Bad Wrong sex, then I cannot be held accountable for any repetitive strain related injuries that may occur as a result of excessive sexual stimulation. My characters are trained professionals, please do not try some of these practices at home (unless you're really sure)

Thank you.

May the reading resume <3

PROLOGUE

The chains above rattle as I jerk in my bonds. My legs quiver, knees trembling, adrenaline pumping.

He circles me. I feel his footfalls. Heavy, purposeful. I can smell him, too. He smells of sex, and sweat, and musk. He smells of sin.

He smells so damn *dirty bad wrong*.

The tap, tap, tap of the cane against my thighs, so gently. I take a breath. The cane comes to rest, pressing against my skin, and he's at my side, his lips at my ear.

"Steady," he breathes and his warm breath sends tingles down my neck.

He trails a hand up my ribs, and my body flinches. Fight or flight.

In my chains I can do neither. And I don't want to.

The glowing heat between my legs gives testament to one simple truth.

I want him... the release he delivers through pain... the silky caress of the abyss beyond fear.

I *want* him to break me.

I *want* him to hurt me.

I *want* him to own me.

And then I want him to love me.

"Tell me what you need, Lydia."

I gasp. His savage hand is on my breast. Gripping, twisting, hurting. My nipples come alive, begging for punishment, and I roll into his touch. It feels so fucking good.

I hear my own ragged breathing, the incoherent murmurs coming from my mouth.

He kicks my feet further apart, spreading me wide. I struggle to keep my balance, but the cuffs pull tight against the chains, taking my weight. Another tap of the cane on my stomach, harder this time, and then his fingers, teasing me open, grazing my clit. *Fuck.*

Two fingers hook inside, pushing in deep. I hear how wet I sound. He groans his approval.

My words catch in my throat, but I force them out.

"Pain... I want pain..."

I gasp again as his two fingers lift me onto my toes.

"I did not ask you what you *wanted*, I asked you what you *needed*."

"Pain ... please, I need pain ..."

He kisses my neck, and I'm lost in him, swimming in his darkness.

"I'm going to hurt you now, Lydia Marsh. I'm going to mark you, and break you, and own you... and then I'm going to make you cum so hard you'll scream my name. Will I tell you what *I* need? I need to see you cry, Lydia. You're so fucking beautiful when you cry."

I screw my eyes shut under the blindfold and take a deep breath.

I'm ready.

CHAPTER I

SIX MONTHS EARLIER

Sicked up onto the pavement of single and homeless at twenty-three years old. I knew I must be hurting, even though I couldn't feel a thing. Shock, I guess. Shell shock.

My toes tapped against the suitcase wedged under my desk. It wouldn't quite fit in the footwell, sticking out like a big red beacon for the entire office to see on arrival. LYDIA MARSH IS SINGLE, it screamed, HER LIFE JUST GOT FUCKED. I died a little at the thought. I've no time for tea and sympathy; the nosey intrusion of strangers in the guise of friendship. Slaverings of pity laid on thick, pitted eyebrows and *there theres*. No thank you.

I breathed in the empty room, soaking up the empty desks in the eerie pre-work silence. It was still dark outside, London only just stirring as the faint kiss of dawn teased the skyline.

Single. Homeless. Screwed.

My mobile buzzed in my pocket, but this time I didn't even

reach for it. I'd no need of his bullshit messages, I already knew what they'd say.

Come home, Lyds, please come home. Please don't leave me.

A twinge of sadness pinched my insides. Home. The home we'd shared, the home in which we'd laughed and fucked and made plans together. The home I'd called ours. But it wasn't ours, not really. When push came to shove it was all Stuart's. *His* name on the mortgage, *his* furniture in every room, *his* goddamn history there before mine. It hadn't seemed a big deal. Why should it? I figured we were in for the long haul, for 2.5 kids and a joint bank account.

I thought Stu would always be there. But no.

One drunken night at a sales conference had put paid to that. I'd been home sleeping while he'd been out fucking. Carly Winters, admin junior. Bottle blonde, with a slightly orange hue and too much mascara. The absolute opposite of me. She looked Barbie-doll fake, plastic and insincere, but I guess *he* didn't think so.

I'd never have known, not if he hadn't been too drunk to put a rubber on it.

Oh my God, Lyds, she's pregnant! She's fucking pregnant!

I should've lost my temper, lashed out and kneed him where it hurts, but anger was a no-show. I listened to the whole sorry string of apologies without so much as a whimper, no hint of breakdown. No all-consuming rage. Nothing.

Don't do this, Lydia, don't block me out! Get angry! Scream, Lyddie, please! Hit me! Anything!

I'd gone to bed. Shut him out and waited for tears to find me. Tears never came, just the itches. Spidery itches, dancing under my scars and begging for the razor blade. It had been years since the calling found me, years since I'd taken a blade to my own skin.

Not again.

Not anymore.

In the early hours, sick of the insomnia, I'd packed a single lowly suitcase while he followed me around, begging and pleading and grovelling for forgiveness. It wasn't a case of forgiveness. Forgiveness I could manage, after all, *all* people do stupid things, even the good ones. I've known that fact as long as I've known my mother... as long as I've been old enough to make excuses for her... as long as I've been old enough to try and make it all better again.

I could forgive Stuart for his stupid indiscretion, but I could never stay. We weren't blood, not like Mum and me. We weren't bound by flesh and bone and years of responsibility. Stuart and I were done, just like that. Over.

He'd asked where I was going, like he didn't know. Work, of course. Keep calm and carry the fuck on; smile through the pain like strong little Lydia always does. Anyway, I had nowhere else to go. Sad but true. One long-term friend from uni in my immediate circle, a couple of acquaintances not worth shit, and my mother back home. I'd have to call on Steph and hope we were still close enough that she'd offer me a sofa until I could get myself straight.

Just stay, Lydia, I'll move out, I'll stay on the sofa, anything. Just until you're settled. Just think about it, Lyddie, you don't need to do this! I don't love her!

I turned off my mobile and dumped it in a drawer, then tried again to shove my case out of sight. It was no use. The thing wouldn't budge, determined to show its big bold face to the world. I gave up and swept the hair back from my eyes, dark, wet strands clinging to my fingers. I was still soaked through from the downpour outside. Cold enough for the chill to break through the numbness, until I was craving my bed at home and the tangle of

Stu's limbs as we snoozed the alarm clock, his sandy hair like a bird's nest against the pillow.

The hitch in my breath surprised me, the unmistakeable wedge of a lump in my throat. I could hardly recall the sensation, hardly remember the last time I'd cried. I broke for the kitchen on shaky legs, driven by desire to outrace the pain. Maybe I could scald it to nothing with a hot cup of black coffee, burn it away before the itches came back for me.

I took out a mug and flicked on the kettle, staring out of the window at the office buildings beyond. My reflection in the glass looked as tired as I felt, sunken eyes peering from sallow sockets. I stepped forward, leaning onto the worktop to check more closely. My eyes appeared even paler than usual, the green of my irises hardly more than a pastel wash, and watery. My eyes were watery.

I tried to choke the hurt down, hawking it back with the grace of an ostrich, unsure of even *how* to let it out anymore, but all I could see was Stuart; his smile bright with laughter, his clothes strewn all over the bedroom floor.

Flashes of our life jarred my senses. So many promises of forever and ever and ever. The only one who'd ever put me first, before all others. He'd loved me. He promised me so.

I gritted my teeth, but still the tears came, spilling from my eyes faster than I could blink them away. I was helpless against the barrage of sobs, which surprised me almost as much as the cheating. Lydia Marsh is a big girl. She doesn't cry.

I jumped a clear mile at the touch of a hand on my arm, spinning on instinct to face my attacker. Humiliation piled on like lead as I recognised the dark brown eyes bearing down on me. James Clarke, Chief Technology Officer. Mr goddamn corporate and perfect at everything. I'd been with Trial Run Software Group over a year, and still I only really knew him by reputation. It was common knowledge he worked long hours, but I'd never been in the office at 6am to find out.

I backed away, sniffing out apologies, but his eyes held me steady without a hint of awkwardness.

"Do you take milk?" he asked me.

I shook my head, wiping my cheeks on a sleeve as wet as my face, praying I wasn't snotty or blotchy, or both. I watched him finish up my half-made coffee and make one for himself. My shaky fingers rattled against his as he handed the mug over, and he held on an extra heartbeat before he let go. I managed to mumble my thanks and he smiled gently. Then there was quiet, with only the low drone of the refrigerator to fill the silence. James leant back easily against the worktop and didn't demand anything in way of explanation. He didn't attempt to fill the emptiness at all, in fact, just sipped his coffee with his eyes on mine. I suspected then that very little on this earth would phase James Clarke.

"I'm sorry," I managed.

He looked me up and down. "You need a change of clothes. I've a spare jacket in my office. It'll dwarf you, but at least you'll be warm."

My eyes crashed into his, a world of pain swimming around my head.

"It's ok, thanks, I have a whole suitcase-full under my desk."

"I see." The look in his eyes told me he did, as well. He saw, alright. "What are you leaving behind?"

"The man I thought I'd grow old with."

"And you're sure this is really where you want to be?"

"No point in moping, right?" I choked on my words even as I said them, and James reached out to place a hand on my shoulder. A firm grip, not too presumptive, just there.

"Get yourself warm and dry before you catch your death. If

you'd like an ear, I'll be in my office. I know how to listen."

"I'm sure you've got more important things to be doing." My laugh came out jagged and hollow.

"No," he said.

My cheeks were burning, even though I was freezing.

"I'm sorry you had to witness my meltdown. How embarrassing."

"You shouldn't be. I've been dragged through the depths myself, Lydia. My offer was sincere, I don't judge and I certainly don't gossip." His dark eyes didn't waiver, not for a moment. They stared straight into mine, an ocean of calm amidst the storm, and there beyond them, was something else. A knowing.

"Thank you. I'll be ok."

"I'm sure you will."

And then he was gone, leaving me to drown in my own mortification. At least there were no more tears.

I HAD ABSOLUTELY NO INTENTION OF SPILLING THE SORRY, DESOLATE guts of my relationship to James Clarke. The extent of our working relationship was limited to the occasional shared meeting. I'm surprised he even knew my name.

I changed into fresh clothes and fired up my computer. No new emails, no reports to file. I'd finished up my outstanding project schedules the previous afternoon, so typically there was nothing pressing to do until regular working hours kicked in. The urge to check my text messages rose up – a morbid fascination to revisit the horror. It nipped at my ankles, begging for attention. That's the only reason I decided to take a coffee up to Mr Clarke. That, and to apologise for my kitchen breakdown.

"Black, no sugar, right?" I said, handing it over.

"I'm impressed you noticed."

"I'm an attention-to-detail kinda girl." I hovered awkwardly, scouting around his office at the certificates and accreditations on his walls.

"Frank insisted I put them up. Apparently it looks the part when clients visit."

"You should be proud of them."

He shrugged. "Most of them aren't worth the paper they're printed on. Sit down, Lydia, take a breath."

The chair across from his was comfortable. I sank back into the leather, all too conscious of my lack of sleep the night before. "I'm sorry about the spectacle in the kitchen."

"You shouldn't be."

"It was unprofessional."

"Professionalism has nothing to do with it. Do you want to tell me what happened?" His tone was even, and calm. He emanated calm.

I considered lying, playing it down to make it sound like a stupid row, but I doubted he would have believed me if I tried.

"My boyfriend had a thing with a colleague a few months ago. A Barbie-doll wannabe with a fake tan. I'd be none the wiser if he hadn't got her pregnant."

James didn't flinch, or rush to console me. "Does he regret it?"

"He wants me to stay. I'm sure he feels worse than I do."

"What do *you* want?"

"I want to go home," I admitted. "Shove it under the carpet and pretend life's still good. But it isn't. What we have together can't really be *it*, not if some other girl's carrying his baby, right?"

"That depends what *it* means."

"In my book *it* doesn't mean getting someone pregnant at a crappy work conference after too many tequilas."

"That's what your head says, what about the rest of you?"

"The rest of me will just have to toe the line and get over it. We're done." I met his eyes, determination bubbling through my spine. "So, how about you?"

He raised his eyebrows. "Me?"

"You said you'd been through the depths yourself. What did you do?"

He smiled. "I made the rest of me toe the line. What we had couldn't have been *it,* right?"

"Your wife?"

"Ex-wife on all but paper." He flashed his bare wedding finger. There was still a faint pale band where a ring would have been. His eyes turned heavy and serious, staring so intensely at me that I had to look away. "It wasn't a pleasant time."

"But it got better? You moved on?"

"It took me a while to lose the ring, but I'm now glad it's gone. Genuinely."

Stuart's face flashed before my eyes again. I pictured him, and Carly, and their tiny little baby. Maybe she'd have a ring one day, the one that should've been mine.

"I can't believe this is happening."

James Clarke moved with purpose, he reached across the desk and took my hands in his, they were warm and steady and so much bigger than mine. The shock of the contact snapped me out of my misery, and I was back in the moment, right there in his office. It was strangely intimate, but I didn't feel the urge to pull away.

"Listen to me, Lydia. Don't beat yourself up. It's ok to fall apart until you piece your life back together."

"That's not really my style."

"I know it's a cliché, but it can be good for you, to cry it out."

"Any other suggestions?"

He stared straight into my eyes. "Suck it up, all the way inside. Put a wall around yourself and refuse to dwell on the pain, not even for a second. Every time a memory comes up just push it away. Slowly, but surely, it becomes second nature. The hurt fades."

"Is that what you did?"

"I should have binned the ring sooner, it would have made the process a lot easier."

I studied the man sat before me, the hard line of his jaw, his confident smile. His black hair was perfectly tousled, making his dark eyes appear even darker. He was certainly imposing in his self-assured calmness.

Women in the office talked about him, a lot. He was the resident 'I would' eye candy of the female Trial Run populous, and up close I could see why. I sensed some darkness spring up in him, and he took his hands away. Whatever had gone down with his ex-wife had got him good, I could tell, but he'd buried it alright, just like he said, buried it deep. My angry ghosts saluted his, waving from the shadows. His waved back before his eyes returned to calm, mask restored.

I looked past him through the window as the dawn broke on a dreary day outside, the first day of life without Stuart.

Back at my desk I deleted the text messages and barred Stu's number. I'd build the wall sky-fucking-high, higher than high, to the ceiling of the whole fucking universe, where the pain couldn't reach me ever again.

It was almost 8am when the ping of my email sounded. I'd never been so pleased at the prospect of something to do, but the email wasn't from a client at all.

From: James Clarke
Subject: Coffee
Should you wish to store your suitcase in my office for the day please do feel free. It may save you some well-meaning questioning from colleagues once 9am hits. You've enough on your mind right now. I don't imagine you'd appreciate their sympathy.
James
James Clarke
CTO, Trial Run Software Group.

A man with intuition.

To: James Clarke
Subject: Re: Coffee
You imagined right. Thank you very much. I'll bring it up.
Lydia
Lydia Marsh
Senior Project Co-ordinator, Trial Run Software Group.

I shoved my drying clothes back in and wrenched the case closed. I'd only just managed to yank it upright when my email pinged again.

From: James Clarke

Subject: Re: Re: Coffee
No need.
James

The office door was already swinging open as I read it, and there he was, mobile tablet in hand on his way to my desk. I took him in as he approached; the confidence of his stride, his self-assured expression, the gorgeous goddamn suit he was wearing. He could have stepped straight off Savile Row. His jacket was pale grey pinstripe, paired strikingly with a dark burgundy tie. Pure white shirt, tailored trousers showcasing solid toned thighs. Even his feet joined in on the show, gleaming to perfection in mirror-shined brogues. He really was Mr Corporate, you could almost smell the senior management title on him. He was tall – really damn tall – commanding an imposing frame without being bulky. I'd heard on the grapevine that he worked out every lunchtime without fail, but he didn't use the shared gym in our complex. The messy tendrils of his hair contrasted perfectly with the hard angles of his face. Mid-thirties, I'd guess. Old enough to be distinguished, but without even a hint of salt and pepper hair. James Clarke was an impressive specimen. Still, it meant nothing to me, nothing at all. He could be anyone for all I cared this morning, just as long as he hid my suitcase.

"I figured you'd lugged that thing far enough this morning already," he said. "Where are you headed when work's done?"

"Islington, I think. I'm counting on a friend."

"Let me know." He leant in close as he grabbed my case, and I caught a scent of musk, almost Arabian, and underneath the smell of fresh linen, and vanilla soap. If that's what a senior management title smells like, it smells damn good.

"Thanks for this, Mr Clarke, I really appreciate it."

"James," he said. "I'm not your boss, Lydia, you don't need to act like my subordinate." He gave me a look I couldn't read.

"Ok, *James*," I smiled. "Thank you."

"I'll be leaving at five on the dot," he said. "If you're later than that I'll leave my office open for you."

I could breathe a whole lot easier once that suitcase was out of sight. With a dab or two of concealer we'd be back to business-as-usual.

James had already gone by the time I went for my case. He'd left it hidden behind his desk, out of sight. Sliding into his seat to retrieve it felt weird and invasive. His desk was immaculate; stationery and papers arranged in lines with perfect precision. There was a letter tray for incoming mail, but outside of that there wasn't a single scrawled note, or post-it, to be seen. Even more notable was the serious lack of anything personal. No photos, no trinkets, nothing. His pens were arranged in uniform, a display of perfectly aligned ballpoints, all black. A black stapler, hole punch and calculator, all standard issue from the stationery cupboard. A metal ruler lay perfectly parallel to the desk edge, and a Trial Run notepad lay open on the first page, unused. Aside from the certificates on the walls there was no touch of the man in the room. A generic leafy plant sat on a bookshelf, which housed only industry-related publications. An empty wastepaper bin, without even a trace of lunch, or discarded paperwork. Nothing.

In a moment of impulsion, I took one of his pens from its position. On page one of his Trial Run notepad, I left my mark.

Islington bound, safe and sound. Thank you.

I signed off with a big scrawly L and a flourish, and

successfully fought the urge to line the pen back up where I found it. A bit of chaos wouldn't hurt him.

I dreaded sofa surfing at Steph's place, but my sharp exit from home had left me well and truly up shit creek without a paddle. Steph is kind and supportive, but I wanted nothing more than to lick my wounds in private without the world in my face. In Steph and Mike's cramped one-bed apartment, that wouldn't exactly be easy.

Steph did her best to act like it was a completely usual Friday visit, pouring me wine and chatting about her day until I wanted to talk. I kept it sparse, outlining what had gone down without delving into the emotional shit.

She listened without interrupting, and then said what any good friend would say.

"He's a jerk. An absolute, motherfucking jerk. You can stay here as long as you want, you know that."

"Thanks."

"I know you aren't going to bawl your eyes out on my shoulder and watch a rom-com marathon, but I'm here if you want to."

"I know." I smiled.

Steph twirled a stray wisp of blonde hair in her fingers. "Have you told your mum?"

"Hell no."

"Maybe she could help?"

"Like she's ever helped," I snapped. "I've got enough of my own shit to wade through without dealing with hers, too."

Steph let it drop. A wise choice.

CHAPTER 2

James

Cara spread her legs like a good girl, pressed tight against the flogging bench with her perky little ass in the air. Just how I wanted her. I knelt down behind, spreading her wide enough to trace my tongue around the tight little ring of her asshole. She squirmed like an eel, and I slapped her ass. Hard. The smack of my palm cut loud across the room.

"I said, don't move."

She stopped squirming. "Sorry, sir."

I savoured my position a moment longer, her glistening pussy just an inch from my nose. I breathed deeply, letting my warm breath tease her. She tensed, but checked herself, keeping still enough to prevent further punishment.

God, I needed this. I needed the heady scent of sex, the musky taste of her against my tongue. I needed to feel her jerk and scream as she came, and even then still beg for more. More tongue, *and* more pain. I'd give her more of both. Gladly.

I buried my tongue, lapping at her slit and teasing a path through the folds to her clit. She tasted so fucking good. She moaned, but didn't move a muscle, not even when I clamped my mouth tight onto her, taking her sweet little nub between my lips.

Her scent hammered my senses, and my dick twitched in my jeans. Fuck yeah.

I stopped.

"What do you want, Cara?"

Her answer came within a second. "Your mouth, sir. Please."

"You will remain quiet and still."

"Yes, sir."

"If you move or make a sound, I will spank you, hard, understand?"

I saw her pussy clench. Horny little bitch.

"Yes, sir. I understand, sir."

"Good girl." I spread her open, stretching her lips wide apart like a pretty pink butterfly. So fucking pretty. I heard her breath quicken, and almost willed her to moan, just so I could punish her. "You have a perfect little cunt, Cara."

I imagined her eyes screwed shut under her blindfold, all her concentration focused on obeying. I wasn't going to make it easy.

I fixed my mouth onto her, sucking her in. She was already swollen with lust, ripe for my touch. I swirled my tongue, gently, my arms wrapped around her thighs to hold her tight to me. Every muscle in her legs was tense, straining for composure. I gripped her flesh in my teeth as I pulled away, savage enough to make her breath hitch. *Make a sound, you filthy bitch, make a fucking sound.* She kept quiet.

I plunged two fingers inside her and she exhaled everything she had. I curled them forward, finding just the right spot. The cuffs on her wrists jangled as I worked her from the inside, but I let her off this once. My thumb balled her clit, pinning her pleasure from both the inside and out. Her cunt made gorgeous wet slurps, slick and swollen from everything she was taking from me. I closed my eyes to savour the sensation.

"I'm going to stretch you open, Cara. You do want more, don't you?"

"Yes, yes please, sir." Her voice was raspy. I slid in a third finger, and her legs trembled. She tightened beautifully, her greedy little slit sucking at my fingers. I worked her into a rhythm, strong steady movements all the way inside her, echoed by my thumb around her clit. "Please, sir, may I come?"

"No."

Her legs shuddered again, another clink of her cuffs.

"Don't make me punish you, Cara."

She was trying so hard, but the sadist in me couldn't resist. I increased the pressure, coaxing the nerves inside. They betrayed her, and she bucked against my hand, wheezing out a string of incomprehensible mewls. I pulled away instantly and her knees almost buckled.

"I said, no."

"I'm sorry, sir," she murmured. "I'm sorry."

I got to my feet, kneading the soft skin of her buttocks in rough hands. "I'm going to punish you now, Cara. You need to be punished now, don't you?"

"Yes, sir. Thank you, sir."

I trailed my fingers up the soft pale groove of her spine, enjoying the way her muscles twitched at my touch. "If you're a really good girl, I'll make you come after."

She groaned and arched her back, jutting her ass out towards me. She's so fucking good.

I didn't go easy on her. My blows were hard, and fast. Slap after slap across her perfect pale flesh. Her ass juddered under the abuse, and soon the sound of her whimpers came loud. Her ass bloomed pink under my hands, rosy and gorgeous, ripening to a deep, dark flush. I coloured her thighs too for good measure, and she let out a squeal as I landed one right on her pussy.

She lay flat to the bench, breathing heavy while I gave her a moment.

"Your skin is so pretty."

"Thank you, sir."

I ran my fingernails down her thighs and she gasped, shifting her legs apart like a wanton whore.

"What do you want?" I asked her.

"I want to come. Please make me come, sir."

Without warning I grabbed hold of her hair, yanking her head back. "You don't deserve it, yet."

I kept hold while I slapped her again, watching the tension in her shoulders as I inflicted her punishment. I observed every twitch, every flinch and every tiny moan, watching her careening to the edge of her tolerance, a slow burning arch of pain. It made my dick throb. I finished up as she made a particularly loud whimper. Perfect timing. I watched the rise and fall of her back as she caught her breath.

"How do you feel?"

"Amazing, thank you, sir."

She wasn't lying. Her face was flushed bright and her thighs were slippery wet, but more telling was the smile that spread slowly across her lips. Endorphins kicking in, no doubt. She was flying high.

I slid my fingers all the way back inside her, saving my thumb for her asshole. She groaned as I forced it in, and bucked back against me with jerky motions. I allowed her movement this time, back and forward against my intrusion as her chains rattled. My free hand curled around her thigh, circling gently around her sopping wet clit, and with steady fingers I brought her to her peak.

I pressed my whole weight against her as she exploded, pinning her to the bench. The restriction sent her wild, and she shuddered against me, squealing like a cat. I didn't stop until she was all done, withdrawing my fingers with a delicious squelch. I touched them to her lips and she licked them clean.

"Good girl."

I unfastened her cuffs and she spun around, reaching for me. I guided her up from the bench and she fell to her knees instinctively, hands aiming for my belt buckle. I let her find it, gazing down at the long dark tangle of her hair. It hung down around her naked shoulders, coiled into damp tails. It reminded me of something. My dick jumped inside my jeans.

Dark, wet hair. Green eyes. So fucking green. Tears, lots of tears. Beautiful pain.

Lydia Marsh.

I reached for the woman on her knees, stroking down her hair and pulling her closer. *Yes.* Her palm against my cock through the fabric, rubbing me. Her mouth already open, wanting.

Green eyes. Tears. Perfect tears.

I raised her blindfold, staring down at her through a haze of lust. Desire pulsed through me, tickling my skin.

But Cara's eyes were brown.

It knocked the wind right out of my sails. I recoiled before I could stop, jolted from the fantasy.

Cara kept her eyes on mine, a hungry smile on her face. Her fingers freed my belt, but it was too late. I took her hands in mine.

"I need a drink, Cara, thank you."

"Are you sure, sir?"

"Thank you, Cara."

She looked disappointed, but it was no good. My mood was broken. I lifted her to her feet and kissed her knuckles before we left the room. She leant into my side en route back to the bar, her naked flesh burning into my chest. It felt good, but it was over for me.

A small crowd retreated from the windows, show over. One of the men patted my shoulder.

"Good scene, Masque."

I smiled back at him. "Yes, it was."

THE BAR WAS QUIET WHEN WE RETURNED, EVERYONE'S ATTENTION fully engaged by the main floor. A couple I recognised, Diva and Cain, were getting down and dirty with a reel of bondage tape and a couple of floggers. I flashed a smile but walked on by, leading Cara by the hand to deliver her into the arms of another club regular. Raven, *Mistress* Raven, to the general club populous, also known as Rebecca 'Bex' Hayfield, but only to me. A real life friend. One of my *only* real life friends, in fact.

I watched Raven's mouth spread into a sly grin as we approached, her kohl-rimmed eyes sparkling. She'd gone for a particularly severe look this evening; blue-black hair twisted tight into a high-pony, topping off a skin-slick latex number which ended just shy of her ass. Thigh-high boots finished the look. She air-kissed me twice to save her lipstick, then turned her attention to the naked woman at my side.

Cara twirled on instruction and Raven nodded her approval.

"Nice and rosy, just how we like it. Good job, Masque." She slapped Cara's ass for good measure, then pulled her in close, roving her tongue up naked flesh to nip at Cara's neck. The obliging sub continued her spin, presenting her cute little tits to Raven's gaze. Porcelain skin with sweet peachy nipples.

"What's this?" Raven asked, raising an eyebrow. "No marks?" She tutted loudly, giving me the eye. "These gorgeous little tits were made for pain, Cara. You want that, don't you?"

"Yes, Mistress."

Cara's silky-soft voice made me hard again, and I glanced away to watch Diva taking a fairly decent flogging.

"Are you going to finish the job?" Raven asked me, pushing her ward in my direction. Cara squeezed her tits together and held them high for me, smiling in invitation.

"I thought I'd leave them for you, Raven. I know how wet you get over nipple torture."

"So thoughtful," she grinned. "Playroom three, Cara, now. Don't you dare touch yourself."

Cara tottered off without hesitation, and I watched her tight little curves sashay away. I turned back to find Raven staring at me, her eyes just inches from mine. She trailed a finger down my nose, pretending to peek under the mask that covered most of my face.

"I'm beginning to forget what you look like under that thing," she laughed.

"Maybe that's the plan."

"So sad. Your face is too pretty to hide, Masque. You used to at least take the thing off between scenes."

"It's growing on me. Besides, I don't really want my face being snapped in this place, regardless of whether I'm flogging the shit out of some young plaything or not."

"Everyone knows the no-camera rule."

"Wherever there are rules they are inevitably broken."

"Fair, but your face isn't exactly your only recognisable feature," she laughed, tracing the tail of the tattoo on my chest. "You can't get a mask for *that* thing."

"Nobody outside of this place ever sees *that* thing." I took her hand in mine as she continued her journey down the beast. "But *this* thing." I pointed to my face. "People see *this* thing all the time."

"It must get so complicated being you, so many lives..." she mocked. "One day you'll wear the mask to the office and the suit to the club, you know that right?"

"And that's the day I quit town and start all over again."

"Such a drama queen..."

"Anonymity suits me."

"*Control* suits you, *Masque*," she grinned. "I think you were born with a crop in your hand."

"It was a cane, actually," I smiled. "And I hope I die with one in my hand, too."

She leant in close, her hand still pressed to my chest. The deep plum notes of *Poison* kissed my nostrils as I breathed her in. She slid her hand down my stomach to the bulge in my jeans, and whispered so softly into my ear I could hardly hear her.

"You didn't come, did you? I know you didn't. You need a proper scene, James, without holding back. Tame doesn't suit you."

"I'm not tame."

"You were a pussycat with Cara, she won't even bruise."

"*Cara* is the pussycat, Bex. I hope for her sake she doesn't say yes to moving into yours, you'd break her in a week. You and I both know she wouldn't cope with the hard stuff."

"You'd better get it on with someone who would then." I felt her lips against my ear.

"Is that a hint? You priming me for your bi-annual foray into the world of submission?"

She squeezed my cock. "Nah. Anyway, you don't have a pussy." She let me go and walked away, tossing me a smile over her shoulder.

"Since when has that been a deal breaker?" I called after her.

"Since tonight." She blew me a kiss.

I'M ALWAYS THE ONLY ONE IN THE OFFICE AT 6AM. I LOVE THE QUIET, before the place fills up with people and the general office bullshit that comes along with them. I made myself a coffee in silence, pondering my workload for the coming week. Sales had just landed a big deal, a bespoke solution for White Hastings McCarthy, one of the top five law firms in the country – a seven hundred seat initial installation across three branches, with seven case management worktypes to scope out. The whole thing was ripe for my desk.

My mind began to assemble the potential project outline. This one would take a lot of co-ordination. A lot of *people*. I hate all that shit.

I leant back against the worktop to sip my coffee. Black, no sugar, just the way I like it. Just how Lydia Marsh had made it. My mind bailed without warning, thoughts unravelling and skittering away. There, in their stead, was a full colour rerun of my Friday morning peepshow. Lydia's tear-streaked face in full focus, and her eyes, so fucking green. Jesus.

Bex was right. I did need a proper scene. The need to dominate pulsed in my temples, thick with the craving for tears and pain and the total surrender of a body underneath mine. Cara had scratched an itch, but the real beast raged on unchecked.

I headed to the men's room, resigned to an early morning hand-job. I pressed my forehead against the tiles as I worked my cock, eyes screwed shut as I summoned up a lightning-quick montage of memories. Women bound tight by their wrists, arching their backs into the pain as the cane strikes. Tears of surrender, and release, and abandon through pain. Their quivering legs as the adrenaline spikes... then the endorphin rush, the point where their bodies turn limp and their eyes glaze in lust. Quiet tears. Acceptance. Absolute, total submission. All for me.

Come on.

Another montage, this one of Bex. She'd fight against her surrender, writhing, kicking and screaming to the edge of release. Spitting curses and fighting against her bonds, until she'd break apart and go toppling into the abyss beyond, screaming out tears and begging for more. She morphed into my Kitty Kat, my Katreya. Her bruised shins running away from me through long grass, begging me to chase her... begging me to hurt her... hurt her in her most tender places.

Jesus fucking Christ, James, just fucking come.

In desperation I let myself go there.

Lydia Marsh, bound at my feet. Staring up at me through watery eyes. Her tits are so fucking pretty, tied up tight in bondage rope, marks of her punishment savage against pale skin. Her mouth is open, ready. Her eyes begging me to take her. I force myself in, and she gags on me. I love the noises her throat makes.

Fuck, fuck, fuck.

I sprayed my load all over the wall, hissing out a string of expletives and already forcing Lydia from my mind. Colleagues were no go. An absolute no-fucking-way.

I had one golden rule. The one I'd never break again.

Fuck no-one you know, and know no-one you fuck.

It was a whole lot safer that way, but damn what I'd give to see Lydia cry again.

Frank and I had the same ritual every Monday morning. He'd knock at my door at 9.15 on the dot, blustering about how time flies, and then ask after my weekend. My answer was invariably the same.

"Can't complain, Frank, how was yours?"

Cue his long monologue of events. Golf, shopping, family meals, some story about the neighbours, and I'd sit and listen, making all the right noises. People like talking, and when they're talking about themselves, they aren't talking about me. It suits me well.

That simple fact has made me an exceptional listener, which also suits me well. It pays to listen. It pays to *understand*.

Frank finally turned his attention to White Hastings McCarthy, gushing at the potential of what the deal could mean for Trial Run. Another of the big boys on our client list. I shared his enthusiasm, and for a few minutes we were colleagues with a single common objective. It was one of those rare moments it felt good to be part of a team.

"Look, James, I know you aren't up for overnighters. There's no pressure on you to go, but Trevor White wants to kick off with a few days onsite once the paperwork's in place. Brighton Head Office, nothing too crazy. A bit of a tour, an initial round of meetings, all the usual. I was thinking you could ask Sam from development in your stead, and send him with someone from project management. I figured maybe Steve Jones or Lydia Marsh, but it's up to you. Lydia headed up the Anderson deal a few months ago, actually, went like a dream. She'd be a good fit."

My throat went dry. "Lydia Marsh?"

"You must know her, pretty girl… tall… dark hair… crazy green eyes."

"I've seen her around." I glanced at my notepad, now cocooned out of sight in my in-tray. Lydia's flowery text: *Islington bound, safe and sound.*

"Great. Do you want me to get Janie to handle it or will you ask them yourself?"

"I'll do it," I said, before I'd even realised.

"Good stuff, James. Good stuff. Let's meet this afternoon, get the team together. I'll send over a calendar invite."

He made to leave, clearly satisfied with our plan, but I called him back from the doorway.

"I'll go to Brighton, Frank."

He shot me a puzzled expression. "There's no need, James. Don't feel obliged, there's no pressure."

"The fact is, we'd be better off if I went. I'll go."

Frank beamed like a cat who'd landed a fat pot of cream. He came back to shake my hand, big solid jerks of gratitude. "I appreciate it, James, and so will Trevor White. I'll get Janie to book you a hotel."

"Make a booking for Lydia Marsh, too," I said. "She'll be coming with me."

"Good choice, James. I'll get Janie on it right away."

I cursed myself once the door was closed, hands in my hair at the absurdity of my impulsion.

What the fuck?!

In frustration I tore out Lydia's Islington note and fed it through the shredder.

CHAPTER 3

Lydia

The senior management team at White Hastings McCarthy stared straight ahead at the man before them, nodding at every smooth point he made. James Clarke was polished, confident, faultless. That's why they call him Mr Perfect, I guess.

My attendance at WHM, smiling and scribbling notes while Mr CTO presented the implementation proposal, was still a surprise to me. Apparently, I'd been first choice. I was just glad he'd looked beyond my little meltdown to give me a shot. This project would be one hell of a gold star on my resume.

James handed me the room at the end of his presentation, and I was dropped right into the chaos of shared calendars and proposed schedules. By the time we wrapped up for the day we'd pretty much achieved sign-off on our timescales. We'd done good.

"That went well," he said as we stepped out into the crisp Brighton evening.

I looked up at him, towering above. He had just the faintest shadow of stubble, his face etched in shadows against the gaudy brilliance of the pier beyond. "It went great," I said. "They loved you."

"They definitely loved *you*."

"I scheduled in some dates in a diary, that's all."

"They liked you, Lydia. You coordinated well for a complex project, considering."

"Considering?"

"Considering recent events," he expanded, dark eyes crashing into mine without even a sliver of awkwardness.

I felt my hackles rise. "My personal shit doesn't make me unable to do my job. I'm fine, James. Thank you."

He laughed, and I gritted my teeth until I realised it wasn't at my expense.

"You sound like me. Knock you down and you're scrabbling to your feet, swinging your fists at the air and claiming it didn't hurt."

"Oh, it hurt," I smiled. "But I'm always straight up on my feet. Always."

We walked along the beachfront towards the hotel in amiable silence. James Clarke was a brooding character, I could tell, but his smile was easy. I felt strangely comfortable in his presence, my steps falling into gentle rapport with his. Every now and again his eyes would catch mine, and I'd see something flash in him, some indeterminable knowing. Maybe it was concern, I dunno, but by the time we reached our venue for the night I felt a calmness I hadn't felt for days. I put it down to the sea air, taking in cleansing deep breaths of salty breeze and thanking my good fortune for being out of the London chaos.

On arrival I paced straight through the hotel foyer, turning in the doorway to the bar to suggest we have a celebratory drink, but James wasn't following.

"There's a good restaurant here, by all accounts," he said. "Have dinner and drinks on my room. I'm sorry I can't join you. I have things to do."

I kept my smile bright despite the major blow out. "Of course. No problem."

"I'll see you in the morning, Lydia." His brush-off panged more than it should have. A rejection-fuelled chink in the Lydia Marsh armour. I elbowed it good and hard, and it fell away into nothing. No big deal.

"See you in the morning, James."

I didn't watch him leave.

I HAD A FEW IN THE BAR. ENOUGH TO REALLY FEEL THEM ON MY WAY to my room. James Clarke hadn't made a reappearance and I hadn't felt the need to keep up my work facade. Hence the large house whites and unsteady legs. I glanced at James' closed door as I passed, right next to mine, trying to be a good neighbour by treading as lightly as possible. I was too drunk for a work night, but hell it felt nice to be in my own space again. A few weeks sharing Steph's shoebox apartment was already driving me crazy. Probably her, too. I took a breath in my own space and caught sight of the pier through the net curtains. Sea-view balconies were a win. Air, glorious air.

The breeze sobered me up enough to ease off the wobbles, and I relaxed against the railings with slightly steadier legs, staring intently down on the people below. I heard a door slide open to my left, but my view was blocked by a partition. A voice cut out in the night, quiet but deep, a low laugh tickling my stomach.

"She said no, then? Probably for the best... what do you mean you *kind of* asked her? You either did or you didn't. You did, didn't you?"

I held my breath, unsure whether to stay or go. Maybe he wouldn't notice if I crept back inside.

"It's for the best, you'd break her and she'd end up moving out again and leaving you in a worse state. Honest, she would... I'm pretty sure it's not love... no, that's definitely not love... Rebecca, that's definitely, definitely not love."

His laugh was so genuine and warm. At odds with the steely professionalism of his corporate persona. I stayed put, committed to waiting it out until he went back inside.

"You could advertise, you know... like most normal people do... you're not *that* weird, Bex, not really. Anyway, some people *like* weird... *weird* people like weird..."

I heard him put a foot up on the bottom ledge of the balcony, and peeked forward to find him leaning out into the night. He was still in his suit, its tailoring hugging him in all the right places. He looked really fucking perfect. *Drunk-speak. Drunk.*

"I've got to go," I heard him say. "Long day tomorrow... Yes, it's going well... Yes, she's good... I can give praise where it's due, Rebecca. She's *good*... Behave will you. It's work..."

She's good. Me? All of a sudden I felt like an intruder. I should have coughed or something, made it obvious I was there. Shit. Too late. *She's good.* I'm good. Of course I'm fucking good. I work really hard... but still. *She's good.* I found I was smiling. Did I really smile anymore? Since Stu? Of course not. Of course not since Stu. His name cut, and I was right back there, at home, packing my things through spidery itches. I tried to rein my thoughts back in, but they wouldn't come. Wine was a mistake.

James was still talking.

"I'll see you on Saturday, ok? Stick an advert online, you'll have probably solved your dilemma by then. Who knows, you might have Cara mark-two already moved in. Goodnight, Rebecca."

He finished the call but stayed still, staring out to sea. I was contemplating a move back inside, regardless of whether or not he'd hear me, but he negated the need altogether by leaning over.

"I hope I didn't disturb you, Lydia."

Crap. So much for hiding.

"I was just getting some air, I didn't mean to eavesdrop." I joined him at the railings, matching his stance. "It's nice out here."

"I like the sea. Clears the mind."

"Yes, it does."

"How was your evening?"

I smiled. "A few too many wines. I'll be fine in the morning."

"I've had a few too many myself. Quite a few too many." He smiled at my lack of response, seeming to read my mind. "Does that surprise you? You think I'm Mr Uptight, is that it?"

"I think you're Mr Perfect. I'm not sure Mr Perfect gets drunk on a work night."

"Mr Perfect?"

"That's what they call you, in the office."

"Do they?" His eyes dug into me, glinting in the shadows.

"Sure do."

"Do you know what they call you?"

"No idea."

"They call you Cat. Short for cat's eyes." He looked me right in the face, staring for long seconds. "It suits you."

"Well, Mr Perfect kinda suits you, too."

"I'm not perfect."

"I dunno, you were perfect today... and perfectly intimidating," I said, moving a little closer as the wind whipped my hair.

"You find me intimidating?"

I smiled. "Perfection is intimidating, is it not?"

"It's easy to be perfect in office hours. It's after that it gets a whole lot harder."

"Yep," I laughed. "Can't say I've got the home shit nailed."

He paused just a second.

"How are you doing, Lydia? Don't insult me with *fine*. How are you really doing?"

I felt my throat tighten, willing me to clam up and slap on the professionalism, but the wine warmed through my veins, loosening my tongue.

"Most of the time ok. Right now not so great. Bad wine." I slapped my wrist.

"I thought a change of scene might do you good."

"Is that why you invited me?"

"No," he replied in a beat. "I'm really not that generous, I wanted you here because you're good. I just considered it an additional benefit."

"Thanks."

"Don't thank me. It doesn't seem to have worked."

"The thought was there."

"On the periphery."

"All the same. Thanks."

"I've had too many wines," he said, "and so have you. We've got a big day tomorrow, we should sleep them off."

"Yes, sir." I mock saluted, sailing my hand out towards him over the balcony. He didn't move a muscle, just stared me out so hard I felt almost uncomfortable underneath the haze. "Goodnight, James."

In a blink he was away from me, stepping down from the railings and out of view. "Goodnight, cat's eyes. Straight to bed."

Turns out Mr Perfect was Mr damn Bossy, too. It suited him.

By the end of day two I'd have sworn we'd been introduced to every single employee of White Hastings McCarthy, including the cleaners. Round upon round of handshakes and tours and polite conversation. I hoped James had a better recall of faces and names than I did, because after about the fourth new person they'd all become a blur. Somehow I expected he did. He didn't seem the type to be lost for a name at a dinner party.

We'd been waved off with fond farewells from the senior management team, and the morning would see our final wrap-up session with the IT department. Then back to London, to more sofa surfing and shared fridge space.

"Tomorrow's just a formality," James said, as we wandered back along the front. "The hard work's been done."

"I think I've got everything clear in my notes. I may just need to reconfirm some of the case management stages."

"Our main prerogative was to cement the relationship, and we've already achieved that. You were invaluable. Thank you."

"We made a good team," I smiled.

"We did."

After my previous evening's rebuttal, I waved James away in the foyer without the suggestion of drinks. He didn't make a repeat offer of dinner on his room tab, so I figured I was out for myself. No big deal. I made a mental note to tone down the wine consumption. Just a couple, nothing crazy.

The first glass slid down my throat like liquid happiness, and Stuart slipped from my mind as easily as he'd thumped his way back in. I was checking out the bar menu when I caught the delicious notes of musk. Musk and vanilla.

"I'm sorry, Lydia, I meant to join you sooner. I had calls to make." James took a seat next to me, leaning in close enough to scan the mains. "Have you ordered?"

"Not yet."

"Excellent," he smiled. "Let's eat."

"What was he like?" James asked, refilling my glass.

I slouched back in the chair to enjoy the ambience of the hotel restaurant, pleasantly tipsy and full of Dover sole. We'd covered all the work talk, and the wine had flowed much more freely than I'd intended.

"Who?" I feigned ignorance and he raised his eyebrows. I dragged out the silence before I answered. "He was nice. Funny. Patient... Safe."

"Safe?"

"What happened to *refuse to dwell on the pain, not even for a single second*?"

"My bad. Forget I asked."

I smiled a little.

"*Safe*. Stu felt comfortable, you know? It was easy. We fitted together."

"It sounds more like a pair of footwear than a relationship."

"Relationships get like that, no?" I took my drink, my eyes on his as I drank it down.

"Maybe some."

"I guess the others must break up before they get that far."

He sat forward in his chair, and that simple movement changed everything. The thrum of cutlery and surrounding diners faded to grey, and there was only him, with his dark eyes so intently fixed on mine. I filed it away, the-James-Clarke-effect, that ability to command the floor that I'd witnessed all day.

"Some relationships offer consistency, others offer challenge. I prefer the company of a woman who'll push me to the very heights of human experience. The kind of woman who'll embrace the same in return. A relationship like that may never feel safe, even if it lasted a lifetime."

"Your wife was like that, was she?"

He took a sip of wine, looked beyond me, to the diners I couldn't see. "She was challenging, yes."

"So what happened?"

"Did you enjoy your main?" he smiled.

"Delicious, thank you, but your subject change sucks. Not even subtle."

"I don't talk about it."

"About *it,* or about you?"

"I listen a lot better than I talk."

I smiled. "That's a terrible cop out."

"Why so?"

"It's lazy," I laughed. "Hiding behind a smokescreen of interest to detract attention away from yourself."

"It's not a smokescreen."

I leant forward, resting on my elbows. "What's so bad about talking about you, Mr Clarke? Are you some big, bad serial killer or something? A secret special forces operator? A stamp collector?"

"I value privacy above almost all other things. I think you understand that more than you're letting on."

"Yeah, I get it. I'm normally the one doing the listening."

"Then I guess we have a stalemate. Two listeners out to dinner, far away from any talkers." His eyes smiled at me, big dark pools of cinnamon. "Were you in love with him?"

"*You* didn't answer *my* question."

"You first."

"Not a chance." I held his stare, unwilling to buckle. The pressure to give into him nipped at my heels, compelling me with an unknown force, strange and unfounded. Finally he smiled, and the tension broke. He shifted in his seat and I felt the bloom of victory in my ribcage, as though I'd won some battle I didn't realise I was fighting.

"Rachel is the kind of woman who thrives on the adoration of others. I gave her plenty of my attention, and for a long time we worked like a dream. Then work got crazy and she lost the spotlight of my adoration every waking minute. I didn't realise she was finding solace in other men until it was too late."

"She had an affair?"

"Several," he announced calmly, then turned the conversation in a heartbeat. "So, were you in love with him?"

I took a breath, itching to pursue the adultery revelation. His expression told me I didn't have a hope in hell. "I thought so."

"Thought so?"

"I *loved* him. I don't know if that's the same thing on reflection."

"Did he make you wet?"

I nearly spat my wine, staring across at the man opposite, at his crisp, corporate packaging, his steady hands, his considered smile. His goddamn perfect poker face and jaw of steel.

"Sorry?"

"You heard me."

I felt my cheeks burning. "I, um... we had a healthy relationship."

"That's not what I asked."

"Stuart is attractive."

"That's not what I asked, either."

"Well, yeah, sometimes. I mean... he could."

"He could, but he didn't?"

I sat agog, waiting for James to crack a smile and admit he was joking, but the smile didn't come.

My words felt so awkward.

"It was nice, but with work, and long days and general life. You know how it gets."

"So, he didn't make you wet. You're a young woman, with your whole life ahead of you. When the betrayal fades you're going to do just fine."

"You aren't so old, yourself."

"Old enough to know what I want, and more importantly what I don't want."

I chanced my arm. "So, what *do* you want?"

"Dessert."

He called the waiter.

CHAPTER 4
James

The splash of cold water did little to bring me to my senses. *What the fuck are you doing, James? What the fuck?* It was her fucking eyes. Cat's eyes. Pale turquoise eyes full of *fuck me hard*. Lydia was a sharp little cookie, a guarded little conker full of pain. Tough, and tight, and aching to be broken apart. Jesus Christ.

Fuck no-one you know, and know no-one you fuck.

She'd driven me crazy this trip. The sight of her reverent gaze as I'd delivered my pitch. Staring up at me like I was the God of fucking everything, standing in front of my PowerPoint deck like some kind of goddamn guru. Sweet fucking Christ. I recalled the gentle swell of her tits as she breathed, the slightest imprint of a lace bra under her blouse. Her sweeter than sweet little handshake, her quiet confidence, her eagerness to please. Yet, Lydia Marsh was clearly a fighter. Someone who bottles it all up inside, buries it deep. I'd avoided everything to do with her in the weeks since Kitchengate. Sworn abstinence and no fucking way. Yet here I was, my cock alive and kicking in spite of my better senses. Would she beg? Would she kneel on her soft little knees and plead for release? Would she sob under the cane like a broken little doll? Not easily...

A far off memory danced across my retinas. The gangly unease of inexperienced youth. The crunch of autumn leaves under my feet as I chased after Katreya. Katreya Moore, just a year older than me, but so much taller. Her white socks gathered messily at her ankles, showing off pale, bruised legs as she ran. Dark hair streamed behind her, tangled in tails. She turned to call after me, her face still streaked with the tears from her scolding indoors. I remembered the skidding halt of her body, long skinny fingers reaching for mine.

"I'm going to run away, James, come with me!" Her eyes pleaded, wide and green, the palest eyes I'd ever seen.

Seen. Past tense.

"Where?" I asked her.

"Who cares."

"What about school?"

"Don't be such a sissy." Her savage eyes teased me. Cut me down before her. She smudged her tears with the back of her hand.

"I'm no sissy."

"Sissy boy, James. You're so fucking good. So nice. Such a good little boy, James Clarke."

"Shut up, Kat."

"Make me."

My throat choked up with childish desire, too young to understand how to really play this game.

"We said we weren't going to do that again."

"So? I changed my mind," she giggled.

"No, Kat. They'll think you've been fighting again."

"Hurt me, James. I know you want to. I'll show you where... places they can't see."

"We said no."

"I've still got the marks from last time... I'll show you... They told me off. Said I'm a bad girl, but I'll be a good girl, for you, I promise. I'll do whatever you say. I'll beg you if you like. Make me beg, James."

Shit... I forced the past aside before it swallowed me whole, smoothing hair back from my forehead while I eyed myself in the mirror. *Get a fucking grip.* This Brighton trip was a whole heap of trouble. *Did he make you wet?* Jesus Christ, what a fucking question. But she answered... her awkward little swallow, the darting of her eyes. So much I'd wanted to say. *He doesn't know how, does he? Doesn't know how to fuck your little asshole raw... Doesn't know how to stretch you all the way open... until you're riding his fist like a wanton fucking whore and grunting for more... Ever had a tongue deep in your ass, Lydia Marsh? Ever had someone force their fist all the way inside you? Ever pissed down someone's throat while they tongue your greedy little slit? Have you ever been hurt, Lydia? Really hurt? Anyone ever fucked you up? Slapped your tight little cunt until you cry? Ever gagged on cock until you puke? Ever seen your tits swell purple? Ever choked for breath until the world turns black? I'll make it feel good for you, Lydia. I'll make you squirt all over my filthy fucking fingers.*

Stop. Just stop.

I was running out of legitimate toilet break time. She'd be waiting, expecting me to come back all smiles and professionalism. Expecting me to steer the conversation back to White Hastings fucking McCarthy and our perfect day's work.

Fuck no-one you know, and know no-one you fuck.

If only I hadn't seen her cry...

I smoothed down my tie, smiling politely and resigning myself to another round of work talk, but Lydia surprised me. She toyed with her sundae, poking the thing like it was alive, over and over with pensive spoon gestures.

"It'll melt if you're not careful," I said, forking up a liberal portion of creme brulee.

Her eyes latched onto mine as she took a mouthful of ice-cream. Unconscious obedience at its finest. She'd clearly been pondering things. She resumed our conversation as soon as she'd swallowed.

"You got me thinking. I think it's really the security I miss. Not him. I mean I do miss him, I love him, but it's not the relationship I miss so much as having that part of my life all wrapped up. You know?"

"That's what you want, is it? Security? The happy ever after of companionship and TV nights?"

Her smile didn't reach her eyes. "I thought that's what I wanted, but a few weeks out of it and I'm not so sure anymore."

"You're a bit young to be settling for the nice steady guy, don't you think? Those guys are normally friend-zoned until at least mid-thirties."

Her eyes did smile this time. "Stuart clearly wasn't as steady as I thought."

"Why did he cheat? It's never just the drink."

"Ouch." She placed a hand over her heart.

"It's not an attack, Lydia, people cheat. I'm just curious why *he* cheated. Comfy slippers man doesn't sound like the kind of guy who'd want to rock the boat for a casual fuck."

"That's a probing question."

"It's a simple question."

"If I answer, it's my turn to ask a question next."

"I don't make deals unless I know all the terms," I stated, bluntly. "I'd need to know the question first."

She raised her eyebrows, gripping her ice-cream by the shaft of the glass to take another spoonful. Firm grip. Nice fingers. They'd look so fucking sweet around my cock.

"Can't you make an exception? We're away, aren't we? Can't Mr Perfect CTO just be James Clarke for one evening?"

The *no* was on my tongue, so ready to slip out and end this silly game before it started, but her fucking eyes sucked me in again. Big and wide and slightly mischievous, twinned with her sweet little mouth clamped tight around her spoon, cheeks hollow as she sucked away the remnants of ice-cream. What the fuck was happening to me?

"James Clarke the man is as guarded as James Clarke CTO, I'm afraid. *He* doesn't make deals unless he knows all the terms, either."

She shrugged. "Ok, so I'll get the first internal meetings scheduled for next week, maybe call Frank in for the initial brainstorm, what do you think?"

I leant forward, fixed her in my stare, the *no* on my tongue fizzing away into fucking nothing. "Why did Stuart cheat, Lydia? What made him fuck some little blonde bitch from the office?"

If she was taken aback by my crudeness, she didn't show it. Her expression stayed constant, determined. She had steel.

"My go next if I answer."

"Fine." My temples pulsed, discomfort at my own sorry predicament threatening to boil over, and yet I knew I'd answer her. Just like I'd always followed Katreya into the bushes. "Talk, before I change my mind."

She didn't hold back.

"He felt things had fizzled. That our sex life had dried up, and I hadn't wanted him since the Anderson project came in at work. He said he was weak and horny and she was hot for him, promising to put her sour little mouth around his dick and suck him good, only that's not the only place he put it."

"Had things dried up?"

"That's another question."

"It's an extension of my earlier question," I said, with a dismissive hand gesture.

"Ok. I'll give you that. I was tired and busy, I thought he understood. He *said* he understood." Her lips pursed in anger, the first real chink in her facade I'd seen since the kitchen. "Has that answered your question? Do you think he was justified now because I wasn't putting out for his bi-weekly demands?"

"Not at all."

"Good, because our sex life *had* fizzled, but it wasn't a few months ago like *he* thinks it was. It wasn't down to the bloody Anderson project and tiredness over a couple of lousy months. It fizzled years ago for me, when we moved in together and he substituted any effort with nights of missionary and the occasional blow job in the living room. It may have fizzled for *him* when I stopped rolling over for the obligatory late night fuck, but he let it go to shit a hell of a lot earlier than that. It should have been *me* screwing some random in an alleyway on a work night out. Not him."

I watched her ease down from the ceiling, regaining her composure in measured little paces. I soaked in the rise and fall of her breasts as she pulled back the rage, and the hurt and the injustice. She grabbed the wine bottle from the ice bucket and poured herself a refill, drinking it down with large gulps.

"Does that feel better?"

"What?" she snapped. "Admitting my boyfriend wanted it

elsewhere even though he was a boring, conservative joke in the bedroom?"

"Venting the pain. Does it feel good?"

"I don't know," she sighed. "It's new. I don't vent, I just deal with shit. I don't even know why I'm talking about it."

"Venting is healthy."

"Says he who doesn't talk either."

"I vent," I said. "I just prefer a more physical outlet for my emotional discomfort. At the gym, or in the bedroom."

"You vent in the bedroom?" She smiled.

"Sex is my preferred choice, although I have to say I utilise the gym more at this present point in time."

"I've heard. Every lunchtime, at the gym down the street."

"People talk about that, do they?" I felt the familiar bristling of the hair on my arms, the rage at the whispered discussions.

"It's hardly a secret. You look sculpted from bronze."

I forced the irritation back behind the veneer. "So, what's your question, Lydia. What do you want to know about James Clarke, CTO?" I forced a smile, an easy one, relaxing back in my seat to diffuse the tension.

"Have you always been like this? Private, I mean."

I smiled at the relatively easy question. Maybe I'd escape this little round of truth or truth unscathed after all. "No. I wasn't private with Rachel. She saw all sides of me."

"Do you miss the intimacy?"

"That's another question."

"It's an extension of my earlier question," she grinned.

I couldn't help but grin back.

"Give someone enough rope and they will hang you with it eventually. Either intentionally or not, the result is the same. I don't miss the intimacy, no."

"So, what happens now? You'll never have a relationship again? Never let anyone in?"

"Not in the conventional sense. I value my sanity far too much."

"I think I shall adopt the same philosophy," she said, raising her glass. "Here's to us. Single and sane."

"Here's to us." I raised mine in return. "Non-talkers anonymous. Private and proud."

"That should be our new tagline. Single and sane, private and proud," she laughed.

"I'll have it printed up and framed for my living room."

"I'll have it printed up and framed when I *get* a living room," she smiled sadly. "I really need to get my shit together."

"Where are you living?"

"On a friend's sofa. It's not the greatest. I need to find a house share or something, but I die a bit at the idea of all the smiles and questions and rigmarole of finding suitable housemates. I need to get a grip."

"You have to allow yourself a bit of slack, given the circumstances."

"A bit of slack won't find me somewhere to live."

The idea was there in a heartbeat. Maybe it had been there all the time, lurking under the surface. *No, James, no. Don't fucking do it, no fucking way.* My mouth turned dry, my throat tightening around the words in my throat.

"I'm sure you'll sort something out."

"I'd better had," she said. "I think Steph's boyfriend is getting sick of me. I hear her shushing him at night and pushing him away. Paper-thin walls."

"Always a bitch, those."

"They should just get on with it. I'm a big girl, I can handle the odd grunt in the night."

I itched to ask her more questions, to scratch at the pain under her skin until I found her soft and raw inside, but the conversation was over. Her head was firmly back on planet Earth, complete with its accommodation nightmares. I tried to convince myself it was for the best, but one flash of her eyes put paid to that.

She'd compelled me to talk, digging into my privacy like a hungry worm. For that small deed alone she deserved to go over my knee. Her perky little ass would feel just right under my palm.

She checked her watch. Game over.

"We should get to bed. Another early start."

"Yes, we should."

I summoned the bill and signed the evening to my room as she watched me. We walked up slowly, the silence hanging heavier with each step. She slid her keycard into the lock and turned to me with cold, cool eyes again. Professional Lydia.

"Thank you, James, I had a great night."

"My thanks for a job well done."

She gave me a smile as she pushed her way into the room beyond, and I was there outside the bushes again, autumn leaves under my shoes.

"Lydia, wait."

She stepped back, eyes full of questions, and there, underneath them was the tiniest hint of potential. I could almost taste the *what-if* coursing through her mind, even if she didn't know it. I took a step towards her, forcing her to tilt her head up to meet my eyes, approaching so close I could feel the heat of her through my suit.

Fuck, I was going to do it.

"I have a friend who's looking for a housemate," I told her.

"She won't pry. No false smiles or interviews, just a room there if you want it."

I watched Lydia exhale a breath, the corners of her mouth lifting as she ran her fingers through her hair.

"I want it. Thank you."

"Don't you even want to know where she lives?"

"Where does she live?"

"Camden."

"That works. What's her name?"

"Rebecca." I stared at her awkwardly, my composure well out of kilter. "Goodnight, Lydia."

I closed the door behind me without even glancing back, fisting my hands in my hair. Jesus Christ. What the fuck? My mind zoomed through excuses, reasons I could give as to why this couldn't happen, but it was pointless.

I already knew I'd never use them.

CHAPTER 5
Lydia

Steph hovered while I scoured her apartment for the last of my things.

"You don't have to leave, you know, not until you've found somewhere decent."

"Thanks."

"You haven't even met this woman, what if she's some kind of psycho?"

"If she's a psycho I'll be straight back on your sofa."

She rolled her eyes. "If you're still alive enough to make the trip."

"I'm sure James wouldn't have suggested the move if she was a complete nut-job."

"Yeah, well, you don't know *him* either. *He* might be a nut-job too for all you know. You know what they said about Ted Bundy? Charming, smart, attractive... I'm sure *he* looked damn fine in a suit, too."

"Ted Bundy wasn't CTO of the company I work for."

"So? Psychos like to hide in plain sight... Look at the whole privacy thing he's got going on. Something to hide, I think. Women's heads in his fridge, maybe?"

"*I'm* private, I don't keep heads in my fridge."

She rolled her eyes again. "Just take care of yourself, will you?"

"I always do."

Steph gave me a tight, strawberry-scented hug and I felt the slightest reluctance to let her go. This was it, my new life beginning for real. I set off into the unknown with my suitcase in hand, destination Camden and the mysterious Rebecca. I'd quizzed James about her, but typically he'd said very little. Rebecca Hayfield. Approaching thirty and *colourful*. Nice and no-nonsense apparently, if a little eccentric, with the ability to mind her own business. She sounded good enough to me. I recalled my crazy enthusiasm for the idea, snapping his hand off without even the proviso of further information. Talk about spur of the moment. Spur of *that* moment, more like it. The memory brought a burn to my cheeks, and once again I fought the urge to face-palm. For the briefest of seconds, as he'd stepped so close in the hotel corridor, I'd thought he was going to kiss me. Of course he hadn't done, the idea was absurd, but just for that one tiny moment, as our bodies almost collided, my breath froze in my chest. Too many wines, too much talk of sex, too fucking fit a man. Even more absurd was the notion that, for that split second, I think I maybe wanted him to. I really never thought I'd get hooked by the rebound shit –overtaken by a ridiculous desire to fuck a hot stranger in a hotel room somewhere. It had been just weeks, jeez. *Weeks.* Not months. Definitely not long enough to be hanging out in one-night-stand territory.

I'd spoken to Steph about it, uncharacteristically desperate to get it off my chest. She'd laughed and given me the thumbs-up, stating a hot, casual fuck would do wonders for my disposition. Maybe it would, but certainly not with James Clarke. An emotionally-devoid fling might let off some steam, sure, but a work rebound? No fucking way. Work flings have trouble written all over them with a capital TROUBLE. James was just hot, that's all. I was merely joining the ranks of the rest of the female populous at Trial Run, worshipping at the altar of his perfect man-flesh. No big deal. *You're a stupid idiot, Lydia, crushing over James Clarke like a silly schoolgirl.* Still, at least it kept my mind off Stuart, that fact alone made it a plus. That fact alone might even just get me through this emotional wasteland and out the other side without adding more scars to my collection.

I changed lines at Euston Station, and was soon hurtling straight for Camden Town. Nerves kicked in; the realisation that I was about to move in with a total stranger churned in my gut. I kept my cool, deep breaths in and out as I cruised through the motions, stepping straight out into a sunny winter Sunday and James' solemn gaze. He loomed tall on the pavement, cutting an awesome silhouette in a fitted black overcoat, double-breasted and clearly tailored, with his collar up against the chill. He could have walked straight out of the office if it weren't for the dark jeans completing his attire. Skinny fit, like a second skin, showcasing the toned brilliance of his calf muscles. I approached with a smile.

"Hey, thanks for meeting me."

"Let me take that." He lifted my case, carrying it easily without the need for wheels. I kept close as he set off at pace, crossing the street to the shops beyond and marching a path towards the canal. He stopped outside a huge-windowed tattoo parlour, pulling me into a recess and gesturing to a bright purple door.

"Rebecca lives above here. It's nicer than it looks."

"That's great," I said, pressing in closer as a crowd of tourists pushed their way past.

"Are you sure you want to do this?"

"Why wouldn't I be?"

He looked beyond me, across the street, unwilling to meet my eyes. "I've known Rebecca a long time. She's funny, and loyal and she knows when to keep her mouth shut, but she's also..."

"*Colourful*, I know," I smiled. "I can handle colourful."

"She's *very* colourful, most of those colours being shades of black..." He leant into me, mouth to my ear. His breath tickled, and not just where it touched. "...Or shades of *grey*. You'll see what I mean, just don't be put off. She's really nice."

"Shades of grey?"

He flashed me a smile before he pressed the buzzer.

"Come on up," a voice sounded, metallic over the intercom. It was followed immediately by the click of the lock, and James pushed open the door, waving me through. A narrow hallway led to an equally narrow staircase, and at the top was a solid red door. It swung open before I was even halfway up, and the woman referred to as Rebecca stepped out to greet us. Colourful was an understatement.

"Well, hello..." she purred. Her voice was invitingly husky, almost posh with an underlying cockney twang. My eyes roved from feet to head as I climbed the stairs towards her. Sloping calves in knee-high boots... slashed black leggings... a tight black t-shirt, with scrawly red print... *Bad girls do it better*. Too many necklaces to count, wound tight around her neck, beads and sparkles and spikes... then her face... pretty and moon-shaped, big dark eyes with crazy lash extensions, dark burgundy lipstick and cat flick liner, and piercings, lip, nose and eyebrow. Her brows were too artificial to be natural, shaped in a perfect villain arch, and softened by the curls of her black mane. She held out a hand as I reached the top, red nails, lots of rings, and tattoos... an explosion of colour as far as I could see... stars and birds and flowers all wrapped together. "I'm Bex," she said. "Pleased to meet you."

"Lydia," I smiled.

She pulled me into wiry arms, air kissed both of my cheeks, then addressed James over my shoulder.

"Glad to see you doing the manual labour, got to use those muscles for something impressive."

"Watch your lip," he said. "You've had me use them plenty enough."

She turned back to me. "James has already moved my furniture around five times."

"Seven," he countered.

"What can I say? I like variety."

She led the way in, revealing a compact, but perfectly pleasant open-plan living space. The place was immaculate, if a little eccentric, all harsh lines and black furniture with a feature scarlet wall. She'd done a great job on the styling. Everything matched, from the red gloss kitchen units through to the prints hanging on the walls. The place was airy and light, yet stamped with the definite imprint of boudoir. It worked. I was relieved to realise I could cope with this space, even like it. James reclined on the corner suite while Rebecca gave me a whistle-stop tour, finally ending up in the room that would be mine. It wasn't like the rest of the apartment. Instead, it was entirely neutral, with a cream carpet and matching magnolia walls. A wrought-iron effect double bed, made up pretty in purple bedding, and light wood furniture. A wardrobe, chest of drawers, small desk and bookshelf. Perfect. I couldn't stop smiling. Mainly with relief.

"You like it?" Rebecca asked, plumping up the cushions on my bed.

"I like it a lot, thank you."

"I made the bed up fresh, but if you have your own stuff feel free to change it about. This is your space, do what you like with it."

"This is perfect as it is, thanks."

James brought my case through, laying it to rest on the floor by the wardrobe. He looked around the room, weighing it up as though he'd never seen it before. That's when I caught the faintest whiff of fresh paint. He smiled at Rebecca.

"I'm done here, I'll be on my way."

She raised an eyebrow. "Not staying for a cuppa?"

"I have a busy afternoon."

She poked her tongue out. "Piss off, then, I'm sure we'll do just great without you."

"I've no doubt about that," he said.

I followed him down to the front door, trailing behind his purposeful steps.

"Thanks, James, for everything."

"You're welcome."

I watched until he disappeared from view, but he didn't look back, not even for a second. I took a breath before going back upstairs, making sure my smile was at full beam for my new housemate. Rebecca already had the kettle on. It was scarlet, like almost everything else in the kitchen.

"Are you a tea or coffee girl?" she asked, holding up both canisters.

"Coffee, please, black two sugars."

"Don't mind James, the disappearing thing's his signature move."

"I got that impression."

"He's good really, despite what he'll have you believe." She smiled, handing me a mug.

I scoped out the space some more while she sat down on the sofa. A collage of photos showed her performing at some kind of event, made up in sequins and feathers and big-holed fishnets. She looked amazing.

"I do a burlesque act," she said, following my gaze. "Not so much at the moment, though. Too much else going on."

"You look fantastic."

"Amazing what a bit of glitter and sparkle can do for you."

I took a closer look at the pictures on the wall. They weren't prints at all, in fact, but originals. I checked out the signature to find a squiggly RH.

"You did these?"

"Sure did. I don't paint so much these days, but I'll do the occasional commission."

"They're amazing." I took my time admiring one of her pieces, a corseted woman, tapping her thigh with a riding crop, stark and stylish and pretty damn sexy. I smiled inside at James' shades of grey reference. "So you don't paint fulltime?"

"Kind of," she smiled. "I work downstairs."

"You're a tattoo artist?" I walked over to another piece. This one was smaller, but more intricate. Some kind of mythical beast, made up of heavy, tribal brush strokes, the head of a dragon trailing into the body of a lion. It was a strange image, dark and brutal, yet strangely beautiful. I couldn't take my eyes off it.

"A chimera," she explained. "One body, two beasts. It was a commissioned tattoo design."

"It's beautiful. For someone's back?"

"Chest, although the tail curls all the way around the ribs to the spine."

I tried to picture the person such a design would belong to, someone like Rebecca probably, someone else *colourful*. I took a seat along from her.

"I love what you've done with this place, it's very cool."

"Really?" She looked surprised.

"Honestly, it's amazingly well done, very stylish."

"The landlady gives me free rein, so if you have any super cool plans for some interior refurb, let me know."

"You sure hit lucky with that landlady."

"Yeah, she's an ex. She owns the tattoo shop downstairs too, so technically she's my boss as well. Means I get special treatment. I don't imagine James would have told you that I sit towards the lesbian end of bi. Is that a problem?" She laughed. "Don't worry. I promise I won't molest you in the night."

"It's no problem."

"Great," she said. "So, you work with James? I bet that's fun for you, his perfectionist tendencies drive me mad at the best of times."

"He's quite a taskmaster. It's good though... he's good."

She smiled at me, bright and warm. "You can ask, you know. It must be on your mind."

"Sorry?"

"How we met. James and I, we're hardly two peas in a pod."

I grinned. "You do seem quite different people."

"I went to school with his wife, known her since we were five. She came to me for an ankle tat a few years back and we got reacquainted from there. Jaz, my ex, and I used to hang out with them, double dates. Then they split up, and we did shortly after. James and I stayed in touch."

"He mentioned his wife."

She raised her eyebrows. "That's a first, he doesn't usually talk about her."

"He didn't say much, only that her name was Rachel and that she was unfaithful."

"Well, that is indeed a turn up for the books. Anyway, enough of James Clarke." She raised her glass. "Welcome, Lydia! Here's to us, and our newfound house-buddy status."

I was happy to toast. All considered, I was pretty damn happy to be there.

James

Rebecca's scarlet lips pouted at me across the table. "So, why am I here?"

"I wanted to spend a lunchtime with my best friend. That's allowed, isn't it?"

"Yeah, right." She smirked. "I'm sure this has nothing whatsoever to do with my new housemate."

"Nothing at all."

"Sure. So, how's life in James' world?"

I smiled. "So, how are things going with Lydia?"

"Good," she said, lighting up a cigarette. I wrapped my coat a little tighter, bracing my collar against the breeze. Our coffees arrived and I sipped at mine while Rebecca took long deep drags, puffing smoke all over me. I'd have vastly preferred to sit inside, away from the wind and passers-by, but Rebecca's nicotine habit put paid to that.

"Spit it out, James, what do you want? It must be killing you to take a day off from the gym."

"I'm an interested friend, curious as to how things are working out. Since it's been weeks already, I imagine you must have some news."

"Have you asked *her*?"

"We *work* together, our conversation generally revolves around *work* things."

"Your choice, I'm sure," she said, then shot me a grin. "You want her, don't you?"

I felt the irritation rising, the desire to shake Rebecca by her intuitive little shoulders pulsing through my temples.

"She's a colleague, which makes her both off limits and disgustingly unattractive."

"I don't blame you, by the way. She's nice. Funny… smart…sexy as hell."

"Can't say I've noticed."

"Oh, *please*. Fuck off with your shit, James." She leant over the table, still wafting smoke at me. "You could have come over, you know, like a normal person, rather than drag me halfway across the city to entertain your private investigator fetish."

"You're trying my patience, Rebecca. Like I said, I wanted to see *you*."

"You could have seen me last night. People have been asking after you… pussies to be spanked, tears to be shed… it's not like big, bad Masque to stay away. Where have you been, anyway?"

"Busy."

"And when are you coming back?"

"When I feel like it."

"Please tell me you finally shot your load in some tight little pussy somewhere? Praise the Lord!"

I met her eyes, conveying my irritation without need of words. "Is she over her heartache?"

"Lydia? She seems to be but it's hard to know for sure. She's almost as private as you, *almost*."

"No sign of reconciliation?"

"Doubt it. From the bits I've heard he sounds like a wet-blanket jerk. She could do a lot better."

"Seems she'll be staying, then." A strange mixture of horror and relief washed over me. It sickened my stomach so much I felt the urge to retch.

"We can hope. I'd sure miss her perky little ass in the mornings." She caught me in her dirty eyes, a sly smile twitching at her mouth. "She's great, James, really great."

I let out a sigh. "So, are you going to talk, or not? I could still catch the gym..."

"Let me see... Lydia Marsh... twenty-three, from Warwick. Tall, dark hair, green eyes, perky little ass... project manager for Trial Run Software Group, you may have heard of them?" I checked my watch pointedly. "Fine!" she laughed. "Her ex sounds a douche, conservative to the extreme, I'm surprised she wasn't the one to fuck around. She must be a fucking saint. I haven't heard him calling, but I gather he's been round her friend Steph's. That's her *only* friend by the way, and she's a class-A fucking idiot. She's only been round once and turned her nose up the entire fucking time."

"Any family?"

"Only child. No daddy from what I can gather."

"Mother?"

"Now, there's a story. I've overheard bits and pieces. Her mother sounds like a real bloodsucker."

"Go on..."

"I'm pretty damn certain she's into drink, and I'm also pretty damn certain Lydia bails her out often."

"How so?"

"Money... support... a sympathetic ear. For all her tough-girl attitude, I think our Lydia's pretty soft. Oh, and get this, she hasn't even told her mother about the break up. I heard her promising to pass on a hello to the lovely Stuart Dobson."

"They don't sound close."

"One way street, for sure. Urgh, victims give me the heebies. I'm telling you now, shit's gone down there. I suspect her mother's crap has screwed her up good." She took a pause, looking at me. "Oh, one more thing. She has scars, James. Self-harm."

"She told you that?"

"She doesn't need to. I'd know them a mile off."

"Whereabouts?"

"Arms, the ones that I've seen. Neat little cuts, wrist to elbow. They're faint, definitely old, but they're there all the same. You'd never notice if you didn't know what you were looking for, but, you know, skin's my thing."

"Intriguing."

"Anyway, she's a model housemate. Clean, tidy and thoroughly well-mannered. She drinks too much coffee and lives on her laptop checking out goddamn work shit 24/7, can't you do something about that? She needs a life. She also needs sex. Hot, filthy, steamy, disgusting fucking sex to loosen her up a bit. She's old way before her time. Maybe you could help her with that, too?"

"I'm not even going to justify that with an answer."

"Whatever you say. I'll give it a shot if you won't, see if she's got any bi tendencies lurking beneath the surface," she grinned. "I've been holding off, but if you aren't interested..."

"I'm *not* interested."

"Suit yourself."

"Knock yourself out, Rebecca. I hope she tastes sweet."

"She's submissive, by the way."

Her eyes challenged me, baiting for a reaction. I didn't give her one, just sipped my coffee whilst staring at the street beyond. Too close to work for this, too fucking close. The idea of prying eyes twitched at my fists.

"How can you possibly know that? Self-harm doesn't equal submission, Rebecca, not every time."

"I've been in this game long enough to know when someone needs a firm hand."

"It's based on fuck-all then."

She cackled at me, an edgy laugh which turned heads towards us. I gritted my teeth.

"She followed me into my room the other night, saw my personal stash of torture implements. You should have seen her face, James, half-apologetic, half-fascinated. I think it was probably the cane that grabbed her most."

"Now you're just taking the piss."

"Yeah, I am, but only about the cane. In my humble experience I've come to know two kinds of control freak. Those like you with the desire to rule the world and everyone in it, and those like her. Control freak through necessity, not by nature. It's not her nature, James, I'm telling you. Something *made* her toughen up, tighten up, hell, probably grow the fuck up earlier than she should've done. Plus, she's a cutter, pain works for her. I bet you any money there's a dirty little girl under that shell, just waiting for someone to tear her open and put her back together again."

She paused in her little monologue, searching my face. "You'd like to see her scars, wouldn't you?"

"No," I lied.

"Oh well. I figured she might be your thing. I've never seen anyone more your type."

"And what is my type? Enlighten me."

"The eyes... Katreya-green, you could say." Another smirk from her, and I must have paled, mortified, staring at her like she was some kind of ghost whisperer. "I do *know* you, James. I've seen you drunk, I've *heard* you drunk, when you're too bloody inebriated to keep your mask up, no pun intended. Besides, Rachel told me years ago, bemoaning the fact she had blue eyes, not green."

"Rachel should've kept her mouth as tight as her pussy. Katreya has nothing to do with anything."

"If you say not. Is that why you suggested she move in? Seriously?"

"Lydia needed a room, you needed a housemate. End of story."

"You hate how well I know you, don't you? Admit it, you hate it."

I called the waiter and asked for the bill. Rebecca didn't seem that surprised, just gathered up her cigarettes and made ready to leave.

"You try my patience to the point of violence, Mistress Raven, but I wouldn't have you any other way. Stay, get yourself lunch since I dragged you out of Camden." I handed her a twenty before I made my exit, stooping down low to ruffle her hair and land a kiss on her forehead.

She tilted her head up, one eyebrow raised wickedly. "I mean it, James. I'll try my hand if you won't."

"I wish you all the luck in the world. I hope she's your new bitch, I really do. A Lydia-Cara ménage à trois sounds exactly up your street."

"Now you're talking."

"I'll see you again soon."

She spun in her seat to watch me up the road. "When?"

I could almost feel the roll of her eyes at my lack of response.

I KEPT MY EYES FOCUSED ON FRANK AS HE DELIVERED HIS MONTHLY motivational spiel. The super-efficient Lydia Marsh pulled at my gaze, wedged in between some girls from admin. I tasked myself to blank her out, forget all about the ripples in the tight mauve shift dress she was wearing. The room was heaving. Lydia was five seats down to my right, squeezed against the table by the guys from sales. I caught them chancing glances over her shoulder, straining for a hint of cleavage.

Lydia always bit her lip when concentrating. I'd noticed it weeks earlier, and every fucking time since. It tormented me daily, that tense little mouth. I could feel her doing it now, sense the tap, tap, tap of her pen against her chin. My mood took a turn for the worse.

"...as you all know, James and Lydia have done a grand job on phase one of the WHM project, we're ahead of schedule and due to go live with the accounts module within the fortnight. They've already recommended us to Salmons, the big personal injury lawyers up in Warwick..."

I'd already heard all this, of course. I cast my eyes around the room, soaking up all the congratulatory smiles from well-meaners. My gaze returned to Lydia, her glittering eyes beaming with pride as they locked onto mine. I granted her the slightest nod. It burst her bubble, and she looked back to her notes as I turned away.

"...Stephen Bryant will be heading to Salmons in a week or two to deliver the first demo. With a fair wind we'll have another top 250 client before the year is done..."

I zoned out.

My balls felt heavy as lead, aching with the need to fuck like a beast. I craved the salty tang of tears, straight from a broken woman's eyes, her tight little cunt mine to abuse. *She's submissive, you know.* Fuck you, Rebecca, just fuck you. *I bet you any money there's a dirty little girl hiding under that shell.*

"...anything to add, James?"

The room looked at me, and I looked blankly at Frank. He was smiling his goofy smile, waiting for me to join in his self-congratulating love fest.

"You've covered it, Frank."

"Great, well, if there's nothing else…" The clock loomed towards end of play, the weekend beckoning. Nobody said a word. "See you on Monday, everyone."

I stayed in place as the room vacated, streams of people filing out like good little soldiers. I stretched my legs under the table, struggling to alleviate the ache in my groin. It didn't work.

The door swung shut behind the stragglers, leaving just the hum of the projector and my delectable project manager. She came closer, leaning over my shoulder to hand me a file. For the briefest of moments her perky little rack grazed my shoulder and my dick leapt to attention, straining towards her with only a flimsy table top for camouflage. The pale swell of her tits was a magnet, the sloping V of her neckline revealing two perfect handfuls. She had two tiny freckles on her right breast. I wondered for a long moment whether they'd match the colour of her nipples. No, her nipples would be dusky pink. Round and ripe and tender. Strawberry buttons on creamy white skin.

"I wanted to give you this."

Her scent knocked me senseless. Black Cherry. She'd applied her perfume like an amateur, carelessly thick on her wrists and no-doubt rubbed to shit, but still my mouth watered. My pulse beat in stereo, both in my temples and my cock. I battled the impulse to tear the fabric from her wrist, hot with the need for scars against my tongue. I forced myself to scan the first few lines of her document.

"Case Management stages for WHM? Already? We won't need these until phase two, it's an inefficient use of your time."

She pierced me with offended eyes. "I did it *after* work, James. Extra-curricular. I'd love to know what you think."

"I leave in ten minutes."

She smiled nervously, her mouth just inches from my nose. "Sure, well, there's no rush."

"Then why give it me now?"

"I was just, um. It was ready."

I flicked through the pages. She'd written a whole fucking tome. "I'll schedule some time next week."

"Oh, okay," she said. I could taste her disappointment.

"Did you expect I'd do it now? I have engagements after five."

"No, not right now. I was just thinking maybe you'd like to come over at some point. See Bex, and me, and we could do it then, or not. Maybe this weekend?"

"I'm busy."

"Yeah, of course, sorry, short notice. It was just a thought. You haven't been over, I thought you might like to see her." She smiled to lighten her words.

"I saw Rebecca today."

Her cheeks flushed pink. "Oh? Sorry, my mistake. I didn't realise."

"Why would you?"

"I guess I wouldn't. We don't really speak outside of work talk. I thought you coming over might re-break the ice."

"I hardly speak to anyone, Lydia, work or no. There's no ice to re-break."

"We spoke in Brighton…"

"Yes, we did."

"...and then nothing. Did it make you feel awkward?"

I watched her unashamedly, revelling in her discomfort. "Why would Brighton have made me feel awkward?"

"I'm not sure."

"You think I'm embarrassed? That I regret asking if your ex managed to get you off?"

"No... yes... do you regret it?" She smoothed her hair behind her ear.

"No."

She looked so uncharacteristically unsure.

"If I overstepped the mark or anything, I'm sorry."

"You have nothing to apologise for." Fuck, now my cock was twitching.

"Just, in Brighton..."

I forced myself over to reason.

"Lydia, we're colleagues. We work well together, do we not?"

"Yeah, really well. I really enjoy working with you..."

"Good. Then all's well."

"I guess there's no issue, then." Her tone was too bright, fake. "You never let me thank you, for Rebecca, either, not really. She's great."

"No thanks necessary." I closed her file, sliding it amongst a pile of others destined for my office.

She took the hint, retreating with just a smile and closing the door behind her.

It was only when she was safely out of eyeline that I retrieved her paperwork, placing it safe in my briefcase for the way home.

CHAPTER 6
Lydia

I WISHED THE UNDERGROUND PLATFORM WOULD SWALLOW ME UP. Blown out by James Clarke, so totally and utterly. I'd hardly be able to look at him ever again. What an idiot. *Hey, James, fancy hanging out sometime, check out my project notes?* Idiot. I stepped onto the train, wedged amongst all the other commuters battling through rush hour. This crush *thing*, whatever it was, was getting ridiculous. Yeah, James Clarke looked good in a suit, yeah, he was smart, and dedicated, and mysterious, and really goddamn talented and so infuriatingly in control of everything it turned my legs to jelly. But so what? Blown out. Time to let it go. I'm good at that.

I really thought I was onto something, really believed we'd had a *moment* in Brighton, whatever that even means. I figured moving in with Bex might be the start of a friendship, or at least the chance to have a conversation outside of work, but nothing. He barely even spoke to me, no questions, no chat about Rebecca, or how life was going, no anything. He'd asked once. *Once.* Weeks ago. I figured maybe he was awkward, maybe we'd overstepped the mark in Brighton, maybe, maybe, goddamn maybe. Who even cared?

I'd asked him over, he'd said no. Not interested. Not in me, not in a friendship. I'd just have to forget about it, just like everyone else in the office that had ever fancied a shot and got nowhere. Hell, it's not like I hadn't got over worse.

It was rebound, of course it was rebound. I probably wouldn't have even done it when it came to it. Work flings are never, ever, ever a good idea. Ever. Just ask Stuart. I wondered fleetingly how he was doing without me. He'd been round to Steph's a few times, desperate apparently, begging to know where I was. He was worried, he said, worried I'd be cutting myself to shit, no doubt. He needn't have been. It felt so far away now, my time with him. Like someone else had lived through the whole thing and I'd been asleep underneath it all. Strange. Maybe one day I'd need therapy, cry it all out and start popping the Prozac. Better to keep it repressed, and keep looking for my perfectly-healthy rebound fling. I mentally erased James Clarke from the list. I'd have to find a new crush now, someone else to capture my imagination.

James had been right in Brighton, Stuart didn't get me off, not really. It had taken James' questioning to make me realise, but realise I had. I'd been giving Stuart a helping hand for as long as I could remember, and eventually I'd lost track of what was fake and what was real. I needed more than that, something hotter, dirtier, grittier. Something all-consuming and wild. Something crazy. Something *real*. Something like the James Clarke of my fantasies. The James Clarke who told me he vents in the bedroom. The thought had whirred around my brain ever since. He was big. Big enough to throw me around like a little doll and use me any which way he wanted. Yeah, sure he would, Mr Perfect. Real life James Clarke was probably as corporate in the bedroom as he was out of it. I consoled myself with that thought.

Bex was already in when I got home, propped in the kitchen with the stereo on, playing thumping tunes I didn't know.

"Hey, Lyds, good day?"

I gave her a sigh. "So-so."

She eased me aside for a path into the fridge, pulling out a bottle of cold white. "Just what the doctor ordered."

I took a glass, let her fill me a large one. "Good idea."

"So what's with your shitty day? James being a nit-picking asshole?"

"He's not that bad," I lied. "He mentioned he'd seen you today."

"That's a turn up. Getting anything from that guy's like milking a rock."

"Tell me about it."

"Don't take it to heart."

I drank my wine. "I don't get him."

"Nobody does."

"You do."

"Sometimes," she smiled. "Did you give him your super-duper project file?"

"Yeah, he said we'll look at it next week."

"Next week?! So much for beavering like a crazy to get that done."

"It wasn't compulsory."

"I hope he was grateful."

"Can you even imagine him with a grateful face?" I grinned at her, loosening up. "It's my own fault, working too hard on something that doesn't mean anything."

"Are you talking about the project file, or about James?"

"The project file!" I said. "Have you been drinking?"

"A few in the studio earlier." Her eyes glinted at me. "He's hot, right?"

"He's attractive."

"And a weirdo... He likes you, Lyds, or he wouldn't work with you."

I finished my drink. "He's private, I get that."

"Sheesh, yeah. It'll take a bloody lifetime for you two to get to know each other, Private and Privater hanging out in Private-ville."

"We aren't hanging out anywhere, it's all about work."

"All work and no play makes James and Lydia very fucking dull indeed."

I laughed. "Am I dull? Really?"

"Nah, just... *focused*."

"That's dull, isn't it?"

"No... yes... a little. But hey, if it floats your pretty little boat."

"It doesn't. I need to get out." I rubbed my temples, willing the blow-out memory away. I left Bex to it, all ready to go ditch the work outfit and veg in my PJs but she called me back.

"Say, Lyds. I'm off down the Dev tonight, if you fancied coming. It's cool there, they even pour pentagrams on your Guinness."

"Pentagrams on your Guinness? Doesn't sound like I'd fit in too well."

"You'd be fine."

I pondered in the doorway, my bedroom cold and still and empty without that bloody project file to keep me occupied. "What would I wear?"

"Little black dress, I'm sure you've got one."

I weighed it up, back and forth in my mind, empty room or goth pub, empty room or goth pub. "I could come for a bit."

The smile on her face told me she hadn't expected it. Was I really that dull? Maybe I was.

Time to put dull, boring Lydia in the bin where she belonged.

Bex had a nudity habit — the constant desire to wander around with little to no clothes on without even the slightest hint of self-consciousness. I'd grown surprisingly used to it, and didn't even flinch when she appeared stark naked and dripping wet, holding up two almost identical looking dresses for my opinion. Her tattoos stopped at her shoulders, leaving her pale skin untouched and unblemished to the belly button, where a Celtic pattern would have swirled down to her pubic hair, if she'd had any. She didn't. I pointed to the dress on the left, a black PVC number with spikes all down the front.

"You sure?" she said. "Spikes not buckles?"

"Spikes. Definitely. You wore buckles last week."

"Well remembered." She looked me up and down, then scowled at my feet. "Lovely dress, wrecked by the footwear. What size are you?"

I looked at my cute little heels, wondering how they could possibly be so offensive. "Seven." She threw me over a pair of obscenely tall knee-highs. "Really?! I'll fall."

"I'll hold you up. Trust me, you'll look hot."

"You going to try and set me up with some sexy, goth stud?" I laughed.

"If you want."

I sighed, bending down to zip up the new boots. "I'm not sure quite what I want."

"You *want* sex. A filthy fuck is a tonic for almost anything, I find."

"I wouldn't know. Things went a little stale with Stu after a few years."

"Then you definitely want sex." She shimmied into her dress, pulling it up tight. Her cleavage looked amazing, like some kind of porn star rack. She layered on her make-up and laced up her boots, then checked and re-checked herself in the mirror from every angle. The doorbell rang, a noise I'd never actually heard. "That'll be Cara."

"Your girlfriend?"

"My sub. She's heard all about you. I'll leave her waiting awhile, she knows the drill."

"Your sub?"

"Submissive. She's kind of like a girlfriend without the girlfriend bit. Sex, basically. She likes me to hurt her."

My mouth turned dry, images of her bedroom flashing before my eyes. "Hurt her, like spank her?"

"Spank her, whip her, paddle her... make her cry then kiss it all better again," she laughed. "Never tried it?"

I shook my head. "Stuart wasn't really that way inclined."

"And what about you?"

"The avenue never really presented itself."

"Shame." She waited a few more seconds, fastened up a studded collar. "Oh, by the way, Cara calls me Raven. Most people do."

"Raven... right." I assigned it to memory.

"You can be Cat. You have cat's eyes."

"Can't I just use my own name?" I said. "Is it some kind of special code or something? Is Cara's name really Cara?"

"No, it's Penelope, but don't tell her I told you. You'll soon get into the name thing. Cat suits you anyway."

My stomach lurched as I recalled where I'd heard that before.

CARA WAS PRETTY LITTLE CREATURE, WITH GORGEOUS DARK HAIR and chocolate brown eyes. She stood waiting in the doorway, knees tight together and head slightly bowed. She had stockings on under her black dress, high enough to see the lace tops. Her skin was goose-pimpled from the cold, arms wrapped tight together under her bolero.

"Cara, you can look up now. This is Cat. Cat, this is Cara."

"Pleased to meet you, Cat." Cara pulled me in for a hug, delicate and light, as she was herself. I smiled at her, trying to think about anything other than her naked ass getting a spanking. I joined them on their way down the street. Rebecca took hold of Cara's hand, a possessive gesture with rough twisting fingers. I couldn't take my eyes off the way they moved together, Cara drifting along so meekly at her side.

The Devonshire Arms was a teeming sea of black. We eased our way to the bar, and while Rebecca whispered not-so-sweet somethings in Cara's ear I stared up at the mosaic of band posters on the ceiling, a mass of colour at odds with the rest of the place. I laughed at the idea of Steph and Stuart finding me in here. Straight-laced Lydia, workaholic, hanging out in a goth bar with two fetish-loving bi girls.

"What's so funny?" Rebecca asked, leaning in close over the music.

"I can't even imagine Stu's face if he saw me now."

"Would you swap? Old life for new?" she asked, fluttering long fake lashes at me.

I pictured myself back in my old apartment, curled up on the sofa in front of the TV, psyching myself up for the weekly, lights-off sex session.

"You know what?" I said. "I'm not so sure I would."

I relaxed into the ambience of the pounding tunes and the theatrics. Hair and make-up I'd never seen before, Mohicans and back-combing, and crimping and undercuts. Piercings and extensions and white, white faces. Rebecca disappeared to the bar to catch up with friends and Cara sidled a little closer, pulling me to her by my elbow.

"What do you think?"

I nodded. "It's pretty cool."

"We love it here," she smiled. "Are you a sub, too?"

I felt the first blooms of a flush. "No... well... I don't know..."

"Never tried?"

"My ex wouldn't have been up for it..."

"You got stuck with vanilla, hey? SUCKS!"

I turned to her, wine-confident and curious. "How long have you been into this stuff?"

"About six months serious. I met Raven in here, and she took me to Explicit. She introduced me to the scene."

"Explicit?"

"Our scene club in Soho. We go every week." Her eyes shone full of enthusiasm, and mischief. "You should come! You HAVE to! You can see for yourself!"

"I'm not so sure about that," I laughed. "What is it? Some kind of sex club?"

"A BDSM club, and yeah, people have sex, you know, but it's not creepy or anything, I promise, nobody's going to hit on you if you don't want it. Come on! Say you'll come!"

I remained non-committal. "Why do you do it? The pain thing I mean."

"Endorphins... adrenaline... fear... trust... the pleasure in letting go... submitting totally to another person. There's nothing else in the world... just you... and them. It's hard to explain. The right dom will know you better than you know yourself, like a God, playing you right on the edge, in the beautiful part of pain. There's this rush, when it hurts, and then a peace. It's so beautiful." Her eyes glazed over as she spoke, disappearing into another world. "Sorry, I'm probably making no sense. You'd have to try it to understand."

It made more sense than I'd like it to. Spidery itches and razorblade kisses. I took another swig of wine. "So, Raven's your dominant?"

"She's my mistress, yeah. There are a few others in Explicit I play with, but I belong to her."

Rebecca appeared behind Cara, wrapping her in possessive arms, and I watched transfixed as Cara turned to her, opening her mouth to welcome Rebecca's tongue. Their kiss was deep and wet, the dominant woman yanking Cara's hair until she melted to her touch, her back arching as Rebecca claimed more and more of her.

"Good girl, Cara," Rebecca purred. "I'll think you'll get the paddle this evening, make your pretty little ass all pink for me."

"Thank you, Mistress," Cara smiled. "I was just telling Cat about Explicit. She should come."

"I'm not sure Explicit is Cat's scene," Rebecca said. I caught the reluctance in her eyes.

"She won't know if she doesn't try."

"Enough now, Cara. Know your manners."

"Yes, Mistress."

It seemed the conversation was officially over. My regret at that fact surprised me.

I LAY IN BED, AS WIDE AWAKE AS I COULD EVER BE. I'D MADE MY excuses, vanishing out of sight while my housemate mauled her girlfriend just feet away. She'd pinned her the minute we landed through the door, forcing Cara over the kitchen worktops and hitching her dress up all the way to the waist. I'd seen a lot more than I probably should have, but neither seemed to give a shit, oblivious to my presence as Cara bucked against Rebecca's advances, yelping little whines as slaps landed hard in tender places.

Noises cut loud through the closed bedroom door. *Still. Quiet. Lower, Cara, bend fucking lower. Hold out your tits, Cara, nice and still. Those nipples need pain, baby, they need so much pain.* I tried not to listen, tried not to wonder what the hell was really happening in there, tried to think about anything but violent sex and how it would feel to be in Cara's shoes. I told myself I wouldn't like it, that Lydia Marsh is no submissive, she's too goddamn rigid for all that shit. I told myself I'd be too reserved, too self-conscious, too uptight. I told myself I didn't want to try it at all, but it was a lie. It *had* to be a lie, because I was burning up in my bed, clammy with nerves and adrenaline, and although I didn't want to face it, I was horny as hell.

Spread it for me, Cara, show me your tasty little pussy. Yeah, sweet girl, that's it, look how swollen you are. I'm gonna make you feel so good.

I kicked the covers away and stared at the ceiling. It didn't work. Nothing I did felt comfortable, not until I gave in to the urge and let my fingers wander between my thighs. I was wet, sodden through my knickers. I pulled the fabric aside enough to reach my clit and it felt so goddamn tender it took my breath away. I played quickly, desperate to orgasm, strumming my fingers as fast as I could just to lurch myself over the edge. I came harder than I had in years, jerking and wheezing out expletive streams of pent-up frustration. It felt raw, it felt right. It felt crazy fucking good.

I came down slowly, orgasm-high and floaty, ragged breath loud in the silence.

The silence.

Shit.

It was quiet enough to hear the footsteps outside my door.

CARA HAD GONE IN THE MORNING. I WRAPPED MY SATIN ROBE TIGHT around my waist and met Rebecca in the kitchen. She made me a coffee without prompting.

"Crazy night, huh?"

I smiled. "A little crazier than I'm used to."

"It gets a whole lot crazier than that."

She was already dressed for work, skinny black jeans and a tight red t-shirt. *Queen Bitch,* it said. She sure was.

"Cara didn't stay?"

She shook her head. "We rarely do the whole cuddle-through-the-night thing."

"I hope I didn't piss on your parade. You know, by being here."

"You can piss on my parade any day, baby. Just say the word." She cackled her trademark cackle.

"She seems nice."

"She's sweet... cute... uber-fuckable. Low tolerance though, life's a bitch."

"Low tolerance?"

"Can't take much of a beating. More a slap and tickle, it's nice, but sometimes a girl needs a little more from her sub."

I grinned at her. "Sounded more than a slap and tickle to me."

She put down her coffee, stared me out straight. "So, what did it sound like?"

I looked away, caught out. "I wasn't eavesdropping. It just carried, you know, through the wall."

"And how did it sound... through the wall?"

"It sounded pretty rough."

She stepped closer, and instinctively I shuffled back, bracing myself against the worktop. "The bed squeaks, by the way, in your room."

I'm sure I flushed crimson. "I.. um..."

She closed the gap, pushing against me to pin me to the counter. "We were right here. Cara arched back right where you are now while I sucked her little clit sore. Did you hear her come?"

"No..." I mumbled, eyes anywhere but on Rebecca.

"Shame," she breathed. "*I heard you.*" Long fingers on my thigh, teasing at the hem of my robe. I could hardly breathe. "What were you thinking about?"

"I wasn't... I don't know..." I said.

Her fingers burned my skin. "Do you wonder what it feels like?" She smiled, mischievous.

"Maybe," I admitted, daring to laugh a bit. "Shit, sorry, how embarrassing. I'm not used to this stuff."

She stepped away, clearing a space. "Turn around and bend over."

My stomach lurched. "Sorry?"

"Bend over, hands flat on the side."

My eyes must have been huge, boring into hers, but she didn't flinch or falter, just shifted position so her weight was all on one hip. My mouth turned dry, nerves sizzling. "I don't know…"

"Bend over, Lydia, stop being so fucking reserved."

Shit. Shit. Shit. My body moved, unwilled, and suddenly my chest was flat to the worktop, palms against the tiles. I heard her position herself to my rear. It tickled as she raised the hem of my robe, hitching it up over my hips. I bit my lip, scorching with self-consciousness… and something else. She ran her fingernails over my ass.

"Ready?" she asked. Her tone was low, insistent. I nodded.

She slapped me hard and I jumped a little, settling down just before she landed another. It sounded worse than it felt, the bite of her palm morphing quickly into a gentle burn. She hit me quick, fast slaps over and over, and soon I stopped jumping and just felt. My breath quickened, the burning of my skin seeming to bloom under her touch. It felt good… great… it felt amazing.

She stopped a moment, long enough to trail a finger down the crease of my ass. "Want more?"

I nodded again, gritting my teeth through the embarrassment.

"I knew it. You're a submissive, alright. Only I don't think a slap's enough for you."

I wrenched my head back over my shoulder in time to see her delve into a drawer. She pulled out a fish slice, and slapped it against her palm over and over – a strange metallic thwack.

"I'm not sure about this…" I said, shifting on my feet but not breaking position.

"I am."

My heart raced, brain pleading no, while my body pleaded yes. I didn't move.

She hit me fucking hard. I leapt up, jigging around with a smarting ass.

"Settle down," she said, simply.

I looked back at her like she was crazy, right until the pain smoothed into a tingle, a really nice tingle, like spidery itches in satin boots, dripping warm treacle over my skin, and there beyond the pain I got a glimpse of the calm place... the place the itches lead to. I settled back against the worktop, hands back against the tiles.

"I fucking knew it," she said, and landed me another. This time I flinched but didn't jump up, and she hit me again, and again after that in the same spot. Pain then tingle, pain then tingle, over and over, and soon I was groaning and whimpering and lost in this crazy sea of self-consciousness and confusion, where the only thing I really knew was that I didn't want to move, not for anything. I just wanted more.

She ran her fingers over me, squeezing tender flesh. I wriggled at her touch, fighting the urge to spread my legs and show her how wet I was. I don't think I needed to. I'm pretty sure Rebecca already knew, well before I did.

"Beautiful," she said. "Shit, I've gotta go to work."

She dropped the fish slice on the side and gave me a pinch, leaving me bent-over, bare-assed and totally shell-shocked, with a face that most likely matched the scarlet of the kitchen. I pulled myself together, yanking down my robe and choking back the shock like it never happened.

Rebecca grabbed her bag and keys and checked her make-up one last time, and I watched her as though she was some strange alien creature that I hadn't spent the past month living with. She turned in the doorway before she left, a huge grin lighting up her face.

"Lydia Marsh, I think we have us a pain slut. Maybe Cinderella shall go to the ball after all."

CHAPTER 7
James

My mobile buzzed in my pocket. Text message.

"*Do you want her or not? Last call.*"

Writing my response was easy. Sending not so much. "*Not.*"

I counted the down the seconds until the second buzz.

"*I don't believe you.*"

"*Believe whatever you want.*"

I cast the phone aside and returned to the paperwork in front of me. Lydia's proposal was virtually faultless. The girl had skill. The phone started up again, rattling against the desk top. It disturbed my pen alignment. I put them straight again before viewing the message.

"*Will I see you tonight?*"

"*No.*"

"*Definitely not?*"

"*Definitely not.*"

"*Positive?*"

"*Fucking hell, Rebecca. NO, you will not see me tonight.*"

A few minutes delay.

"*Spoilsport. Cara says she's forgotten what your palm feels like.*"

"*I very much doubt that.*"

I needed out of this Lydia Marsh shit. The suggestion that she move in with Rebecca had been a bad one. A rash decision made purely by my cock. Now she was there to stay, holed in tight with the only person I called a friend. I'd shit my own bed by courting a ridiculous fantasy. Bad form, James, bad fucking form.

Fuck no-one you know, and know no-one you fuck. I held on to my mantra daily, gripping it in white knuckles every time she entered my room, every time the ping of my email sounded with her name, every time she crossed my path in the fucking corridor.

She brought me coffee every fucking morning, just how I liked it. Just like we were friends, placing it on my desk with the same shy smile every motherfucking day. And the meetings, countless fucking hours of watching Lydia Marsh watching me, oblivious to the torment of her pretty green eyes. Lydia Marsh who didn't think I cared shit for her. It's better that way. Definitely better for me.

I'd given Explicit a wide berth for weeks. The club regulars dulled to grey once I'd seen the pain in Lydia's eyes. Even sweet little Cara, even Rebecca. What I'd seen in Lydia was real. Beautiful, hot, raw pain – her broken soul peeking out through the cracks in her armour for just one single helpless moment, and I'd seen it. I'd seen *her*. Even if I bleached my retinas she'd still be there, sobbing her hard little heart out in the kitchen.

I slammed the file shut and smoothed down the edges. Perfect order. Just how I liked it.

I DIDN'T TELL BEX I'D CHANGED MY PLANS. SHE'D FIND OUT FOR herself soon enough.

In my craving for a distraction I'd done the unthinkable. I'd pulled out the little black book. The *virtual* little black book, of course, full of email addresses and online dating profiles all tagged together nicely with photos of my encounters. I'd checked them out one by one, browsing for the perfect Lydia Marsh antidote. Several were off the radar, status *relationship* or no longer active at all, others I'd red flagged as emotional no-gos. I only hit one lucky jackpot. A submissive known as Violet from over in Kent, far enough away to avoid 'just passing' or suggestions of coffee, but close enough to make it in on short notice. She'd been good last time around. Nicely experienced. Really fucking dirty but a little too fucking keen. Still, we'd passed the six month cool-off, she was green light status all over again.

I'd dropped her a message, making it perfectly clear what I wanted from her. She'd taken the bait, just like I'd hoped. I used the opportunity to check out Masque's profile. It was still relevant. Sparsely populated, unrecognisable and entirely untraceable.

Interests - Everything. Every. Fucking. Thing. No vanilla.

Seeking - Sex only. Casual encounters.

Not in a hotel bed, with the cute little coffee trays and in-room satellite TV. Not in some random woman's living room surrounded by domestic trinkets and family photos, and sure as hell not in mine. One venue only. Public, casual, impersonal. No strings, no questions, just filthy rough sex. They'd never even see my face.

It's amazing how many women want it that way.

I TOOK UP MY POSITION AT THE SHADOWY SIDE OF THE BAR, watching for my guest. I was invisible from the main entrance, well placed to enjoy her nervousness as she looked around the room for me, jittery and unsure as the stepped amongst the club regulars. I saw Violet's hair first, redder than I remembered, piled up high on her head in a vintage wave, her long neck sloping down into narrow collarbones. She was older than me, hitting just the other side of forty and blessed with both a high pain threshold and a deep-seated desire to be abused in public. She was a gusher, with a pussy long ripened for punishment, conditioned for the hard stuff by two rough labours and a special-interest side income. Pay-per-minute webcam, fucking herself raw with any crazy implement her public paid for. It was her edge over the younger competition. Good news for her bank balance and good news for me. She'd take my whole fucking fist without so much as a whimper. Dirty bitch. My cock twitched. Thank sweet Jesus for that.

I made my approach without speaking a word. She sensed my presence, turning to look up at me with hungry eyes.

"Masque, hi. I didn't think I'd see you again."

"Hello, Violet." I took hold of her chin, forcing her face from side to side as I checked her out at close quarters. "You look good."

"Not for long, sir, I'm sure."

I tipped my head to the main floor, to the cuffs hanging down from the ceiling centre stage. "I'm going to hurt you in the spotlight, for the whole club to see. Do you consent?"

She didn't even hesitate. "Yes, sir, thank you, sir."

"I'm going to fuck you up bad, do you understand?"

"Yes, sir." Her eyes lingered on mine, dark as night in the shadowy hollows of my mask. "Please, sir, if you would, please bruise me bad. My regulars would like that, sir, very much."

"And where would your regulars like to see these bruises?"

"Everywhere, sir."

"Tell me where, Violet. Where do you want me to hurt you?"

I watched her gulp, her chin still tight in my grip. "My ass, sir, and my thighs."

"And?"

"And my tits, sir, please… and please hurt my pussy, too."

"The regulars want to jack-off to your gaping, bruised cunt, do they?"

Colour bloomed right across her cheeks. "No, sir, that's just for me."

I couldn't help but smile at her.

"Good girl, Violet. Good girl. Let's get a drink."

Lydia

CRAZY, CRAZY, CRAZY, I'M FUCKING CRAZY.

I'd officially lost my mind, leaving the Dev at gone midnight to trail along with my new weirdo friends to their weirdo-wacko sex bar. All I really knew was that it was located in Soho. We took the Northern Line to Tottenham Court Road station, and I followed them in silence, my mouth dry as parchment as I tottered along behind in crazy high stilettos. I'd been the subject of a total makeover, dressed at Rebecca's whim for my debut appearance at sex club central. She'd laced me up tight in black leather, fastened me into fishnets and suspenders, then turned her attention to my make-up. Sweeping flicks all the way out from my eyes, burgundy lipstick and false lashes, with just the slightest hint of rouge. I didn't look like the usual fit-for-the-office Lydia at all, and I'd felt strangely well for it. At least I had back at the apartment. A change is as good as a rest, so they say.

My guides stopped outside a pair of unmarked wooden doors, and my nerves jangled around my stomach so hard I considered running, but Rebecca had my elbow locked tight in hers, no hope of escape. She knocked and two huge men stepped out, smiling in recognition once they caught sight of Bex and Cara.

Bex pulled me forward. "This is Cat. She's my guest tonight."

They waved us on through and I was in, just like that. We stopped at a shadowy red reception bar to leave our coats, handing them over to a skinny little creature with so many piercings I could hardly make out her features.

Rebecca grabbed my hand tight as she climbed the main staircase, stopping dead before we stepped through into the main club. "Remember your name, Cat. Lydia doesn't exist in this place."

I nodded, then followed her in, looking this way and that as I struggled to orientate myself. It was a bigger space than I'd imagined, a gulf of standing area lined with dimly lit seating. Plush booths lined with rich scarlet brocade and occupied by small clusters of people, some of which appeared to be particularly well acquainted. I tried not to pry, forcing my eyes to remain on Raven alone as she led the way. The main bar was a crazy spectacle, flashing bright in a neon hue – all pinks and greens and electric blues, with bar staff to match. I sat down beside Raven, noticing Cara following up the rear, saying her hellos to the groups in the booths.

"Well?" Raven asked. "Are we staying?"

"Yeah. But I'll need a large glass of something."

"I'm sure we can sort that out." She leant in close, breathing into my ear and directing my gaze with a finger. "Toilets are over in that corner. There's a ladies', a men's and an anybody's'. So take your pick when you go. There's also a wet room off to the side, but I wouldn't recommend you head in there unless you want a face full of piss. It's where the edge players get it on." She gestured further along. "Main stage area. They have a selection of cuffs from the ceiling, with an electric wrench for suspension play. There's also an X-frame propped at the back and sometimes they'll set up a flogging bench if it looks as though it's needed. Mainly the stage is for the hardcore players, so be warned, things really can get fucking hardcore up there. You'll soon know about it if someone's starting up a scene, they'll fire up the main spotlights and turn it into a show. Don't be surprised to see people getting it on from the sidelines, it's like real-time porn, only better if you're into the whole pain-pleasure thing. Nothing like the sound of a screaming sub in live audio."

"Will there be a show tonight?"

"All depends who's in. Sometimes I go up there, but *I'm* babysitting *you* this evening." She winked. "As you can see, in terms of general ambience some of the seating is in darkness, some spotlit, depending on your penchant for exhibitionism. There's a chill-out room to the back of the main floor, but there's not all that much chilled out about it. Lastly, down the corridor you have the playrooms. That's where a lot of the fun and games happen."

"Playrooms?"

"Yeah, for smaller scenes. They have a variety of furniture in them... benches, racks, cuffs, frames, cages... this is a members only club, and each member is assigned a locker off to the side of playroom one." She jangled some silver keys in front of my face. "People tend to collect what they need and choose a room for their scene. Some are big enough for multiple pairs or groups, others more for one on one play. They all have internal windows, so you'll get spectators looking in, but playroom four has blinds if you want a bit of extra privacy." She smiled. "I'm not sure you'll need to know the etiquette, but an open door means people are welcome inside and will sometimes be invited to join in. Closed door means watch but don't enter, unless you're in a separate scene and want to use the free equipment. Everything gets hosed down and sterilised at the end of every night, but we're all pretty responsible and we clean up after ourselves. There are wipes in every playroom, and a selection of rubbers. Safe sex is standard here, this isn't a dive."

"Nice to know," I smiled.

"There are some toys available for sale under the bar, vibrators and butt plugs and shit like that, as well as batteries, lube and bondage tape. Sometimes they stock rope as well, but you can't count on it. If you have any issues there are always hostesses about." She pointed at a tall woman in white PVC leaning against the wall to the side of the bar. "That's Delicious, she's on duty tonight. If you ever get any problems, unwanted attention or some kind of medical issue they're always around to help, and they hang out with the newbies if they feel nervous. You're with us, of course, so it's not so relevant to you."

"And how much does this cost? To be a member, I mean?"

"Why, you thinking of joining?" she grinned. "It depends. If you want to come every week you pay for VIP membership, which is four hundred a month, with a fifty percent discount for a partner if you have one. You can also invite one guest a month in addition. Occasional members pay five hundred for the year, but they also pay another hundred on the door each visit, and don't get a discount for partners."

"So you pay four hundred every month to come here?"

"Sure do. Why do you think I needed a housemate?" she nudged me in good humour. Cara slid over a couple of drinks, cocktails from the looks, bright blue and topped with an umbrella. I mouthed thanks.

"There you have it," Raven rounded off. "Explicit in a nutshell. Everyone uses a name here, for privacy, hence the Cat thing. Oh, and there's a no-photography rule, things like that. There's an official list of dos and don'ts but everyone generally knows what they are. Anyone leery gets asked to leave pretty sharpish, so generally it's ok to relax and it's always ok to say no if you don't want to do something. You'll get offers, I'm sure."

"How long have you been coming here?"

"Five years or so. I started coming here with Jaz, but she doesn't come so much these days. Any more questions, Sherlock?"

"I think you've covered it. Now to see how long I can hack it without running home safe to suburbia."

"Suburbia? You're talking about Camden as suburbia?! You're getting wild in your old age, I'm sure there's a deviant little Cat in there somewhere, after all."

"I guess this is the place to find out." I raised my glass for a three-way toast. "To new experiences."

"We're always up for that," she smiled.

MAYBE IT WAS THE DRINK. MAYBE IT WAS THE TENSION IN THE ROOM – the shadowy glimpses of couples making it all the way to last base without a care in the world for who saw them. Maybe it was the vicarious buzz from the people heading to the playrooms for more hardcore action. I can't say for sure what made me so excited when the spotlights on the main floor lit up, but my heart raced in my chest so damn hard I thought it would thump right out through my ribcage.

"Action," Raven said, giving me a hefty nudge. "Let's go."

Alcohol made me brave enough to follow her lead, holding

onto her for dear life as she wove her way amongst the spectators. Cara pressed in close behind, pointing out a spare pew in the shadows with a decent view of the stage. My jelly legs were relieved to be seated, wedged between my two guides to watch the action unfold. I dared to cast my eyes around the other viewers, but most were cloaked in darkness beyond the glare of the lights. I couldn't deny the adrenaline. The whole room was buzzing, and me along with it.

"Who's up?" Cara whispered to Raven behind my back.

"No idea," she replied. "Maybe Tyson and Trixie?"

"They're in playroom two," Cara said. I saw Raven shrug, then turn her attention back to the floor as a woman took her position under the spotlights. She was pretty. Older than any of us, maybe early forties. A shapely redhead with her hair piled high, trussed up tight in a simple black PVC dress. She was breathing deeply, staring out beyond the crowd at the darkness. There was a serenity to her. A calmness in her stance despite her agitated breath. She swayed gently in her own little trance, her arms graceful like a swan, oblivious to all around her.

A shadow appeared at her rear, looming large through dark drapes. A man. A huge fucking man. Electric nerves pulsed on sight of him, fear and excitement mashing into one heady concoction. A ripple went through the crowd, an excited murmur that fizzed up my spine.

The man was as toned as a gladiator, ripped and raw and ready to fight. My eyes bowed down to his feet on instinct, and slowly I worked my way back up. Heavy black boots. Tight black denim over sculpted legs, hanging low enough to showcase the muscular V of his hips. His abs looked forged from steel, tense and tight under bronzed skin, and his chest, oh my God, his chest. My eyes widened in recognition. A huge tattoo in jet black, curling all the way around his ribs. A multi-headed beast, tribal and malevolent, dancing on his flesh as though it owned every part of him. So *this* was the man with the chimera, the design on Rebecca's wall. The design I'd looked at every fucking day since I moved in. My eyes shot to his face, searching for the identity of the man who wore such a mark, but there were no answers to be found there. The man was masked, most of his features hidden behind black leather. His eyes were only shadows, dark and sinister, and his hair was slicked back to his scalp, as dark as the rest of him.

I had no idea who the fuck this man was, but I'd never seen anyone so beautiful.

Cara broke my trance, leaning right across me to speak with Raven. "I thought you said he wasn't coming?"

Raven put a finger to her mouth to hush her submissive, and I caught a flash in her eyes that meant business. Cara sat back in position, content to let the conversation drop, but me not so much. I leant into the silenced Cara, putting my mouth right to her ear.

"Who is he?"

"Masque," she whispered. "He's a God here... seriously hardcore. He's so fucking dirty bad wrong."

"Dirty bad wrong?"

She smiled at me. "Dirty. Bad. Wrong. So wrong,... but so right."

Raven grabbed my elbow, pulled my ear to her mouth. "We should go now."

My stomach lurched. "Why?"

"This isn't for you. We need to go."

My words were out at lightning speed. "I want to stay."

"You don't know what you're getting into. This scene, here, right now, really isn't for you."

"I don't care. I want to stay."

We stared each other out for long seconds, and I felt the uncomfortable urge to plead like a child. She looked away as the man known as Masque made a move. He pressed up against his woman and she melted into him, relaxing her head against his shoulder in complete compliance to his will. He wrapped his arms around her, tugging down the zip at her breast. She was surprisingly heavy-chested, loose flesh hanging low against her ribs. I felt my cheeks burn as I watched the path of his hands. He took the zip all the way down, offering her naked body to a roomful of eyes. She was shaved, like Raven, and even from my position I could see how wet she was. I shifted in my seat, burning but fascinated. She looked so raw, so vulnerable in her nakedness before the crowd. Pinned bright in the spotlights, every part of her bared to the world. She looked so real, so authentic. She looked *free*. My mouth dried to paper.

Raven leant in again. "We're leaving straight after. No arguments."

I nodded.

Masque tossed the woman's dress aside, then trailed his fingers down her arms. Her skin goose-pimpled, and she let out a moan as he took hold of her wrists, raising them high above her head. She held them as instructed, not even flinching as he fastened her into the leather cuffs hanging from the ceiling. Her breathing quickened as he retreated to control the hoist, winching the chains up tight until her arms were stretched and spread above her. He returned to test the chains, pulling down on them to check their resilience. They took his weight easily. He pressed his lips against her ear, whispering words I couldn't hear. She spread her legs, giving more of her weight to the chains above, and he tapped his fingers against her thighs to indicate even wider. She did as he wished, gripping tight to the chains for support as she spread herself as far as her legs would go. He moved to her front, and she tilted her face up towards him, eyes still closed. Her lips parted in silent offering, and he moved in closer, teasing her mouth with the slightest touch of his. I heard a moan as she inched forward, straining for more. He gave her what she craved, a harsh, hungry kiss, all tongue and teeth. Her lipstick was smudged when he broke away, her lips full and puffy.

"He's a God, isn't he?" Cara whispered. I could only nod.

He took Red's breasts in rough hands, kneading her with brutal fingers. She had big nipples, dark and ripe, and huge areola, like saucers. She rocked into him, sucking in breath as he pinched her nipples. He twisted them, hard, and she flinched, biting down on her bottom lip as he twisted harder still. Finally she cried out and he lowered his head, sucking on her teat like a hungry baby. A hungry baby with teeth. She groaned and shifted in her chains, arching her back into him as he gobbled at her flesh.

"His teeth hurt so bad," Cara said. "He's a real biter." I felt her eyes on me as I shifted again in my seat. "Does he turn you on?"

"I... um... I'm not sure." I was lying and I knew it, a stranger to myself, compelled by alien desire.

"He'd do it to you, you know... I know he would," she smiled. "Do you want him? His pain feels so good."

Raven leant across, to yank at Cara's hair. "Enough," she hissed.

I focused back on the stage. Masque retreated behind the drapes, returning with a long length of cord which he hung loosely around Red's neck. He took a breast in his hand, and proceeded to bind her, loops of cord cutting in until her soft flesh turned hard, swollen with blood. He repeated his efforts with the other, then bound them together where they turned darker still, jutting out like two pink warheads. He grunted his approval, teasing and flicking her thickened nipples until Red was twitching on the spot.

"That feels so good," Cara breathed. "You wouldn't believe how amazing he makes that feel. You can come from that, you know, if it's done right. A nipple orgasm. He's done it to me."

"Cara!" Raven seethed. "One more word and I swear you'll be one sorry fucking bitch."

I heard soft squelches from a couple to our rear, the scent of sex heavy in my nose. Cara leant against my shoulder, positioning herself out of Raven's view. She whispered so quietly I could hardly hear her. "Play with yourself if you like. Everyone does... or we could do it for you." She placed a hand on my knee and I clamped my legs shut instinctively, embarrassment burning my face.

Masque upped the ante on stage, brutalising Red's swollen breasts. He slapped them hard, and loud. Hard enough to make Red whimper. She jerked under his assault, her head lolling back in pain, but she was smiling. He ceased his attack long enough to slide his hand between her legs, and she moaned like a whore, grinding herself against him. He played her for long seconds, and I saw his fingers disappear inside her, four of them. *Four.* I sucked in breath at the sight. More words in her ear, then she was nodding. A smile. Deep breaths, her chest rising and falling in anticipation of something. He retreated once again behind the drapes. I strained for sight of him.

"Here we go," Cara breathed again.

When Masque returned, he came armed. A collection of implements like the ones I'd seen in Raven's room. I recognised some of them. A flogger and a horse whip, and some wooden paddles that looked as thick as chopping boards. And a cane, a long, thick cane with a leather handle.

"The cane's his favourite," Cara murmured. "I can't take it though, hurts too much."

He brandished a flogger with long suede tails and knotted ends, flicking her back gently before starting up his momentum, big arcs over and over, building up speed until they connected. She moaned at the first hit, but relaxed into it, adjusting her weight to steady herself. I heard the swish as the tails hit, over and over. Sometimes they'd curl around her body to lash at the soft skin on her ribcage. She'd jerk then and hiss out all her breath. She began to rock in her chains, losing herself in the rhythm. She cried out as he changed target, whipping the flogger hard between her legs to bite at her pussy. She squealed when he caught her clit, clenching her legs tight against the assault.

He yanked her head back by her hair, his mouth at her ear. I caught his low bark, the most dangerous sound I'd ever heard.

"Your cunt is mine, Violet. *Mine.* Don't you dare fucking hide from me."

Her name ricocheted around my brain. *Violet.* She spread her legs wide again.

"I'm sorry, Master, I'm sorry."

"Good girl."

Another direct hit and this time she squealed like a banshee but didn't clench. Her knuckles turned white as she gripped the chains above her head, taking everything he dished out. He landed a particularly nasty blow and she really wailed, gulping in air like a fish as her knees trembled underneath her. Still, she didn't shield herself from him.

I felt heady, dizzy, reeling at both the scene before me and the pulse between my thighs. My hands felt clammy. *I* felt clammy.

Finally, he stepped forward enough to soothe her with his

fingers. She wheezed at his touch, murmuring words I couldn't decipher. He asked her a question and she nodded.

"Please, Master. Please."

He buried his fingers inside and this time he ploughed her rough. She loved it, moaning for more as he stretched her open, and moaning harder still as his other hand strummed her clit at the same time. He stopped as she began to peak, and she wailed out a groan of disappointment.

"Tears first, Violet," he barked. "Cry for me."

My stomach turned over itself, and there underneath the nerves was a primal need I'd buried for years. I checked either side to find both Raven and Cara engrossed by the show, and then, slowly and ever so quietly, I slid my hand between my thighs.

James

THE BEAST RAGED, TWISTING THROUGH MY MUSCLES. IT BAYED FOR tears, and beautiful, beautiful pain. It bayed for Violet's broken flesh. She strained her head as I swished the cane, eyes wide with anticipation, and fear. A gorgeous combination.

"Master... I..."

"Tears, Violet. You'll cry for me." I hardly recognised my own voice.

She took long, deep breaths and I took a moment to feel the room. It thrummed all around us, alive with sex. Violet tensed her shoulders. "I'm ready, Master."

"Tell me what you need."

"Pain, Master, please. I need pain."

"Beg."

I paced to her front, slow and deliberate. She couldn't take her eyes from the cane, flinching every time I let it flick in my grip. I'd planned a long warm-up, priming her with both paddle and crop until she was floating on endorphins and ripe for the strokes, but no. The beast had his own plan.

Her tears would taste so much fucking better for it.

Her tits were colouring nicely, swollen with blood, long rubbery nipples jutting out at me. They made the perfect target for the tip of my cane. I flicked at her, mottling her skin plum with the early promise of bruising. They'd come up so fucking pretty. Shame I'd never see it.

"Please hurt me, Master."

"More."

"Please, Master, please. Hurt me, please. I need pain."

I fought the urge to bury my cock in her dirty little asshole. I could punch-fuck her cunt at the same time, make her gush her filthy fucking juices all over the floor. *Later.*

I completed my circuit, taking up position to her rear. I let the cane rest high on her buttocks. *Tap, tap, tap.*

"Beg."

"PLEASE, MASTER, PLEASE!" she yelled. "HURT ME!"

I landed the first blow before she'd even finished. It landed hard, and she jumped a clear mile, straining at the chains. I let her settle back into position. Her legs were already shaking.

"More," I hissed.

"Please hurt me," she wheezed.

"Good girl."

I landed the next two in quick succession and she cried out, dancing on one leg like a wounded ballerina. Instinct took over as

I read her movements, leaving her just enough time to regain her balance. Again, and again, and again. I savoured her stripes. Savage white flashes of punishment on tender skin. Neat lines from a steady hand, a practised hand. Her ass looked so fucking pretty.

Her breathing grew frenetic, pain flooding her body with adrenaline. She started swearing, hissing out filthy obscenities. It only made me punish her harder. I increased the pace of my strokes and she started to flail, losing her fight for composure. She twisted and turned, howling like an animal until her throat was raw. I gave her a moment, moving close enough to finger the ridged stripes on her backside.

"Cry for me," I whispered. "Let it all go."

I hit her again and she wailed like a butchered pig, flapping her useless arms around in her cuffs. The next stroke buckled her knees, and she swung in her chains, wailing without breath, just one long, desperate wheeze. It sounded so fucking good. She got to her feet, knees knocking, and her shoulders began to bow, hunched. I ran the tip of the cane down her spine and she straightened.

"Ready for more?" I growled.

"Yes please, Master."

"Good girl."

She screamed through the next few. It's that beautiful final stage, the one before they break. I love that part. Feral cries of torment, skin on fire. I eased up slightly as her chest began to heave. Tears. Beautiful fucking tears. I made sure to land two hard strokes in the same spot on her ass, and it sent her right over the edge. Sobs. Loud, desperate, gorgeous fucking sobs. I pressed myself against her back, wrapping my hands around to squeeze her poor, sore tits. She liked that, I could tell. They always like that. Sore tits make wet pussies.

"That's right, Violet," I whispered. "Let it go."

She cried freely, resting her head back against mine. I nuzzled the tender spot at the nape of her neck and her breathing calmed, slowly. I turned her face in my direction, eager for my prize. She was even more beautiful than I imagined. Black rivers of tears ran thick down her cheeks, make-up spoiled so perfectly. I licked them up, all the way from her jawline, running my tongue right the way over her puffy eyes, digging for more. She groaned, straining for my mouth on hers. I gave it to her, wide open and wet, forcing my tongue in as far as it would go. When I pulled away her eyes were glazed, high on endorphins. She smiled at me.

"I'm going to really fucking hurt you now, Violet," I breathed.

"Please, Master, please more," she said, and she really meant it.

There were no more screams. Only tears. The soft yielding of a body hungry for punishment. She took it well, like the true pain slut she is, until I finally rewarded her with my whole fucking fist where she takes it best.

The beast inside savoured every fucking second.

CHAPTER 8
Lydia

MASQUE. SCULPTED FROM SIN, AND SEX AND SWEAT. HIS BRUTALITY, so measured. The beast on his chest, pain embodied. He was all I could think about. He was all I *had* thought about, through the early hours of Sunday morning with the taste of Explicit still ripe on my tongue, and on still through the day, *all* day, without reprieve. I had endless questions about the man in the mask, all to which Rebecca replied one damning phrase.

No, Lyds. Not him. He's way too dirty-bad-fucking-wrong.

But she couldn't know. How could she? She couldn't possibly know the way I'd thrummed to his darkness. The way his body had called mine across that room. The way every part of me ached for liberation in his chains.

I jumped in my seat as a thwack boomed loud. Metal on wood. A metal ruler slamming onto a desk, more specifically.

"Jesus Christ, Lydia. Are you even here today?"

James Clarke didn't look happy. His brows were heavy with annoyance. His jaw set in a grim line.

"Sorry, I am listening."

"So, answer the question."

Shit. "Sorry, what question?"

He sighed. "Get with the plot or take the day off, I've got no time for this."

I thumped back to reality. "Sorry, James. I'm listening now."

I watched him place his metal ruler back in position, unable to avoid the observation that his hands were big and strong, and ripe for brandishing implements – or for sitting on. *Like Masque's.* Thoughts of what the Explicit beast did with his fist made me shudder, I could almost feel him inside me. Goddamn it, I was actually screwed. Masque, Masque, Masque, everywhere I looked. I shoved chimera-man and his strong hands back in the closet and forced my eyes back to James.

"What was your question?" I asked him.

"Are we fully prepped for the phase one sign-off visit? We're going on Thursday, unless you've been sailing so high in fairy-land you haven't checked your email this morning."

"Thursday? To Brighton?"

"Well, that answers my question," he groaned. "*Yes*, Thursday, *yes*, Brighton. Another overnighter, returning Friday evening. If it goes well we can begin your phase two project plan next week. It was good, by the way."

Suddenly I was right back on planet Earth. I couldn't help but smile. "You read it? Already?"

"Finally, some sign of intelligent life. Yes, I read it." He slid the file across the desk to me, careful not to disturb his pen alignment. "There were a couple of typos on page thirty-nine, you should run spellchecker on the next one."

My pride took a knock. I could have sworn I'd used spellchecker. "But it was good? Apart from that?"

He fought back a smile that twitched at his mouth. "It was

excellent. I don't even want to know how much time you spent learning WHM's case-management processes, but it paid off. You did well. Gold star for Cat's eyes."

I flicked through the file, at his pencil notes in the margins, all positive. "I didn't think you were going to read it yet."

"I'm pleased to surprise you."

"Thank you," I grinned. "And yes, we're ready for the phase one sign-off visit. I spoke to Trevor White this morning and he was very happy with how we handled their accounts migration. *Fantastic* was the word he used."

"Trevor White is calling *you* now, is he? I thought he'd gone a bit quiet at my end."

"On my direct line. I think we've developed a good working relationship."

He gave me another of his unreadable looks. "I'm sure he's very *impressed* by you, Lydia."

"Thanks."

"Enough of this love-in. You need to be on your game with WHM, and this morning you haven't been. Anything I should know about?"

"Anything... like?"

"You tell me. It's not like you to be so... distracted. I need you on point." His gaze was razor-sharp. "Is it Stuart? Has something changed?"

I tried to fight back a smile but my mouth wouldn't listen.

"No," I said. "Nothing's changed with Stuart. I'm sure he's happily hanging out in Babies-R-Us choosing rattle-toys with Carly." *And I'm happily hanging out in Freaks-R-Us with Rebecca*, my brain added. "Everything's good."

"Then I'll put this morning down as a one-off. Keep focused, Cat, I need you with me."

"I'm with you," I said. "You can rely on me, James."

His smile was all genuine this time, tension forgotten, and all over again I noticed how fine a cut he made in a suit. Musk and linen and dark, dark eyes, brooding and smoky and goddamn gorgeous.

Masque, James, Masque, James. Between the two of them my sanity stood no hope in hell. I never recalled singledom feeling this damned crazy before.

"Cara said *she's* been with him, and *she's* not got a high tolerance. You said it yourself, *a slap and tickle.* He hasn't fucked *her* up, has he?"

"Fucking hell, Lyds, not this again." Rebecca fake stabbed me with dramatic hand gestures, scowling like a lunatic. "Seriously, Masque is NOT for you! There are a shitload of men out there who'll give you a slapped ass and a fucking good time."

"But I want *him.*"

"You don't know what the fuck you're talking about or what the fuck you'd be up against."

"I'm not asking you to set it up, I'm just asking that you take me there again."

"Sign up if you want, it's a free country."

My heart dropped. Four hundred a month, not likely with Mum's track record of emergencies.

"You can take me as a guest every month, you said so. Or Cara could."

She sighed. "So, I take you back to Explicit. Then what? You're going to march up to him and say *'Hey, Masque, I saw you beat the fuck out of some redhead on stage the other week, how about you slap my pretty little ass and tell me I'm dirty?'* Is that your plan?"

"I dunno," I admitted.

"You have no idea who the hell that man is. He'd eat you for breakfast, Lyds. He gives Cara a slap every now and again as a favour to *me*. Do you want to be a favour, too?"

"No. I don't want to be a *favour*." I choked back the irritation. "Do you think I'm too ugly for him? Is that it?"

She got up in my face, eyes deadly serious. "No. I don't think that. That's ridiculous."

"What then?"

"I'll slap you *myself* if you keep going on, Lyds."

I brushed her aside and put the kettle on. "There's something in me. I can't explain it. I need this, I need *him*."

"You don't need *him*."

"The way he was with that woman, it did something to me. I've never felt anything like it."

"He'll hurt you, Lydia. Bad. Really bad. Dirty fucking bad."

"Maybe that's what I want," I snapped.

She took the coffee mugs from my hands, placed them on the counter and dragged me from the kitchen, right the way through into her bedroom. My insides tickled at the sight of her torture implements, but it wasn't them she was taking me to see. She fired up her laptop, plugged in an external hard drive from her desk drawer.

"Have you ever seen proper marks, Lyds? I doubt it. *This* is what Masque does. *This* is what he'd do to you."

I watched over her shoulder as she enlarged a thumbnail, and there he was. My heart pounded at the sight of his perfect chest, the chimera dancing on his skin. There was a blonde stood facing away from the camera. Her back was a mess, red-raw welts criss-crossed over each other, and below that her ass was purple. Literally purple. Bruises like I'd never seen before.

"He did that?"

"The welts are fresh, the bruising is days old. You want to look like that when he's finished with you? You'll hardly be able to sit down for a week. That's what redhead is feeling right now, don't doubt it."

"That's supposed to put me off, is it?" I asked, crossing my arms.

She spun back in her seat to face me. "Doesn't it?"

"No."

"Sure, well how about these?" She flicked through some more until she found what she was looking for. On this one the blonde's face was cut off, the picture stopped at her shoulders. Her breasts were bound and swollen, blotchy with deep red bruising. She had needles threaded under her skin, rows of them leading right up to her nipples.

I felt the pulse in my temples. "What else does he do?"

She shrugged and exhaled all her breath. "Fucking hell, Lyds."

On the next the woman was spread-eagled, bound tight to a wrought-iron bed like the one in my room. Again, I couldn't see her face. The picture was focused on her pussy, red and puffy, between purple-streaked thighs. Masque was knelt over her, ready to strike her again. On this one he was naked. I felt my cheeks burn. His stiff cock was as threatening was the rest of him, a weapon in its own right. His implement of choice in this picture was a metal ruler, his target her poor swollen clitoris.

"You can't even imagine how much that hurts," Rebecca said.

I recalled the thump as James Clarke had landed one on his

desk. Ow wouldn't even begin to cut it. I stared at the image, willing it to burn into my memory forever since I doubted I'd ever get to see it again.

Rebecca sighed. "I shouldn't be showing you these, Lyds, it's purely to knock some sense into you. Most doms stick to the ass or the thighs, the fleshier parts, you know?"

"But not him?"

"Masque isn't most doms. He's dirty..."

"I know, dirty bad and wrong."

"Yes, dirty bad and wrong." She slapped my arm. "You're getting too bloody cocky."

"Maybe," I smiled. "I appreciate what you're trying to do here."

"Clearly you don't," she said. "He gets off on proper pain. He craves submission, like all doms, but it's more than that with Masque. He needs you to break, that's what gets him off. Could you break for him? Would you cry? Beg him to stop? Let him lick your tears? Would you fall apart enough to sob in his arms like a broken little doll?"

I felt my heartbeat between my thighs. "I don't cry..."

"He'd *make* you cry, trust me."

"Maybe that's what I need," I spoke aloud.

"Or maybe Explicit has sent you round the twist."

"I need to find out."

"Don't do this!" she said. "Don't put me in this position."

"Please, Bex. Just give me a chance!" I yanked the arm of her chair until she was facing me, forcing her to meet my eyes. "Just one chance. If I get hurt, it's my own fault."

"You *will* get hurt. It would be irresponsible and downright fucking stupid." She crossed her arms, resolute.

I paced away from her, Masque's image burning at the corner of my vision. "You took these pictures, right?"

She raised an eyebrow. "Yes. Why?"

"So, you must know him pretty well, yes?"

She paused awhile, eyeing me suspiciously. "Yes, I know him well. He's the only dom to ever leave me with scars. I'll show you them, if you like."

"He's hit you?"

She rolled her eyes. "Yes, he's hit me. Hard. I've subbed for him a few times, when the mood takes me. Occasionally, I'll add, it's very occasional."

"So, you'd know if I could cope with him, right?"

"Just where the fuck are you going with this?"

She knew damn well where this was going. I could see the spark in her eyes.

"We have a month, yes?" I said. "Until you can take me as a guest again, I mean."

"Yes..."

"So, use it! Test me! Train me or something, whatever you call it. If I can convince you in one month that I've got what it takes to cope, then take me back to Explicit. If not, then I'll forget all about him and never mention him again. I promise."

A sly grin crept across her lips. "Are you propositioning me, *Cat*?"

I'm sure I was the colour of beetroot but I kept going. "I want to prove I can cope. Please, Bex."

She stood up from her chair, closing the distance between us. My heart raced so hard I could have sworn she could hear it. "It's *Raven*. Have you ever been with a girl, Lydia?"

I shook my head. "Not yet."

"Good answer," she smiled. "On your knees."

"Now?"

She took my chin in her hand, gripped me rough. This wasn't

the Rebecca I knew, but it wouldn't be, because this wasn't Rebecca at all. This was Raven. *Mistress* Raven.

"Don't ever question me again. I speak, you obey."

I dropped to my knees without hesitation. "Sorry, Raven."

"*Mistress,*" she hissed. "You'll call me Mistress."

"Sorry, Mistress." My pulse raced like a jackhammer, nerves on fire.

She hitched her skirt, bunching it high around her waist to reveal just a tiny pair of lace panties. She swept the hair back from my face, holding a hand possessively against my scalp. "You're going to eat my pussy now, Cat, and if you want any fucking chance of this plan of yours working out, I'd better believe you're fucking hungry for it." She spread her legs, and yanked my head towards her. I breathed her in, a musky smell of sex so familiar and yet so alien. "Pull my panties to the side."

I did as she asked. Her pussy was smooth against my fingers.

"Do you want this, Cat?"

My throat made a strange moan as I answered. "Yes, Mistress."

"Good girl. Now lick my fucking pussy."

I licked her fucking pussy.

I BRACED MYSELF AS I TOOK A SEAT, TENDER FLESH KEEN TO REMIND me of Raven's paddle. She'd hit me good. She'd hit me hard. And I'd loved every single minute of it. I brushed my fingers across my nostrils. I could still smell her. I smiled to myself.

"You seem happy today, Cat's eyes," James said, handing me the itinerary ahead of Thursday's meeting. "If you can think of anything to add, now's the time to say."

I scanned through it, leaning back into the leather chair I'd been spending more and more time in of late. "Looks good to me."

"Fine. I think it's all there from our end, I'll send it over to Trevor White for his final approval."

"This is really it, huh? Stage one sign-off looming, the minute all our work becomes worthwhile."

"I never took you for such a sentimentalist," he said. "Anyway, don't get too carried away, we've still got stages two and three to pull off. Plenty can go wrong yet."

"I think it will go great," I said, idly.

"That kind of assumption leads to complacency. We need to stay on the boil."

"Yes, sir," I smiled. "Lydia Marsh on the boil, sir."

His look was stern, but there was amusement behind it, I could tell. His eyes glittered like black diamonds, and I fought the urge to poke my tongue out at him, revelling in a high I'd never felt before. Cara hadn't been wrong. *There's this rush, when it hurts, and then a peace. It's so beautiful.* She'd missed out the euphoric afterglow, the excitement, as though your soul is bursting through your skin.

"Are you mocking me, Miss Marsh? I don't take well to mockery."

"I'm not mocking you," I said. "I'm just happy."

"And what can have possibly made you so happy between Monday evening and Tuesday morning?" he asked, leaning forwards with his elbows on the desk.

My eyes glanced to his metal ruler, just to the side of him. Images of Masque flashed into my mind all over again.

"I guess I'm finding a whole new me. A happier me."

"Nothing like a break-up to aid a little self-reinvention."

"Seems not," I grinned. "I'm beginning to think maybe Carly Winters did me a favour after all."

"That's a bold statement for such early days."

"Sure is." I turned the pages of the itinerary, scouting the notes beyond. An email from Trevor White with some earlier amendments. A suggestion of a management round-up after lunch and a proposed evening meal. The evening meal had been crossed out in biro. "Was this you?" I asked, holding it out for him to view.

"Yes."

"So, we aren't doing the social with WHM?"

"No. Is that a problem?"

I shrugged. "No, not at all. Just curious."

"Trevor White was keen to take us out, but I think we'll have had enough of the corporate face by that point, don't you?"

"I guess," I said. "Whatever you think."

"It's been taken off the agenda anyway. I said we'd be busy catching up on other project updates."

"Sure," I smiled. "That's fine. I'm sure we'll catch them again."

"We'll have enough to discuss amongst ourselves, without Trevor White trailing you around all evening."

"I'm sorry?"

"He likes you, Lydia. Professionally *and* personally."

I flushed. "I don't think you can say that based on a few calls to my direct line number, I'm his project manager."

"I'm not basing it on a few calls to your direct line number, I'm basing it on a few emails he sent to my inbox yesterday afternoon."

"What emails? What did he say?"

"Never mind what he said. I just don't want him creeping around."

"You don't need to worry about me, I'd be very professional," I assured him. "I'm not going to be flirting with clients. Work and play don't mix."

He leant forwards even closer, until musk and vanilla danced across the desk to me. "No. They don't. Just so long as you remember that."

"I think I'd find it hard *not* to remember that in light of recent circumstances, thanks very much."

His eyes softened. "I'm just being cautious."

"It's fine," I said, but it wasn't. My hackles were up, my foot twitching under his desk.

"Don't worry, we'll still get a social, a treat on me. You deserve it after everything you've put in. I really do appreciate it."

Too little, too late. I handed him back his itinerary, and got to my feet.

"Was there anything else?"

"Well, I was thinking we could go through the..." he paused, weighing me up. "No, there's nothing else."

"Then I'll see you in Brighton," I said. "I've got a lot to prepare over the next few days."

"Of course."

I didn't linger.

The ping of my email sounded as soon as I was back in my seat.

From: James Clarke
Subject: Professionalism

Lydia, I've offended you. It was unintentional, and I assure you it's much more about Trevor White than it is about you. I would

never question your professional integrity. You conduct yourself faultlessly.

James Clarke
CTO, Trial Run Software Group.

Flawless instinct all over again.

To: James Clarke
Subject: Re: Professionalism.

Do you mean 'sorry'?

Lydia
Lydia Marsh
Senior Project Co-ordinator, Trial Run Software Group.

I waited.

From: James Clarke
Subject: Re: re: Professionalism

Yes. I mean *sorry*.
Nothing like making someone work for it. I'll remember this should the boot ever be on the other foot.

James Clarke
CTO, Trial Run Software Group.

His awkwardness made me smile. Maybe James Clarke was human after all.

To: James Clarke
Subject: Re: re: re: Professionalism.

Apology accepted.

Lydia
Lydia Marsh
Senior Project Co-ordinator, Trial Run Software Group.

I didn't hear from him again, and the day was much worse for it.

I guess a girl can always make room for two crushes in her life.

Masque or James, James or Masque. I found myself hoping I'd never have to choose, but then scrapped the silly thought pretty damned quickly.

I breathed in the scent of Rebecca on my fingers. Just what the hell was happening to little old Lydia Marsh?

MY HEELS SCUFFED AGAINST THE LEATHER SOFA, STRUGGLING FOR grip as I bucked up against Rebecca's mouth. Her fingers were still inside me, her lips still tight around my clit as I tumbled over the edge of orgasm. A proper orgasm, not like the ones I'd faked with Stu after every half-arsed effort he'd ever made. It felt so good. Bex kissed my stomach on her way back up, lingering long enough to flick at a nipple. I struggled to catch my breath, mouth still open as she assaulted me with her tongue. I could taste myself on her.

She draped her arm across my chest, the lively colours of her tats matching the mottled shades of my bruises. I looked down at myself, admiring the welts of my punishment. Just three nights in and I was already getting better at this, a ripe canvas for her abuse. She was colouring me in so pretty.

"You taste seriously fucking good, Cat," she husked. "I could lick your sweet little slit all day long."

"And you, Mistress Raven," I whispered.

"Oh yeah?" she asked, dipping her fingers back inside me. "So, you like pussy, do you?"

I grinned. "Yes, I like pussy."

"Good." She kissed the corner of my mouth. "You're turning out to be quite the little pain slut, baby. I'm impressed."

I felt a bloom of pride in my chest. My descent into insanity really knew no bounds. I rolled into her, until we were eye to eye. "You think I could handle Masque now?"

"We're a way off establishing that, sweet thing," she said. My heart dropped and I collapsed onto my back, struggling to hide my disappointment. "Hey, don't take it so bad. We're only three fucking days in."

"I just want to know I can see him again, that's all."

"Ok, ok," she said, nuzzling my neck. Her lips drove me crazy, trailing their way up to my ear. "I get it, he's driving you loopy, you need to see him again, yada yada fucking yada. So how about we up the stakes?"

"How?"

"Well..." Her fingers teased at me all over again, working their way back inside. I groaned as she pushed all the way in, my tender clit craving both more and less at the same time. "I think you need to get back on the horse, show me you're ready for cock again. *Real* cock, not the plastic shit I've been giving you these past few days."

"I'm ready," I said. "Ready for *his* cock, anyway."

"Your tight little cunt needs cock *now*, Cat, not in a month." She smiled at me, a smile full of deviance and sin. "Show me you're ready for him. Show me how well you'll convince him to fuck you."

I moved against her fingers. "How can I do that?"

"Let's set a challenge. Pass it and I'll introduce you to Masque, no more tests, no more games, no Explicit even, just you and him and whatever the hell becomes of it."

My eyes widened, and I squirmed to check if she was being serious. She was. Her eyes were hooded, high-on-sex and sparkling with mischief. "What do you want me to do?"

"Tomorrow night, in Brighton. I want you to seduce a man, take him to your bed, and make him fuck you senseless. I want you to ride his cock all fucking night long."

"Tomorrow night?! But it's work!" My stomach churned as I ran through my options. Trevor White flashed before my eyes, but that would be so unprofessional. Shit. Maybe a barman after James had gone to bed, maybe some random in a club. My head swam with nerves. "I've never picked up a stranger before. I don't even know if I can."

She rolled onto me, pinning my arms above my head. "Not a stranger, my sweet little Lydia. I want you to seduce James Clarke."

My breath caught in my chest for one long second before I sighed in her face. "James?! You want me to seduce James Clarke? Mr Mysterious? You said it yourself, getting anything out of him's like milking a rock. How on earth would I initiate that kind of shit? He'll blow me straight out the water."

"But you don't object in principle?"

I looked away from her, cheeks on fire. "James is very attractive. He's hot, he's strong, he's clever and driven... he's goddamn gorgeous," I admitted.

"Yes, he is."

"But he doesn't want me."

She pulled my face back to hers. "What the hell makes you say that?"

Embarrassment burnt, and I craved the safety of my bed, hidden under the duvet away from all this craziness. "I asked him over last week. He said no."

"You asked James on a date?" she grinned. "You kept that quiet."

"Don't I always? And no. I asked him over here, to hang out with *both* of us and check my project file."

She laughed, and it sliced like razors. I pushed her off me and she took it in good humour. "Jesus, Lyds, you asked him to come check out your *project file*? That's a new name for it."

"Laugh if you want, he said no, anyway. I'll have to try and seduce Trevor White instead, he's a client."

She shook her head. "James Clarke, Lyds, that's your challenge."

"He won't fuck me!" I wailed. "Seriously, Rebecca, it's not possible. You're setting me up to fail!"

"I'm setting you up to test your resolve, there's a difference. Seducing James will be an easier bag than seducing Masque, believe me."

"It will be impossible!"

"No, it will be *difficult*. That's the point. He's a tough cookie, you'll have to be persuasive. Succeed and you'll get your time with Masque, that's a promise. Cross my heart and hope to die."

I weighed it up. Whichever way I looked at it felt completely unobtainable. James would blow me out again and I'd look a fool, and then I'd lose my shot with Masque altogether. All bad. I sighed. "You're such a bitch, Rebecca. You know I'll fail."

"If you want Masque enough, you'll make sure you don't."

"Have any date rape drugs lying around I could borrow?"

Her eyes twinkled, and she pulled me in for a kiss. I resisted at first, mouth fixed in a stubborn little line, but she won me over. She pulled away, smiling. "You won't need date rape drugs, Lyds. He's tough, but he's not that tough. Just be yourself, and don't let him escape before he's given you his cock."

"I'm myself every day, he hasn't offered it so far."

"I'll give you some advice. James likes to be confided in, he likes vulnerability. Open up to him as sweet little Lydia on a night out in the big bad world, and you'll get your guy."

"I can't open up, Bex, you know I can't."

"And there's your challenge."

"Like I need any more hurdles on this ridiculously impossible quest of yours." I rolled my eyes. "He won't want me."

"That's up to you. It's your future with Masque at stake, take it or leave it."

"Why do you even want me to fuck James anyway? Does the idea get you off or something? Mr corporate screwing your new little pain slut?"

"You've got me there. Yes, it does," she laughed. "I think you'd be good for each other, you both need to let off some steam."

"Oh, so it's a two-way mercy mission now, is it? Get us both laid at the same time? You're really serious, aren't you? I can't believe you're doing this to me!" I removed myself from her arms, leaving the sofa to check myself out in the full-length mirror. "And what about this?" I pointed at my battered body. "How the hell would I even begin to explain this, if I ever even got that far?"

"Be inventive. Lights out... panties off only... Use your imagination."

"When I fail at this, and lose my job in the process, you're giving me another shot at Masque, Bex, as well as free rent until my life is sorted again. This is totally unfair." I marched away to the sound of her cackling.

"You won't fail, Lyds, I have every faith in you."

I shot her the finger before I slammed my bedroom door, and only just caught sight of her poking her tongue out at me.

CHAPTER 9
James

TREVOR WHITE WASN'T LISTENING TO A FUCKING WORD I WAS saying. He nodded in all the right places, but his beady little eyes were fixed well and truly on Lydia, and Lydia alone. She stared ahead oblivious, hanging on every word I said. I was relieved. A two-way street and I'd have struggled to hold myself back from throat-punching the sonofabitch. This Lydia Marsh shit was becoming unbearable to the point that I'd been checking out employment ads. A decent management position, far away from London and far away from my cat-eyed temptress. I don't think she even realised the effect she was having. The girl had no fucking idea how sweet her perky little ass was, or how one watery flash of her eyes could drive a man to insanity. Her humble oblivion made her even more fuckable. I had to get out of this. *Calm down, James, keep it together.*

I took a sip of water and continued my presentation, making every effort to ignore Trevor and his grubby little advances. Lydia was better than him, out of his league, even if he did own a shiny gold Jaguar and a part share in a racehorse. Wanker.

I was about to break for lunch when a mobile started bleeping in someone's handbag. I gritted my teeth in annoyance, and gritted them harder still as I realised it was Lydia's phone that was going off. She blushed, and shot me a look of apology, scrabbling to put the thing on silent. Trevor leant in close to catch a glimpse of her message, and I found myself thumping the projector screen behind me with a falsely-elaborate point. It got his attention and for a moment I stared him out with eyes of death. He raised his eyebrows in surprise before I yanked myself down enough to shoot him a smile. He lapped it up, moment forgotten.

Finally we broke for lunch and I virtually marched Lydia down the corridor for a 'five-minute-co-worker-catch-up'. Trevor hovered, keeping a shifty eye on us from the meeting room doorway.

"I'm really sorry about my phone," she gushed. "I was sure I'd turned it off."

"Clearly not," I snapped. "Is he bothering you?" I tilted my head in Trevor's direction.

Her eyes widened, naive and oblivious. "Who, Trevor? No, why?"

"He's practically slavering over you. It's an embarrassment."

She burnt up, the perfect amount of rouge flooding her cheeks. "He just seems friendly."

"He's more than friendly. He's like a dog sniffing a bitch on heat. He'll start humping your leg if you're not careful."

"It's ok, honestly. I'm fine. I can handle it."

I sighed, forcing a lighter tone. "I think it's going well in there."

"You're doing great," she smiled. "Really great. You've covered everything from our end perfectly."

"The phase two section was all from your project plan. It's your success too."

"Wow, thanks." Her eyes glowed with life. "I'm really glad you liked it."

"Shall we grab a sandwich? Get out of here?"

She grimaced, knotting her hands together. "I already agreed we'd eat with them, I'm sorry. I didn't know not to. Trevor told me they were putting on a buffet the minute we stepped through the door."

It didn't surprise me. I forced a smile. "No problem. They are the client after all."

I led the way back up the corridor, dying inside as Trevor took my Cat's-eyes by the arm and schmoozed her on into the dining hall. I should have been grateful to him, relieved at the possibility of her disappearance from the open market, but all I felt was hate.

FINALLY, WE WERE OUT OF THERE. I SANK A DOUBLE-SCOTCH AT THE bar and ordered in a bottle of red. The afternoon had dragged like a bitch, every second leading up to the inevitable moment that Trevor White would make his move to hijack our evening. I'd stepped in before Lydia could even blink.

"Sorry, Trevor, we'd love to, we're back-to-back with office catch-up calls until nine. Some other time, though."

He couldn't argue, feigning politeness and waving us away for a 'pleasant evening'. It would be. Now.

"I really thought he was coming with us," Lydia said, eyes sparkling in amusement. "He looked so put out when you said we were busy."

I handed her a glass. "Did you want him to?"

"Did I want Trevor White to join us this evening?" she smiled. "No. Why would I?"

"He's the senior partner of one of the largest law firms in the country. He's got a gold Jag, part share in a racehorse and a villa on the Spanish coast. Plus, he's still got his own hair and most of his own teeth. He could be your next Mr Comfortable."

She rolled her eyes at me. "Another Mr Comfortable is the last thing I want."

"Really? Why so?"

"Didn't I tell you? I'm the new-model Lydia. *This* Lydia is wild and free and single. She doesn't want TV nights or lights-off sex on a Tuesday evening."

"I guess she doesn't want Trevor White, then."

"No, she doesn't," she grinned. "She doesn't want a relationship at all."

"Welcome to the club," I held up my wine and she clinked my glass. "Single and sane, private and proud."

"You remembered," she said. "Is it up in your living room yet?"

"Sure is. I had it printed in Stencil font, 180 point size. Takes up my entire mantelpiece."

"Liar," she laughed. "I might get Rebecca to make it up as an art print for you, when's your birthday?"

I nearly choked on my wine. "Sorry?"

"Your birthday, when is it?" Her smile was sweet and unsuspecting. Interested. Only Rebecca knew my birthday, if she even remembered. Maybe my sisters, if they could ever be arsed to send a birthday card.

"June Nineteenth."

"Gemini," she said. "The twins. Multifaceted and complex."

The beast burnt beneath my shirt. She had no fucking idea. "Yes, I'm a Gemini. If you want to believe in all that mumbo-jumbo."

"I'm a Scorpio. Born on Halloween."

"I really did pick the right housemate for the lovely Rebecca, then, didn't I? It doesn't get much more goth than a Halloween birthday."

"Quite true."

"Aren't Scorpios supposed to be the weirdo star sign? You don't seem all that weird to me. I think it's all baloney."

A sly smile lit up her face, hitting me straight in the dick. "Looks can be deceiving."

I raised my glass. "Quite true, Cat, quite true."

Once again, she had no fucking idea.

I DRANK QUICKLY AND LYDIA MATCHED MY PACE. WE'D RETIRED TO A table at the far end of the restaurant, nestled amongst some oversized ornamental plants, and the dim lighting dilated her pupils perfectly. She looked divine, naturally sexy, dazzling with life, a different girl entirely to the one I'd found in the kitchen all those weeks ago. The conversation flowed much more easily than I was accustomed to, glossing over anything too personal and landing on a healthy dollop of work talk mixed with personal history, ambitions, funny stories. *She* was funny, and sharp, and interesting, battering me with questions without being invasive. I found myself sucked into her, compelled by her strange green eyes.

We ate heartily, and happily, complementing the chef on his fine culinary talents, but after dessert Lydia's demeanour shifted a gear. She became nervous somehow, edgy. Her dainty little fingers played with her wine glass, twirling it round and round in front of her. She was a puzzle I'd love to solve, an enigma that vexed me, snaking up my backbone like a creeping vine.

"Is something troubling you?"

Her eyes widened as they met mine, and she swallowed nervously. She smiled to hide it, but I caught it anyway. "I'm fine."

I let it drop, pouring out the final dregs of wine between our glasses. "I've enjoyed this evening," I said, in an attempt to smoothen her disposition.

"Me, too, very much. Thank you."

"You're welcome. You deserve it."

She seemed to be about to say something, edging a little closer and pursing her lips in that way she does when she concentrates. I knew her mannerisms far too well, too many hours spent studying her in the guise of professionalism. I waited for it, but her mobile cut us off, chirping away with some generically irritating ringtone.

Her face paled, and for a horrible moment I figured it was Stuart or someone equally unwelcome.

"It's my mum. I need to take this." Her face was apologetic, even though it shouldn't have been.

"Take your time, I'll get another bottle," I smiled. I took our empty glasses back to the bar, moving slowly. She held back, avoiding conversation until she was certain I was out of earshot. I made sure to head for the side of the bar out of her eyeline, so she wouldn't observe my return, I ordered quickly before taking up position at the side of some foliage by our table. I could just about see Lydia, but was positive she'd never see me. I could hear her just fine from my location. I soaked up every word.

"Calm down, Mum. Just breathe... breathe, Mum, I can't hear you... Colin? You mean the new Colin? Left where...? Oh, Mum! He did what...? Well, how could he?" She leant forward against the table, fisting a hand in her hair. She looked pained, agitated, scared. My tongue felt too big for my mouth. "Please say you didn't give him all of it? Oh God, Mum. Why? You'll be ok, I promise, just calm down, okay? We'll sort it out. *I'll* sort it out. I'll call them tomorrow, I'll set something up... they aren't going to throw you out, not over a few arrears. How many?! Jesus, Mum, why didn't you tell me?"

So, Rebecca was right. Lydia looked around, clearly keeping an eye out for me. She returned to her call, satisfied I was still at the bar. "You'll get over him, Mum, you will... Don't say that! He wasn't right for you. If he was, he wouldn't have done this... He's just another loser, ok? You'll meet someone better... You said you wouldn't give him any money. You promised after Steve! I'm not angry... I'm not shouting... Mum, I'm not, I promise. I'll sort it out, I'm away with work right now, but I'll try and get some time in the morning... It's not like that! I can't come home right now, you know I can't, I have meetings tomorrow, but soon, I promise... Don't be like that, you know I care! Mum... Mum? Mum?" She sat with her face in her hands, shoulders hunched in misery for long, slow seconds before she pulled herself together and looked around again. Her breathing was frantic. I watched her chest rise and fall in short bursts. She tried her phone again, calling and recalling over and over. I found I was burning up, gripping the wine bottle in a vice, our two fresh glasses clamped tight in my fingers. I composed myself, pasting on a smile before I reappeared, as though I'd just sauntered back from the bar.

"Sorry, they had to go to the cellar," I said. She smiled but it was empty, fragile. She looked on the edge, a delicate little sparrow dithering on a twig. "Are you ok? What's happened?"

"It's um... it's nothing," she pretended, waving away my question. Her breathing was still shallow. "My mum is having some problems."

"Nothing serious I hope?"

She smiled a horribly sad smile. "It's *always* something serious."

"I'm a good listener, indulge me." I handed her a fresh glass, poured the wine. She drank it down quickly and held her glass out for a refill. I topped her up. "Talk to me, Cat's-eyes. Maybe I can help." A shiver ran up my spine as I realised my offer was genuine.

She was about to wave it all away, I know she was. Her eyes sharpened as she choked back the upset, and I was losing her, losing the moment. I resigned myself to the inevitable public-facing Lydia, who pushed the pain deep inside and offered up nothing but slick-smooth persona, but something seemed to change in her. She stared me out for long seconds, so intensely it was almost uncomfortable. I kept quiet, sipping at my wine while she worked out her next move. It surprised me.

"I'm not good at talking," she said, "but I'll give it a try."

"Please do."

"My mum is a very emotional person, always has been, as long as I can remember. She has problems coping with life. She's a good person, but she makes stupid decisions."

"What kind of stupid decisions?"

"Men, usually," she said. "She falls in love every other week, normally with losers with no prospects and loose morals. I guess they see an easy ride, easy prey. They move in and use her up, then leave again when she's all spent out. She falls apart every time, says she can't take it. She's suicidal at least four times a year, depending on how many relationships go down the drain. If I'm lucky she'll be happy for six months straight, but that's unusual. Her men don't usually stay longer than a few months. She'll replace this latest one with another, and another after him. I give it three weeks tops, but in the meantime she'll be a wreck. She drinks and she gambles her money away on the slot machines.

She claims she doesn't, but it's always the same. I bail her out and she falls apart again, over and over and over." She paused, looking across at me with honest eyes. They pounded me in the stomach so hard it almost pained. "So, there you go. That's my world."

"How do you bail her out?"

"Money mainly, time when I can. For a while I was paying her bills direct from my account, just to make sure it got done. She seemed to be getting better at it, so I gave her back control earlier this year and just gave her money when she needed it. A big mistake. She's now three grand in rent arrears and they're threatening to throw her out. She claims Colin needed the money I sent her, to fight a custody battle for one of his kids or some shit. He promised he'd pay her back before she got evicted, only now he's done a runner."

"So she blew your money on some loser named Colin?"

She flinched, eyes narrowing to shards of pain. "It's not the first time. I've tried to get her professional help but she won't take it, says *I'm* the only one who can help her, but I'm too far away living it up in the big city. She hates that I moved here, wants me to go home, but I couldn't go home, even if I wanted to. The money's better here, and she always needs all I can spare. One day I hope I'll be earning enough that I can get a bigger place and have her come live with me, if she will, that is. At least then I could keep an eye on her."

"You said she's been like this as long as you can remember, was it the same when you were growing up?"

"It was *worse* when I was growing up," she said. She looked away, but not in time enough to hide the sheen in her eyes, the threat of tears. She choked it back well. "When I was little I couldn't help her, I'd just have to watch and tell her it would be ok. Weak words from a seven year old, of course. She'd cry all night, say she couldn't cope and kiss me goodbye, telling me that I'd have a new family soon, with a mum who could take better care of me. I'd be so scared, watching from the stairs all night while she drank herself unconscious. She never seriously attempted suicide, but she got out the pills a few times. I hid them in the end, in the cupboard under the stairs, she'd shout at me when she had a headache, but I'd never tell her where they were. I was too scared. I used to pray every night that God would help me save my mummy, but God never answered, only a string of losers, with foul mouths and fouler manners. I lost count of how many men I should call *Daddy*."

"Did any of them hurt you?" My mouth was dry as sand, no matter how much wine I sipped. I inched my chair closer, holding back the urge to reach across the table for her.

"Hurt me? Like physically? No. I wasn't abused or anything, most of them ignored me entirely."

I breathed out in relief. "You shouldn't have had that on your shoulders, Lydia. You were too young, much too young. Did nobody help you?"

"Mum had a friend I called Auntie Sylvia, she'd come round often, try and help out. She's still there with Mum now, living round the corner. I'd never have been able to leave if she wasn't. She'd cook for us sometimes, when Mum was too depressed, and bring me toffees and a pat on the head. She's nice, Syl. She helped." I heard her breath hitch again and this time she struggled to bring it back in line. She put her hand to her mouth and her fingers were shaking. "I shouldn't talk about this, I'm sorry. You'll think I'm a right freak."

"I don't think you're a freak. I think you're a bloody saint. A lot of people would have cut that shit off long ago."

"I can't cut her off," she said. "She's my mum, she needs me. I promised myself I'd be able to save her, just as soon as I was old enough... brave enough... clever enough... I'm not any of those things yet, it appears."

"You are *all* of those things," I said. "But you can't save other people, no matter how much you want to. People will always walk their own path, dance with their own demons."

"I have to try," she wheezed. "I have to try harder. I let her down again. I always let her down."

Her pain broke my resolve, and I was off, dragging my chair to her side, so close. Her delicate little hands in mine, so small. Bright eyes staring up at me.

"No, Lydia. You didn't let her down. *She* let *you* down."

"She let *herself* down. She's worth so much more than this, if only she could see what I see. Why can't I make her see?" Her eyes were pleading, searching, open and raw.

My heart raced, buckling under the pressure to touch her, to pull her close.

"People only see what they want to see, and they only do whatever they want to do. You can make excuses for them all you like, but you'll *always* be making excuses for them. Always." I lowered my head to hers, eye to eye. "It was the same with Rachel. She had different men every week, and then she'd cry and say she was sorry, that she'd try and be better and she needed me to love her, that I was all she had. I blamed her for letting *herself* down, blamed *me* for trusting too much, but ultimately she let *me* down, and *your* mum let *you* down, too."

A single, lonely tear slipped from Lydia's eye, trailing a slow path down her cheek. I wiped it away before she could, choking on the urge to taste her pain.

"Thank you, James," she said, squeezing my hand. "That means a lot." She leant forward to land the softest little kiss on my cheek. I closed my eyes to blank her out, fearing I'd kiss her back. "I think I've done enough talking now," she said. "Can I have another wine?"

I released her tiny hands from mine and reached for the bottle.

I didn't pull my chair away from hers, not even when the conversation lightened and we were back in the realms of friendly colleagues. Lydia perked up well, firing off a couple of text messages to her vampiric mother with the promise that she'd sort her life out in the morning. I could have throttled the woman. The image of a scared little girl peeking through the bannisters at her drunkard mother twitched at my fists. The girl was made of steel. Steel housing a whole load of pain. Years of pain and fear and desperation. It made her all the more beautiful to me.

Cat's eyes danced in the candlelight as we finished up the second bottle. She leant forward in an uncharacteristic display of closeness, resting her forehead on my shoulder. "I'm drunk," she said. "But I had a great night."

I rested my chin on her head, breathing in the scent of her hair. Coconut and lavender. "As did I."

She sat herself back upright, smiling. I knew something was coming before she even opened her mouth. "Was Rachel your true love? The only one for you?"

I raised my eyebrows. "Hell would usually have to freeze over for me to answer that question."

"But not tonight. You'll tell me tonight, won't you? It's that kind of night, and I told you about my mum."

"So, it's tit-for-tat now, is it?"

She laughed. "Kind of. I dunno."

"I loved a girl before I loved Rachel, a crazy girl who dreamt of running away with the circus. She was a livewire."

"Tell me about her."

"She was young, crazy, reckless, gifted... free... passionate. Beautiful."

"She sounds quite special."

"She was *very* special."

"What happened to her?" she asked, eyes boring into mine, eyes just like the woman she spoke of.

"She ran away and joined the circus as far as I know," I smiled. "I went to university, and she flew away. She begged me to go with her, I begged her to come with me. Neither would have worked, not really."

"That's a shame."

"Maybe," I said. "Maybe not. I thought it was a shame for a long, long time, until I met Rachel."

"Where did you meet?"

I sighed. "It's time for bed, we have meetings in the morning."

She pouted, and the urge to suck on her bottom lip made my mouth water. "Can't you just answer that one final question?"

"What difference will it make?"

"It will make a difference to me," she said. "Just one short answer, please. Indulge me."

In my mind I saw Katreya's smile as she disappeared out of sight, goading me to follow her. I took a breath. "I met Rachel at work. We worked together."

"At work?!" I could see the surprise in her face, as surprised as everyone else had been by my deviation from the corporate persona.

"Yes, at work. It was a mistake, it's always a mistake."

"But she was worth it? Worth making a mistake for?"

I smiled, standing to leave and pulling her with me. "Sometimes mistakes are worth making. But only sometimes."

We rode just three floors in the elevator, but it took forever. Lydia leant gently against my side, her hand curled around my waist to burn at my ribcage. I knew I should push her away and regain at least some marginal distance as professional associates, but I didn't. She felt too fucking good – her soft form melting so perfectly against the hard lines of mine. She'd be sleeping in the room next door, mere metres away. The thought made my dick twitch, but my resolve held firm as she rooted her bag for her keycard, placing my own firmly in the lock and preparing to say my goodbyes.

She looked over, eyes pale as moonlight and so fucking pretty. Her toes were turned in, one foot tapping gently on the spot.

"I guess this is goodnight, then," she said.

"I'll see you bright and early. Breakfast at seven-thirty."

"Sure, yeah, seven-thirty."

I turned away, destination my empty hotel room, but in a heartbeat her hand was on mine, pulling me back to her.

"James, wait. I just wanted to say that I'm not a talker. Nobody knows that shit about my mum, not apart from my friend Steph, and Stu, he knew too."

I smiled. "You don't have to worry, Cat's-eyes, I'm a silent witness."

She pinned her bottom lip. "I didn't mean that. I trust you. I just wanted to say thanks, for listening. It really helped."

"I'm glad I could help." My mouth was turning dry, a pulse in my temples. *Go to bed, James, go to fucking bed.*

"I really enjoyed myself tonight," she continued. "A lot."

"Me too." I opened my door again and she stood watching me, her toes resuming their tapping. I feigned ignorance, turning back only to wave her goodnight. She looked crestfallen, retreating with rosy cheeks. Her keycard danced in her hands like a fish, skittering to the floor. She cursed under her breath and dived on after it. Her skirt hitched up, outlining the gorgeous perky swell of her ass through the fabric.

Fuck no-one you know, know no-one you fuck.
Fuck no-one you know, know no-one you fuck.
Fuck no-one you know, know no-one you fuck.

I looked into the silence of my room. The perfectly-made bed, the case unopened on the dresser, the cute little tea and coffee tray, and satellite TV, and then, stupidly, I looked back. I looked back at my green-eyed Cat.

She was still watching me, her door half-open.

"Goodnight, James," she whispered.

"Goodnight, Lydia," I said, but still I hovered.

We stared at each other, the air thick in the corridor, so fucking thick I could hardly breathe. Finally, she disappeared, sighing as she went and leaving only the creak of her door as it eased its way closed.

I caught it just before the lock clicked.

She spun in shock at the intrusion, but didn't have time to respond before I was at her, my mouth on hers, hot and heavy and horny as sin. I paced her backwards while she grappled for balance, conceding to my force until she slammed into the wall. She let out a moan, opening her pretty little mouth. Her tongue danced with mine without reserve or restraint, as though she'd been waiting for this moment all evening. Maybe she had.

She tasted fucking gorgeous.

"This is a mistake," I growled, my mouth still on hers. "A big fucking mistake."

Her hands fisted in my hair. "Some mistakes are worth making," she wheezed.

Her neck smelt of Rose, and White Lilly, and a hint of Amber. I licked at her skin, and she shuddered against me, tilting her head back to grant me access. I roved my way up to her ear, teasing at her earring with my teeth. I heard her murmur as I nipped the lobe, enjoying the short, raspy song of her breath.

"Yes…" she moaned. "Please… I like it rough."

I pressed her tight enough to mash her tits against my chest. "How rough?"

Her eyes fell to the floor. "I'm, um, I'm trying to find out."

"Let me help you with that." Her fingers gripped my shoulders, her head lolling back as I grazed my teeth down her throat. She groaned at my touch, bucking against me for more. Sweet fucking Jesus. My dick strained in my suit, craving the silky soft heat inside her.

I backed up enough to palm her breast, a perfect handful, the hard little nub of her nipple ripe for my mouth. I dipped my head, sucking her through the fabric.

"Use your teeth… please," she hissed. An explosion of white heat behind my eyeballs, the beast crying for savagery. I bit her as hard as I dared, a full mouth of delicate flesh begging me for pain. Her breath hitched, and she shuddered, arching her back to give me more.

I admired my work, her rosy nipple dark through her wet blouse, jutting just high of the lace of her bra. I wanted more. Fingers at her buttons, desperate for skin, but she stopped me, scratchy fingers on mine, plucking me away from her. I eyed her, full of questions, but she didn't answer, just skirted sideways, taking me with her, her hand reaching across the wall. For the light, she was going for the light. I grabbed her wrist on instinct, pinning it above her head with more force than I intended.

"No fucking way, Cat. I want to see you."

She bit her lip, and this time I did what I'd thought about doing a million fucking times before. I clamped my mouth over hers, hungry and feral and desperate, crazy for the beautiful fucking creature who'd driven me insane. I felt her unravel, bucking against me, her thighs either side of mine, needy for cock. I let her wrist go free, gripping at her ass through her skirt, curling my fingers under the hem. My balls ached at the promise of her tight wet slit, the sight of her spread and exposed and so fucking vulnerable.

"And I want to see you, James," she said, yanking at my tie. My stomach clenched, the beast flaring on my ribs. *The beast.* I'd gone fucking mad already, dancing with disaster in my colleague's hotel room.

"There's something you need to know," I said. "Something you won't expect..." But it was too late, she'd already picked at my shirt, pulling it open to my nipples. Her eyes widened to saucers, her hand at her mouth as she paled before my eyes. Motherfucking hell, was it that much of a shock? I looked down at the head of the beast, its inky black tendrils, seeing it through fresh eyes, just as she was. Of course it was a fucking shock.

Fuck no-one you know, and know no-one you fuck.

Mr Corporate had fallen apart right in front of her fucking eyes. My balls bellowed in frustration, stilted lust twisting a knife in my gut. I backed away with a growl of obscenities, buttoning up my shirt before she could blink.

"Shit, Lydia, this wasn't supposed to happen."

She didn't speak a word, just gawped like a slack-jawed idiot. I fought the urge to choke the breath from her, shake her into submission until she fell to her knees and worshipped my cock to teach her manners. I grabbed my tie from the floor, smoothed down my hair.

"I hate fucking clichés, but can we forget this ever happened, please?"

I didn't wait for an answer, pacing my way to the exit as fast as my legs would carry me. I'd almost made it when she called out, her voice all weak and pathetic.

"James... wait."

"I'm sorry, Lydia, this was my mistake. I'm very sorry."

"Wait... please. Just wait a minute."

I rested my forehead against the door, ears ringing with regret and embarrassment and self-recriminations. Fuck this shit. I went for the handle, breaking for the corridor, one foot in no-man's land before I heard her speak again.

"Masque! Please, for God's sake, just wait a minute!"

Now it was my turn to gawp like a slack-jawed idiot.

CHAPTER 10
Lydia

James stopped dead in his tracks, one foot still inside the door.

"What the hell do you know about Masque?" he asked me.

"I saw him... you! I saw *you*! At Explicit, last weekend, I was there with Rebecca and Cara, and I didn't know it was you, I swear!"

He edged back inside. "Rebecca took you to Explicit? Why the fuck would she do that?"

"I wanted to go... I wanted to see."

"Well, now you've fucking seen. I need to go. I shouldn't be here."

"No, no, no!" I hissed. "Please, Masque... James... don't go."

His eyes met mine, and this time they were the shadowy eyes of the man in the mask. I couldn't help but smile. *Seduce James Clarke and you'll get your time with Masque. Cross my heart.* It was so fucking obvious. His bulk, his manner, his perfectly chiselled jawline, his relationship with Rebecca.

"I'm glad this is amusing you," he said. "It's not looking so funny from where I'm standing."

"I'm not laughing, it's just all falling into place."

"You'll have to enlighten me."

I sat on the bed and put my head in my hands, deep breaths in and out.

"I heard Rebecca and Cara, you know... in the kitchen. I didn't expect to feel anything, but it turned me on, ok? And Rebecca knew, she heard me, and she took me to Explicit, just to see. I didn't think it would even be my thing, but then there was this guy... this incredible guy... commanding this redhead on stage like she was the only woman in the entire universe, and this man, with the chimera tattoo from Rebecca's wall, was so powerful, so compelling, I couldn't take my eyes off him."

"I'm glad you enjoyed yourself," he said. "I need to leave now. Let's call it a day."

My heart pounded. "You don't understand!"

"What's there to understand? You saw a freak in a club, it was me. End of story."

"I didn't see a freak," I wheezed. "I saw a God, James. I wanted to be *her*. The woman on stage. I haven't stopped thinking about that man, not for one single second. Ask Rebecca, I've been driving her mad." I looked up at him, desperate for his reaction. "Please don't leave. Not yet."

He came to the bed, got down on his knees, placed hot hands over mine. "I hurt people, yes. But I wouldn't have done that with you, not here, not tonight. This was just about you and me, two people in a hotel room. I wouldn't have hurt you, Cat, I promise."

I smiled at him, at the absurdity of the whole situation. "You're not listening to me, James. I *want* you to. I *want* Masque. I want James Clarke too, but I'm crazy about Masque, I can't get him out of my head."

He squeezed my knuckles. "You don't want either, trust me."

I felt my temper flare a little.

"Don't tell me what I want, ok? Don't treat me like an idiot who doesn't know anything."

He sighed. "I'm not treating you like an idiot, I'm telling you the truth."

I hated the way he looked at me, like some cute little dolly who doesn't know shit. Not like the *proper* women from Explicit, not like Rebecca and Cara and all the other perfect minxes he hung out with every bloody weekend. I pushed him away and got to my feet.

"You think I don't know what I'm talking about? I'll show you. It's why I was going for the light, James, I didn't think you'd like it."

I unbuttoned my blouse, shaky but resolute, slipping it from my shoulders and unclasping my bra, revealing my bruised tits. His eyes widened as I jiggled out of my skirt, presenting myself in just a small pair of lace panties, nervous but unrepentant. I twirled slowly and I caught him swallow, soaking in every wheal and bruise.

"Rebecca's work," he said calmly, a smile twitching at his mouth. "I should have guessed."

"I *asked* her to," I insisted. "I *wanted* it."

"Why?"

I felt my cheeks flush, and folded my arms over my breasts. "Practice," I mumbled.

"Practice?"

I looked at the floor, anywhere but at him. "For *Masque*, I was practicing for Masque."

"And good old James Clarke, was he practice for Masque too?"

My mouth clammed up. "No... yes... I don't know. I wanted *you*, I wanted you before I even saw Masque."

"Tut tut, that's a dangerous game, playing one man's lust for the sake of another's." He got up, took the TV remote from the dresser and flicked through the stations until he found a late night comedy show. I watched in silence as he turned the volume up loud, wondering what the hell he was doing. He took a seat on the edge of the bed. "You're a bad girl, Lydia. Do you know what happens to bad girls?" A whirlwind of tiny butterflies fluttered around my stomach. "Come here."

His hands reached out, pulling me forwards by the waist. I sucked in my stomach, trying to cut a better picture, but he shook his head.

"Don't ever do that again. I want to see you exactly as you are. You have a beautiful body."

His fingers travelled up my ribs, to my breasts. He gripped tight, rolling tender flesh in heavy palms. "You've been a *disgustingly* bad girl, Miss Marsh. Take your panties off."

I did as he asked, sliding the flimsy lace down over my hips to drop to the floor. I gripped my legs together, blushing under his gaze, but he shot me a look of disapproval. "Don't hide from me."

I shuffled my feet apart and he placed his hands on my thighs to guide them wider still, studying me so intently I flushed with embarrassment. I suddenly wished I was shaved like Rebecca, but he didn't seem to care. "You have a gorgeous pussy. I can't wait to stretch you open."

I pictured the woman on stage, her animal groans as his fist pumped all the way inside her. "Will it hurt?"

"I could *make* it hurt... if that's what you need." He took my arm, twisting it in the light. I could have died on the spot, pulling away from him to hide my scars. It took Stuart years before he figured what they were, but James wasn't Stuart. He was another animal entirely. He raised my wrist to his lips. "I don't want you adding any more of these, there are much better ways to savour pain." Canned laughter sounded loud in the room as he peppered my skin with kisses. "I'm not going to hurt your pussy tonight, but bad girls *do* need to learn their lesson. Over my knee."

My heart raced as I lowered myself onto his legs, the hard ridge of his cock pressing into my stomach. It added to both my nerves and excitement in equal measure. He tweaked my position, pushing my head down low and placing a strong arm across my shoulder blades. I steadied myself as he tickled my thighs. "You will not make a sound. The last thing we want is anyone calling the police. They will hear only the TV, agreed?"

"Yes," I said.

"Good girl."

He hit me harder than Rebecca ever did, much harder, landing blows right on top of my bruises. I sucked in breath for the first few slaps, jiggling around on his lap as best I could, given his grip on me. He paused after ten and slipped warm fingers between my legs. "You're a dirty girl, Cat. So fucking wet. Your cunt smells fucking gorgeous."

Another ten, and the tingling well and truly kicked in. My breath came out hard and ragged as he began to vary the blows, landing some on the soft skin of my thighs. I couldn't stop myself grinding against his cock jutting beneath his trousers, even though he'd curse and hit me all the worse for it.

"You're on dangerous ground, Cat's eyes," he said, accentuating the words with the thwack of his palm. "Playing with the beast. I'd love to see you striped by my cane, your tits all bound-up sore for me." I could hardly breathe, my pussy was on fire. "I'd love to break you open, but not tonight. Not tonight..."

He released his grip, leaving me sprawled across him as I caught my breath. I twisted my head to meet his eyes. "What now, Masque? What are you going to do to me?"

He massaged my ass with firm fingers, heightening the post-spanking glow. "You're with *James* tonight, not Masque. I'd quite like to do what I came in here for."

"What did you come in here for?"

He twisted me in a heartbeat, pulling me up to straddle his legs, his face in mine. "I came in here for *you*, Lydia, my green-eyed temptress. Not for kink, or bruises, or gaping pussy and tears... just you."

His mouth was on mine in a flash, hands in my hair. His tongue was so fierce, knocking me right off kilter. This wasn't like with Stuart, the twist of his tongue around mine was primal, raw... it was amazing. I kissed James right back, wrapping my arms around his neck for extra balance as he got to his feet, taking me with him. He laid me on the bed, barely breaking contact, covering the whole length of my body with his. I grappled with his shirt, desperate for skin on skin, desperate for the chimera.

"Please let me see you," I begged into his mouth. "Please." He raised himself up, straddling me with solid thighs, the outline of his cock thick through his suit trousers. I sucked in breath as he took off his shirt, and there, in all its glorious darkness, was the beast upon his chest. I traced its lines with shaky fingers, all the way down his ribs. "It's so beautiful."

"Rebecca's a fine artist."

"Did it hurt?"

"Some of it. Good pain, though, Cat, some pain feels so good."

"I'm learning that."

"You'll learn a lot from Rebecca, she's extremely experienced."

I dared to meet his eyes, wrenching my gaze from the beast. "I want to learn from you. From Masque."

"This isn't a conversation for now. I'm ravenous." He lowered himself onto me, sculpted muscle hard against my tender breasts. I loved his skin against mine, the chimera scorching, just like I'd wanted... just like I'd imagined. He worked his way down with his mouth, stopping to suck at my nipples. I awaited the pain of his bite, but it didn't come. "I knew you'd have perfect tits." He met my eyes as he flicked his tongue. "They'll learn to love pain, I promise."

"You can hurt me," I moaned. "I'm ready."

"I have other plans." He carried on down, slowly, and my stomach knotted as he positioned himself between my legs, tickling the soft line of hair with his breath.

"I should have shaved... like Rebecca."

"Your pussy is divine as it is. Don't be shy." He growled in the back of his throat, and pulled my lips apart, stretching them wide with his fingers. I closed my eyes, fighting back the embarrassment. "Look at me, Cat." I did as he asked, and his eyes were so honest, so raw. "I wish you could see how pretty your cunt is, you're so fucking beautiful like this." He ran his tongue over me, darting ever so lightly over my clit. I squirmed and he gripped my thighs, holding me still. "I'm going to make you come, and you're going to let me. You will not fake, or exaggerate, or rush yourself for the sake of dramatics. You must relax and let it happen. Am I clear?"

I nodded.

"Deep breaths. Relax."

I did as he instructed, regular, rhythmic breathing while he kissed his way around the soft folds of me. I moaned when he sucked my clit into his mouth, and it was all genuine. He took his time, soft growls of pleasure ramping up my own, and I soon forgot about any embarrassment, writhing against his mouth as he played me with expert care. I let out a hiss as he slid two fingers inside.

"You're tight, Lydia, so fucking tight. You're going to feel so fucking good around my cock." A third finger took my breath, and I started to jerk against him, adding friction. "This may feel strange, relax." He curled his fingers inside me, pressing tight, and the pressure felt so weird, almost a low ache, but not quite painful. He worked his hand in a solid rhythm, slowly at first, until the beat overtook me and I was reaching for him, consumed by primal need I'd never felt before, and then the unthinkable happened. I needed to pee. Really bad. Really, really fucking bad. I gripped at his wrist, but he didn't ease up.

"I need the toilet," I rasped. "Sorry, I need to go."

"You don't, trust me."

Panic bloomed beneath lust. "I do. I really need to pee."

"You don't."

I whimpered as he picked up pace a little more, pressure building. "James…"

He smiled as he pressed a hand hard on my lower belly, right on my bladder. "Piss, Lydia, if you need to, don't fight it. Let it go."

"I can't…"

"You can. It isn't piss, believe me, but even if it is…" He pressed harder, and pumped his fingers with renewed urgency until something inside me went crazy. My feet thrashed about on the bed, scuffing at the sheets for grip. "Let it go, let it out."

I didn't recognise the noises coming from me: weird groans and wheezes as my hands gripped at the bed, at him, anywhere I could reach. "James!"

"That's it, Cat, that's it…"

The noises, oh my God the noises, slurping wet noises, all from me, but I couldn't control it, couldn't stop. I exploded, swearing and gritting my teeth and hissing out air, bucking and jerking and kicking at the bed. My hands flattened against his back, fingers desperate for grip. He kept playing me, all the way through, keeping up a perfect rhythm until I flopped down lifeless, gasping for breath.

"Oh my God," I said. "What the hell was that?"

He smiled. "That, Lydia, was a vaginal orgasm, which I can only assume you've never experienced before. A bit different from strumming your clit, don't you think? I can only imagine Rebecca was saving some prime cuts for me, since she could have done this to you in her sleep."

"She didn't do that, no," I wheezed, suddenly all too aware of wet sheets clinging to my thighs. "Did I piss? I'm so sorry!"

"That's not piss. That's the beginning of a squirt. Give it enough practice and you'll be gushing across the room like the porno squirt queens."

"Are you serious?"

"Deadly." He licked his fingers. "And it's delicious. *You* are delicious."

I felt a grin spread across my face, endorphins dancing through me. "Can I taste *you* now, please?"

"Later." He moved from position, standing to loosen his belt, I reached out my hands as he lowered his trousers, desperate for a touch of him. He looked just like his picture, thick and meaty, with a glorious dark nest of hair at the base of him. All man. He climbed up to me, stroking his length just out of my reach. "You're so ripe for cock." He looked at his strewn clothes, then at the bedroom door. "Pissing hell, I don't have a rubber with me."

I smiled, propping myself up on an elbow to look at him. "In my bag, on the chair."

He handed it over, and I pulled out a pack of three. He raised his eyebrows and I laughed. "They were already in my bag when I set off this morning, I didn't notice until lunchtime."

He smiled back. "Rebecca, the dirty cow. I guess she knew what you were up to?"

"It was her idea. She was insistent actually, made it a condition of me seeing Masque again."

"Clever bitch," he said. "So, she put you up to this, did she?" he climbed up to me, taking the pack from my hand.

"She knew I wanted to, she just upped the stakes. She upped them quite a lot..."

"I'll bet she did." I watched him tear open a packet, stomach fluttering as he rolled one on. "One thing can be said for our Bex," he said, eyes on fire. He held up the other two packets. "She knows me pretty well. We won't be sending her any returns."

I could still feel the thump of my heartbeat between my legs. "I'll be having major words with her about all this when I get home."

"I'm sure she'll be ready for it. Roll over, Lydia, spread wide for me." I shifted onto my front, nerves alight as he settled himself over me. "Remind me what you said, when we arrived?"

His cock felt huge, resting tightly against my slit. "I, um... I like it rough?"

"I hope you were right."

I squealed as he forced himself all the way in, lurching forward at the strength of his assault. He was as big as he looked, stretching me wide, but even though he fucked me like a punishment, slamming me with deep guttural groans while I whimpered like a baby, it felt so good I begged him for more. He was happy to oblige.

He obliged all night long, and even then I wanted more, losing my nerves, losing my inhibitions, losing everything until there was only the way he felt inside me.

I COULDN'T STOP LOOKING AT HIM, STARING LIKE A DUMBASS. I MEAN I *always* stare at him like a dumbass, but I was like a dumbass on steroids. I finished up yet another coffee and Trevor White was right on hand to grab me the pot. He poured a refill with a smile, edging his chair closer to mine in the process. James had been right, there was a definite thing going on there.

I made to meet James' eyes, to see if he'd noticed the invasion of personal space, but he wasn't looking at me. He hadn't looked at me all morning in fact. He'd missed breakfast and walked briskly to the office, speaking barely a word other than to confirm the day's itinerary. I'd let it slide, but my heart was in my stomach, all churned up. Horny, and happy, and exhausted, and scared. I was scared. What if I wasn't good enough for him? Why wouldn't he look at me?

We had lunch with the WHM team, and James stayed embroiled in conversation with their data warehouse manager, leaving me with Trevor. I made polite conversation, easing away from anything too personal, and trying to avoid gazing at James' back like some lovesick puppy.

"So, when will you guys be down again?" Trevor asked, a hopeful sheen in his eyes. He pushed his glasses up his nose and leant in close, swatting my elbow with an over-friendly hand. "We sure like having you around."

"I don't know yet," I said, honestly. "Phase two begins next week, so I guess whenever we're ready to go live."

"Soon, I hope. Next time we'll have to do that social, I'll show you the Brighton nightlife."

"I look forward to it," I lied, thanking the heavens that James was ready to resume.

Once again, he didn't meet my eyes.

THE TRAIN BACK TO BRIGHTON WAS RAMMED, AND IT TOOK ME A while to get a seat with James. He stayed glued to his tablet, checking emails, until finally I plucked up a voice.

"Are you ok?"

"Fine, thank you. And you?"

He wanted me to lie, I know that, but words tumbled out of my mouth without censor. "Not really, you've been weirding me out today. Are we screwed now? Is that it? Do you hate me after last night or something?"

He looked around, scowling at the proximity of other commuters. "Not now," he hissed. "Not here."

"Well, where then?" I hissed back. "I want to know we'll be ok. We work together."

"You think I don't know that? *That's* the problem. Work and play don't mix. We made a mistake."

"Some mistakes are worth making..." I whispered.

He smiled, but it was so muted. My heart sank. "I enjoyed that particular mistake very much, but it *was* a mistake. Now we have to find a way to resume normal relations."

"Ok," I said. "If that's what you want." My hands were clammy, I knotted them together.

"I'm being sensible, Lydia, and so should you. We both knew this was a bad idea."

"And this occurred to you between seven and half past this morning, did it? You were fine when you left me."

"A cold shower works wonders for rational thinking."

"I won't mention it again, then. I'll be your *mistake* and we can forget it ever happened." I tried to sound less hurt than I really was.

He leant in close, his mouth to my ear. "I won't be forgetting it ever happened. I couldn't if I tried, I promise."

I looked out of the window the rest of the journey, and let him get on with his emails.

I HATED MYSELF FOR IT, BUT I COULDN'T LET HIM WALK AWAY. ONCE he was gone, that would be it, I just knew it. He'd batten down the hatches and never speak about it again, and me and Masque and everything I'd fantasised about would be ruined. I trailed him through the station, even though we'd said our goodbyes and were off in different directions. He turned to face me, shrugging his shoulders.

"What can I say, Lydia? What do you want me to say?"

"Just listen a minute, please, surely you've got that for me, after last night."

"I've got all the time in the world for you, I'm just trying to be smart about this." He pulled me around a corner, to the side of a portable coffee truck. "We need to do this, we need to be professional."

"I know, I get it!" I wheezed. "But last night was amazing, I've never felt so alive. *You* were amazing. Please don't ruin it now, not yet."

He sighed. "This *thing* can't work. We work together, a *professional* relationship, we can't cross that line, it gets too messy, believe me."

"We crossed it already, I'm just saying we may as well cross it again."

"And I'm saying James Clarke and Lydia Marsh, co-workers at

Trial Run Software Group *have* to be co-workers, I said it before, I'm not cut out for a relationship. Especially an office romance. I'd never make it work. I'd try and I'd fail, and you'd quit, or I'd quit, or we'd both quit and lose the excellent working relationship we've built up. I don't want that. I want you at my side, on my team, happy and stable."

I bit my lip, concentrating so hard I felt my brain could explode. "What makes you think I want a relationship? I'm straight out of a shit one, you think I want to trade in my new life for another stab at domesticity?" I was burning up, I could feel it. "Because I don't. I don't want that! I don't want an office romance, or hearts and roses and shared sandwiches at lunchtime, James, I want Masque! I want what we had last night."

He reached out a hand, just for a moment, just long enough to run a finger down my cheek. "I know you don't want another Mr Comfortable, but you don't want this either. You think you do, but you don't. I know you don't want your career getting messy any more than I do. I know you well enough to know that. We have to draw a line under this before it gets out of hand. Can we go back to being James and Lydia, please? I know I messed up. I know it was me who barged my way into your room last night and I'm sorry for that."

"I'm not," I said, simply. "I'm not sorry at all."

"You will be, when it fucks your career."

I clutched my hands to my temples, thinking, thinking, thinking. Sensible Lydia agreed with him, tried to regain some perspective. "You're right, of course, you're right."

He smiled, a faint smile, part relief, part something else. "I had a great night, an excellent night."

"So did I," I said, preparing to walk away. He took a step aside to let me pass, but I placed a hand on his shoulder on the way.

Please, Lord, let this work. "Look, no hard feelings, I'm sure Rebecca will set me up with someone else at Explicit, she's been trying hard enough."

His eyebrows pitted, mouth clamping instantly. "You're planning on going back to Explicit?"

I smiled. "Well, of course. I want to explore this new side of me... where else would I go? It seems pretty cool there, I like it. I guess I'll see you around." I took another step forward but he pulled me back, pinning me to the side of the coffee stand.

"Don't do this, please."

"Do what?"

"Don't make this impossible for me."

I stared him out. "Don't make *what* impossible for you?"

"*This.* This *sensibility*. It won't work if you're at Explicit every weekend, it just won't work."

"I'm not going to ignore my fantasies, just because *you* don't want to fuck me again. I'm going to Explicit, James, just as often as Rebecca will take me. It doesn't have to be a problem. I'll meet someone else, don't worry about it." I tried to make my way past him, but he blocked my route, barring me with the solid muscle wall of his chest. I could only imagine the chimera below his suit, taut over tight skin.

"Jesus Christ, Lydia, don't you fucking get it?" he seethed. "I don't fucking want you to meet someone else at Explicit. I can just about cope with seeing you in the office every fucking day, but *this*, this Explicit thing is totally unviable for me."

"Well, what do you suggest then?" I snapped. "That I just totter off like a good girl and never darken your door again?"

"No, of course not."

We stared at each other, both fiery and tense and seriously

pissed off. Stalemate. I shrugged, lost for words. "I dunno what I can say."

"Neither do I."

Thoughts ticked by slowly, struggling for resolution. I decided to take my chances. "Ok, so let's back up a bit. The work thing is bad, right, I get it. I agree with it. Fucking co-workers is a disaster waiting to happen. It couldn't work."

"Most certainly," he said. "It's not feasible."

"Fine, so James and Lydia are no more, we keep it professional, we do our job, we keep things straight between us and get back to normal."

"That was my thinking on it, yes," he said, warily.

"But what about Masque and Cat?" I said. "What about their personal time?"

He raised an eyebrow. "Where are you going with this?"

"Just think about it a minute. We're both private people, right? We both know how to keep our business to ourselves. So, what if Cat and Masque did their own thing, completely outside of our normal lives. No crossover, no awkwardness, no mention whatsoever of Explicit, not even the vaguest hint that there is anything extra-curricular about James and Lydia."

"You propose Masque and Cat have an Explicit-only relationship? Is that what you're saying? And you really think that will work?"

I nodded. "I think it might."

"And Cat is really happy to fuck Masque in a public-only environment, is she? No strings, no late night cuddles, no in-bed sex with warm sheets and cosy pillows..."

"Cat's happy to fuck Masque wherever she needs to."

Seconds ticked by so slowly. I could see him weighing it up, running it through his mind. My heart pounded, waiting for his verdict.

"I guess Cat will have to speak with Masque when she sees him at Explicit, see what they can work out."

I breathed out in relief, a smile blooming on my face. "Cat and Masque will have to wait a few weeks, until Rebecca can take a guest again."

He cocked his head. "I think Cat might find herself on the guest list tomorrow night. Masque has platinum VIP membership, he can take a guest whenever he wants."

"Then Cat will be there." I beamed.

I walked away before he could change his mind.

CHAPTER II
James

"Ah, James! I was expecting your call. I wondered which one of you would get me first. How was Brighton? Good, I hope?"

"Cut the crap, Rebecca. Just what the hell have you been doing?"

She cackled so loudly I moved the handset from my ear. "Was three enough? I thought a twelve-pack may have been overkill."

"We didn't have any spare afterwards."

"I should hope not. Our lovely Lydia deserved a good session of cock. Please tell me you managed to make her cry? She's such a guarded little cookie, that one... no tears at all, and believe me, I've been trying."

I ignored her completely, filing her revelation for later. "What the fucking hell were you thinking? That little Explicit stunt could have cost me my entire fucking life."

"Must you always be so dramatic? She's not a blabber, James, it would have been fine."

"That's my career you're being so blasé about."

"If you hadn't taken the bait last night, I'd never have taken her back to Explicit, ok? She'd never have discovered the identity of the elusive Masque. Anyway, if you'd have told me you were going to be beating the shit out of some random, I'd have picked a different night to bring her along."

"I'm *allowed* to change my mind as to when I frequent Explicit, Rebecca, or are you going to fill the place with more of my professional associates every time I take a fucking night off?"

I heard her slide her balcony door open, light up a cigarette on the roof terrace. "You *wanted* me to do this."

"I really didn't."

"Lie to yourself all you want, but deep down we both know you wanted her. It's why she's here, *Masque*, you wanted her at Explicit, you *knew* this would happen."

"You seem pretty fucking sure of that."

"I'm beyond fucking sure of that. You like her, and you *should*. She's awesome." She took a long drag. "You know I always tell you the truth, James, even when it's rough. That's why I'm your friend."

A flash of remembered gratitude dulled the flames. "I know that, Bex. I haven't forgotten what you did for me."

"So, I'm doing it again, only this time it's a shitload more pleasant a task... You *like* her. Deal with it. I'm sure I'll get a thank you in time. Jewellery or boots are always appreciated."

"Now you're pushing it," I snarled, but it was a front and she knew it. I heard her soft laughter and struggled not to smile.

"Will I see you tomorrow?"

I made her wait a few seconds. "Yes, you'll see me tomorrow."

"Praise the Lord! Masque is back in town."

"It would appear that way," I said. "Oh, and Rebecca?"

"Yes, James?"

"Please make sure our lovely Lydia wears plenty of eyeliner, she *will* be crying tomorrow night, I assure you."

She was whooping before I could reach the end-call button.

I took up my seat at the side of the bar, tipping my glass at the regulars passing close enough to catch my attention, and I waited for Cat's eyes. Raven appeared first, head to toe in red latex, with Cara just a moment behind, shimmying in a tiny pink tutu. I held my breath as my guest followed them in, rational James springing up to bludgeon me with my own stupidity, but it soon passed. Lydia looked sensational, standing tall in stiletto knee-highs, stocking tops visible under a plush-velvet mini-dress. Her hair was styled in a natural wave, sweeping down around her slender shoulders, and her eyes, sweet Jesus, her eyes... Raven's work, certainly, heavily lined with kohl and swept out to a feline arc. They looked paler than ever, dancing with the light as they searched the room for me. Giving up, she joined the girls at the bar, sucking up sex-on-the-beach through a neon-pink straw.

I finished my scotch as Raven whispered in Lydia's ear, pointing over in my direction. I stepped into clear view, sinking right into those jade green pools as I made my way over. I took a stool to her left, close enough to breathe her in. Amber and Rose, and something else. Some kind of body scrub, Cherry Blossom. My knee pressed into hers, the simple contact buzzing like static.

"Good evening, Cat."

"Good evening, Masque." Her hand dithered nervously between her leg and mine until I made the decision for her, snaring her delicate little fingers and pulling them to rest on my thigh. She smiled, edging her way closer. "I was worried you wouldn't be here."

"It would be a rude host who'd put a name on a guest list and not arrive to greet them."

"You know what I mean. I'm really glad you showed." She

squeezed my thigh through my jeans, eyes finding mine in the shadows of my mask. "You look so different."

Cara caught our attention with a shrill little squeal. Raven was twisting at her nipples through her crop top. I watched Lydia's breath quicken, a tense little gulp of air.

"Are you sure you want to be here?"

"Dead sure." She jumped as a trio of regulars took up position behind her. Tyson leant to the bar across her shoulder, dazzling her with a smile.

"A new face," he said. "Hey, pretty lady."

"Cat," she said, smiling.

"Tyson. So, you're here with Masque on this fine evening?"

"She is," I replied.

"Don't start without me," he grinned. He ordered his drink and resumed conversation with the women at his rear. Lydia's hand clutched at my thigh for dear life. She waited until they were out of earshot.

"Does he want to join in?" she whispered, voice croaky.

I revelled in her awkwardness. "He's a watcher. He'll be at the window, you can count on it."

"The window? You mean when we..."

"When you're bound at my mercy and I'm pounding your tight little pussy, yes, he'll be watching."

I waited for her reaction, for her to wimp out and walk away, but she didn't move a muscle.

I LET HER RELAX, BUT NOT FOR LONG. THE PLACE HAD FILLED NICELY, the main floor busy enough to thrum. Just as I was debating my next move, the spotlights struck up. Perfect timing. Lydia looked over my shoulder, straining to see who was on stage. I watched the rise and fall of her chest, her adrenaline starting to flow.

"Shall we?" I asked, rhetorically. I helped her down from her stool, leading her over to the main floor. People made way, letting us straight through to the front; a benefit of being so well known in this place. I found us a decent vantage point, taking a seat on one of the benches and pulling her down onto my lap. We were on the edge of the spotlight, visible to anyone who cared to look. Many did, curious as to the new, beautiful lady-friend I had in tow. "Keep your eyes on the stage," I whispered. "It should be a good one." I ran my fingers down her bare arms, enjoying how she shivered at the contact. She reached back for me, gripping at my hips.

"You were amazing up there last week," she murmured. "I loved it."

"You'll love this one, too," I said. "That's Cain, and his girlfriend Vix, they really know how to play." They took up position, Vix submitting meekly to the cuffs above her head.

"Is he going to cane her?"

"Would you like him to?"

"I think so."

I kissed her neck. "More likely the flogger, the cane is too harsh for a lot of tastes."

She squirmed as the scene started up, making herself comfortable. I held her close, my hand on her ribs to feel her breath. The flogging was a good one, nice and hard and really fucking thwacky. Vix lurched forwards in her chains, howling with every lash, while Lydia watched, transfixed, gripping hold of my thighs underneath hers. I felt her breathing turning shallow.

"Horny isn't it?" I whispered. "So fucking horny." I ran my fingers down the smooth line of her throat, across her collarbone to the strap of her dress. She tensed as I slipped it from her shoulder. "Relax, Cat, don't fight me." I slid my fingers inside the fabric, smiling to find she was naked underneath. Her nipple was already hard, a little bullet crying for my touch. "Keep your eyes on the stage."

I freed her from her other strap, warm lips against her neck. She let out a squeak as I pulled the fabric down, offering the perfect swell of her tits to anyone who cared to look. She let go of my thighs, hands flailing against the exposure. "No," I whispered, firmly.

I heard the softest groan from the back of her throat as I raised her tits high in my hands, rolling her nipples between my fingers while she writhed against my chest, compliant.

"Good girl." I raised my knees between hers, hooking her legs to spread them wide. She moaned, fighting my efforts but only for a second. I squeezed her tits with savage strength to punish her, loving the way her shoulders hunched at the pain. "Touch yourself."

She ignored my instruction at first, nervous enough to flash her eyes around the room. The gaze of strangers met hers, and instinct made to clamp her legs shut. I blocked her efforts, reaching down to wrench her panties to the side.

"Play with your dirty wet cunt, Cat, before I put you over my knee in front of this whole fucking room. Is that what you want?"

Slowly she slid her hand between her thighs, rubbing so softly she was hardly moving. I swatted her hand away in frustration, and she whimpered as I plunged two fingers inside her. "That's what you need... show the world your pretty little pussy."

The action on the stage ramped up a level, Cain lowering Vix's bonds enough to slide his cock into her mouth. He shoved his hips forward and she gagged on him, chest heaving and retching as he forced his way all the way in. I felt Lydia clench around my fingers, a soft little mewl hissing from her lips.

"You like that?" I teased. "Like the way he fucks her mouth?" She nodded, so slightly it was almost unperceivable. "Ever had someone use you like that, Cat? Choke you up real fucking good?" She shook her head. "That's going to change real soon, my sweet little Cat's eyes, you're going to retch on my cock until you're sick."

My good little Lydia lost the plot in my lap, whimpering and bucking and riding herself stupid on my thick fucking fingers. Sweet Christ, she was a dirty bitch after all. I pulled out to strum her clit, playing her fast, straight over the edge of orgasm. She arched herself against me, wrapping her arms back around my neck for leverage as she came in my hands. I smiled into her neck as she floated back down, trembling in the aftershock. She came to her senses, covering her tits back up and closing her legs tight, all too aware of the eyes staring at her.

"That was insane," she whispered.

"It was *hot*," I breathed, grinding my crotch into her ass.

I pointed her attention back to the stage where Vix was still getting her face fucked, rivulets of tears and spit dribbling down her chin. Beautiful.

Lydia turned to face me, eyes wide and so fucking gorgeous. "Were you serious?" she said. "Are you really going to fuck my throat like that?"

"No," I said. "I'm not going to fuck your throat like that." I smiled at her confusion. "It's going to be a whole lot worse."

I wasn't joking.

Lydia

I NEEDED THE NEXT WINE, AND THE ONE AFTER THAT. I WAS BURNING with embarrassment, crazy shocked that I'd let Masque finger me in front of a room full of strangers, but hell he'd got me off. He'd got me off so good my insides were still reeling, and I'd *liked* it. I'd *loved* it. He sipped at his scotch on the rocks in silence, brooding and dangerous. His eyes were in the shadows, hidden in the hollows of the mask, yet I knew he was staring at me. He hadn't stopped.

He ordered another whisky, but didn't give me the option of more wine. Instead of alcohol, which I could have desperately done with, he ordered me a pint of water, and placed it firmly in front of me.

"I'm ok," I said. "I'm not drunk."

"It's not because you're drunk. I want you to drink that pint for me, as fast as you can."

I raised an eyebrow. "Why?"

"Do as you're told. You'll see why."

I took a long swig, glugging back as much as I could in a single effort.

A woman in white PVC made her way over, leaning down into his ear. I strained to make out what she was saying over the beat of the music. He smiled his thanks and waved her away. "That's our call, you'd better drink up."

"Our call?"

"Playroom three is empty."

"Oh." Nerves flared, dancing around my spine, but my clit was on fire, pulsing between my legs.

He got up in my face, his breath hot on my lips. "If you want to back out, now would be a good time."

I swigged back the rest of my water, gulping it down as fast as I could swallow, then slammed the empty glass on the bar. "I'm not wimping out, Masque, I want you to fuck my mouth."

"It's going to be rough, Cat, and real fucking dirty." He placed a hand around my throat, surveying his vessel.

"I hope so." I dared to smile, wishing I was as half as brave as I sounded. "That *is* why I'm here."

He planted a solid kiss on my lips, cupping my chin in his hand. "That's my girl."

WE PASSED RAVEN AND CARA EN ROUTE TO PLAYROOM THREE, AND Masque took hold of Raven's wrist, pulling her in close to his mouth. Cara smiled at me, offering me a sweet little wave as they whispered out of earshot. I smiled back, blushing at the thought that she'd been watching earlier. I guessed it should have been the least of my worries, since I was about to do it all over again. The corridor was teeming with observers, pressed up against the interior windows of playrooms one and two. They turned to look as Masque opened room three for me, and my heart skipped a beat as faces moved over to our window. My eyes shot around the room, trying to distract myself. There were a couple of benches, with cuffs dangling all over the place, but Masque was stood instead upon a simple gym-style mat, waterproof and springy. He beckoned me to join him. I glanced over my shoulder to find more faces at the window.

"Ignore them," he said. "Look at *me*."

I looked at him gladly. His jeans were slung low on his hips, the hard lines of his torso towering above me, even in my heels. The chimera looked darker than I'd ever seen, moving as he moved, alive on his skin. I stared into the dark pools of his eyes, soaking up the shadowy strength of his features. He was beautiful, magnificent. He was perfect. I took a few paces forward, catching his musk in my nostrils. It made my mouth water.

I jumped as the door opened, breathing in relief to find it was only Raven. It soon became obvious she was staying.

"Raven's going to be helping me," Masque said. It was clearly not up for discussion. "On your knees."

I positioned myself in front of him, dropping to the soft padding of the mat underneath. Raven moved to my rear, pulling my hair into a makeshift ponytail. I considered asking questions, but Masque's hands were already on his belt. He dropped his jeans, kicking them off to the side and his cock rose free, huge in front of my face. He slapped it against my cheek, packing a hefty thump.

"Deep breaths," Raven said. "In and out."

I did as she said, taking in all the air I could like some kind of deep sea diver. Masque tilted my head up to him, and Rebecca held me firm in position. "Open your mouth," he said. "Wide. Tongue out." He smiled at my compliance. "Good girl."

"Hands behind your back," Raven added. "You will keep them there."

I knotted my fingers behind me, determined to obey, managing just two more breaths before Masque slid himself between my lips. He aimed at an angle, and his cock bulged out from my cheek. He growled, straining until it popped free again. "So fucking pretty. Spit on me, Cat, make me wet."

My first effort was pathetic, years of good manners counteracting the instruction. It was Raven who reacted, grabbing his length in her hand and leaning down next to me. "He *said* spit on his fucking cock," she snapped. "*This* is spit." She spat like a llama, and it landed right on target, dripping down the underside of his shaft. "Now you," she ordered. "Do it properly."

I did my best, hawking out as much as I could, even though some landed short. "Better," she said. "Again."

Attempt number three was the best of the lot, leaving a long slimy trail between his cock and my chin. "Quick learner," Raven purred.

I pulled away, cheeks on fire, but Masque gripped my chin, guiding me back. "Do you have a problem with spitting, Cat?" he asked, voice low and dangerous. I shook my head even though I didn't really know the answer. "Speak."

"No," I said, my chin still pinned in his grip.

"No *what*?" Raven hissed.

"No, *sir*," I corrected, hoping it was the right etiquette. It seemed to appease her.

"You need to break, Cat, understand?" Masque said. "All the reservations you've ever known will fall in this place."

"Yes, sir."

"You will learn to be dirty here, obedient without restraint. That's what I offer. Do you want it?"

"Yes, sir."

"PLEASE, sir," Raven snapped.

"Please, sir, please!" My mind was unravelling, knees quivering underneath me, but I was strong, determined. I wanted this.

"Look at me," Masque ordered. I raised my eyes to his, sucking in breath. "You're mine in this place. Mine to command, mine to control, mine to protect. You will give yourself to me."

"Yes, sir," I rasped.

"Open wide," he said, and I did it. I opened wide, ignoring the faces at the edge of my vision, the faces clamouring to witness my humiliation.

"You will say thank you for this," he told me.

He leant down, hooking his fingers behind my teeth and stretching my jaw as far as it would go. My lips splayed around his grip in a truly degrading manner, but I didn't pull away, not even when he hacked up a healthy gob-full of spit straight into my mouth. I fought the urge to retch.

"Lucky girl," Raven purred. "Say thank you."

Good Lydia Marsh screamed from the sidelines, screamed that she didn't want this, but as the horror subsided it left something else. Something uncoiled in the pit of me, and it wanted all of this, it wanted all of *him*.

I swallowed his filthy gift down and opened my mouth wide for more. He obliged, dribbling a thick strand of drool all the way from his mouth to mine. I took it all from him, and he stroked tender fingers down my cheek, his eyes full of pride. It made my heart swell, blooming through my chest in a wave of bliss. My mind twisted, wondering what the hell was happening to me, but the serpent in my gut uncoiled, demanding everything he had to give.

"You are so fucking beautiful, Cat," he hissed through gritted teeth. "So fucking beautiful."

He rammed his cock inside my mouth so hard I gagged on impact, cheeks billowing out in desperation for air. He didn't let up, forcing his length right the way to the back of my throat while I retched and spluttered and strained against him. I felt my eyes watering, tears streaming as I fought for breath. He fucked my mouth like a man possessed, hissing and groaning in effort while Raven held me tight. My hands moved from their position just long enough for her to yell at me. I put them back.

"Relax your fucking throat," Masque said. "Let me in."

He shunted Raven from position to place his hands at the back of my skull, wriggling deeper into me. He groaned as he found the perfect angle, and my lips slammed into the hot flesh of his groin, his balls mashed tight against my chin. He held the position for long seconds while I blinked away tears, then pulled out with a low growl, leaving me free to cough and splutter and gasp for air. My chin was dripping, streaked with spit and tears and God knows what else.

"Beautiful girl," Masque whispered, presenting his cock for round two. I gave him my mouth gladly, feeling the familiar warmth of Rebecca pressed into my back. Her hands snaked between my legs, teasing at my clit.

I gagged harder at his assault this time, every muscle clenching in a bid to expel him, but he didn't retreat a single inch, solid as stone. I felt a fluid-rush churn up from my stomach, and choked it back in panic, coughing around his dick like a flailing fish.

Rebecca's voice at my ear, soft, soothing. "It's ok, baby, it's ok... let it out."

I swallowed it down, determined not to retch again, but he pushed in too damn hard. I paled in horror as fluid surged from my mouth, drenching Masque's stomach and running down his thighs in a river of pure embarrassment. My vision blurred, dizzying in my mortification, but he smoothed my hair back unfazed.

"It's water, Cat. I made you drink it down, remember? Don't worry, I like it this way."

I stared up at him through streams of tears, eyes stinging with smudged make-up, and right there, underneath him, with Raven's fingers in my pussy, I let it all go – every single scrap of reservation, every tiny sliver of self-control, and it felt like the road to Heaven. I let Masque support my head, surrendering myself absolutely. He moaned his approval, slamming himself into my throat over and over again. When I retched I let it go free, soaking him with stream after stream of gagged-up fluid, and it only seemed to spur him on. Finally, I felt the ascent of orgasm, Raven's fingers working my clit in perfect rhythm. I grunted with alien noises, squelching and groaning and snorting without restraint, a strange croaky quack gurgling from my throat. Masque shifted with the approach of his own climax. I could feel it in his cock, in his thighs, in the balls against my chin. His cock started to twitch in my throat, preparing to spurt.

"Now, Raven, now," he hissed. She heeded his instruction, ramping up the efforts on my clit until my body exploded, shaking and twitching and jerking in her arms. Masque bellowed loud, pressing his cock to my tongue as he erupted, his salty cream filling my mouth.

His taste was all the reward I needed. The nectar of recognition for a job well done. Raven backed away as Masque dropped to his knees, gripping my shoulders in hot clammy hands. He didn't even give me chance to swallow him down before his mouth was on mine. *Dirty bad wrong*, they called him, and they weren't lying. Not one fucking bit. I smiled as he licked up my tears, *his* reward, no doubt, just like Rebecca had warned me. He flicked his tongue across my eyes, digging for every last trace, and then he held me tight, my head against his chest where I could feel his heartbeat booming loud.

"I'm so fucking proud of you, Lydia," he whispered. "So fucking proud. I've never seen you look more beautiful."

I sighed against him, floating on endorphins, smiling to myself as I realised he'd used my real name.

"So, what brings you around these parts?" I handed Steph her cappuccino, sliding into the seat opposite.

"I came to see *you*, of course," she said. "I hardly hear a peep from you these days."

"Sorry," I said. "I've been really busy at work."

"You look different. I guess this is *her* influence?" Steph rolled her eyes at me, unimpressed. I looked down at my outfit, not quite sure of what she was referring to. "The dark clothes, the eyeliner, the crazy choker… you look like some kind of goth, Lyddie."

I couldn't resist laughing. "Seriously? You think *this* is goth? You haven't been out in Camden. It's just a black blouse and some eyeliner, chill your beans."

"You can come back to mine you know, if things are too weird there."

"Things aren't weird," I smiled. "Things are good."

She raised her eyebrows. "Good?"

"*Very* good," I beamed.

"Good like, a *man* good?!"

I sipped my espresso, trying to rein it in. I'd been doing so bloody well, keeping a business-as-usual face at the office for days on end, acting like James Clarke was nobody in particular and it didn't give me goose-pimples to stand within fifty yards of him. I deserved one little outburst, surely?

"Maybe *man* good, yeah."

"Bloody hell, Lyddie, you kept that you to yourself."

"It's early days, totally casual," I said. "No big deal."

"Whatever, missy, you're grinning like a lunatic. Is it suit man? Washisname? James, big CTO boss guy?"

I looked around, paranoid about colleagues since we were just a stone's throw from the office. "He's not my boss, not really."

"So, it *is* him." She grinned. "I'm assuming he doesn't have heads in his fridge, then?"

"I haven't seen his fridge, but the signs are good." If only she knew.

"I'm happy for you, honest I am." She stared into her coffee, an uncharacteristic quietness taking hold.

"But?" I added for her. "What did you really come here for?" I folded my arms, waiting.

"Well, your news kind of makes mine redundant, but I figure I'll tell you anyway," she said. "It's about Stuart."

My stomach knotted, his name an unwelcome sound. "What about Stuart?"

She sighed. "He's been round, a lot, desperate to see you."

"So? Shouldn't he be at home with the mother-to-be? Tell him to get stuffed."

"That's the thing… she isn't there. He isn't even sure the baby is his, she admitted as much to him. Seems he isn't the only contender for biological father status."

My blood froze in my veins. "Why are you telling me this?"

"Because he misses you. Honest, he does. He was round every night until we finally let him in, now he hardly leaves, just spends his time moping over you."

"He needs to move on, I have."

"Have you, really? It's only been weeks."

"Months. It's been months," I snapped.

"Barely."

"What happened to *he's a motherfucking jerk*? *He* cheated on *me*, remember?"

"I know he did! But he feels awful for it, Lyds, I promise you.

He was a jerk, an absolute jerk, but he knows that. He's desperate to make it up, hun, he really loves you."

"Love doesn't do that. It doesn't sleep around in an alleyway at a work conference."

"I can't argue with that, but I promise you, the guy's crazy about you. Maybe it was just a stupid mistake?"

"Have you heard yourself?" I spat. "*Maybe* it was *just* a stupid mistake? He fucked some little slut and got her pregnant."

"Maybe."

"Oh, piss off, Steph, of course he did. It's totally over."

She looked crestfallen, and it annoyed the shit out of me.

"Ok, I'm sorry. I thought I'd try. You two were good together."

"We weren't good together. Honestly, my eyes have been well and truly opened. I've never been happier."

She broke the tension with a smile. "And this is because of suit man, is it? This spring in your step?"

"He's part of it. A *small* part of it."

"Or all of it," she let out a low laugh. "I never saw this coming, I really didn't." She leant in close across the table. "So, tell me... is he, you know... is he good?"

At that exact moment I saw James' outline stroll past the window on the street outside. His hair was wild in the wind, face flushed from his hour at the gym. I lowered my head, avoiding any chance of eye contact. My skin tingled with life, excitement blooming in my stomach.

"He's better than good," I grinned. "He's goddamn-fucking amazing."

CHAPTER 12

James

I knew her knock. The dainty little rapping of the knuckles against my door. It always made my pulse race, my dick twitch, my fucking mouth water. I played ignorant.

"Who is it?" My voice was gruff, dismissive.

She turned the handle. "It's Lydia, have you got a sec?"

I beckoned her in, keeping my eyes fixed on my monitor and pretending to be engrossed in development-team appraisals. She took a seat in the chair opposite, shuffling papers in her lap like a true professional.

"And what can I do for you, Miss Marsh?"

Today she didn't play along. "James, please, can we really talk. Just for a minute?" She was biting her lip, fiddling with her chin. She looked thoroughly awkward, in fact.

My heartbeat pounded in my stomach at the thought of the bruises under her skirt. "What's the problem?"

She kept her eyes firmly on the paperwork in her lap. "It's Salmons," she said. "The deal's landed, right?"

"Yes, it has," I confirmed. "Frank's calling a meeting about it later on today, sharing the good news. We got it on the back of WHM, Lydia, you should be proud."

"I am proud."

"So, what's the issue? Spit it out."

She finally met my eyes. My pulse raced, adrenaline pumping. Those fucking eyes, every fucking time. Weeks of fucking her senseless at Explicit had only made it worse.

"I just got accosted by Emily Barron, by the photocopier. You know Emily?"

"Emily Barron." I pretended to think, an inkling of where this was headed creeping up my spine. "Blonde girl, yes? From your team?"

"She was angry, with me. Do you know why?"

I shook my head, smooth. "I have no idea."

"She told me you've blown her out of the Salmons project, that I've been assigned to it instead."

"And?"

"Is it true?"

"So what if it is?"

She sighed. "Emily's been working on the Salmons' deal for weeks. She did all the pre-sales prep work with Tony Carter. It's her deal, James, she wants to project manage it."

"I don't give two shits what she wants, I'll pick the team *I* want for a deal that size."

Her eyes widened. "So, you *are* assigning me to Salmons? With you?"

I choked back irritation. "*Yes*, I'm assigning you to Salmons. Frank's already signed off on it, we're good to go once phase two of WHM gets wrapped up."

"I think you should give it to Emily," she announced, arms folded.

"On what grounds? That she's worked hard? Give me a break, Lydia, that doesn't mean shit."

"It means shit to her. She hates me for it."

"Let her hate you for it. It's not your call, and it's not your fault."

She looked behind her, checking the door was closed. "We're supposed to be playing this cool, yes? Keeping things really low key, no waves, no personal relationship. You wanted that just as much as I did."

"Easily as much as you did," I snapped. "And you shouldn't be talking like this. We had an agreement."

"Then why are you ruining it?" she hissed. "Putting me on Salmons is a dumb move, it draws attention, makes us look closer than we should be. Explicit-only, you said. Now Emily's mad with me and the whole fucking team know about it. Don't think I don't realise WHM is almost up, no more cosy coffee mornings and nights over in Brighton. If you wanted more time together, you could have just said. You didn't need to pull Emily off her project, James, it was unfair."

My hackles were smoking, breath fierce. "Have you quite fucking finished?"

She smoothed her skirt down, nodded her head. "Yeah, I'm finished."

"For your information, Miss Marsh, this decision had nothing whatsoever to do with our personal relationship. I picked you for Salmon's because *you're* the best, because *we* work well together, because *you* have experience on large personal injury case-management implementations." I shot her a look of fire, jaw tense. "Emily Barron is scatty and disorganised. She worked with Tony because she had an ideal personality for a rapport-build with the Salmons team in the early stages. I never had *any* intention of letting her work with the implementation, and neither did Frank. Not even Tony wanted her to handle it, if you must know." She flushed beetroot, eyes like saucers. I was on a roll. "And as for your little monologue about coffees and hotel nights, I'm Chief fucking Technology Officer. I make decisions that are best for this whole company. If you think having you on the other side of this desk takes priority over me doing a good job for this business, then you are way off the mark. Way, way off the fucking mark."

She rubbed her temples. "I don't think that."

"That's not how it sounds."

"Really, I don't. I was just stressed, she kicked off at me, ok? And I didn't know anything about it. I felt like an idiot."

"Frank was going to tell you, since *he's* your boss."

"I'm sorry, James."

I rubbed my palms against my thighs, clammy hands. "Your minute's up, Lydia, I'm really busy."

She stood without a word, edging her way to the doorway. I didn't look up from my screen, cock rising at her humiliation, despite my anger.

"I guess I'll see you later," she said, letting herself out.

I didn't indulge her with an answer.

My email sounded a few minutes later. My cock responded in its usual fashion, jumping on sight of her name in the preview box.

From: Lydia Marsh
Subject: Professionalism

James, I've offended you. It was unintentional, and I assure you it's much more about feeling bad for Emily Barron than it is about you. I would never question your professional integrity. You conduct yourself faultlessly.

Lydia Marsh
Senior Project Co-ordinator, Trial Run Software Group.

I smiled despite myself. It was amusing to have my whole earlier email spouted back at me.

To: Lydia Marsh
Subject: Re: Professionalism.

I know that's my email. Switching the names doesn't make it an original piece of work.
In light of this fact, I feel entitled to plagiarise yours:

Do you mean 'sorry'?

James
James Clarke
CTO, Trial Run Software Group.

Her reply was through in a heartbeat.

From: Lydia Marsh
Subject: Re: re: Professionalism

Yes. I mean *sorry*.
Nothing like making someone work for it.
You said you'd remember, should the boot ever be on the other foot. I guess you did.

So, how does it feel to be the injured party?

Lydia Marsh
Senior Project Co-Ordinator, Trial Run Software Group.

I stroked my cock through my suit, the thought of her smug little smile driving me to insanity. I was pissed off, fuming, but still she amused me.

To: Lydia Marsh
Subject: Re: re: re: Professionalism.

Come and find out.

James
James Clarke
CTO, Trial Run Software Group.

I waited for it.

From: Lydia Marsh
Subject: Re: re: re: Professionalism

???

Lydia Marsh
Senior Project Co-Ordinator, Trial Run Software Group.

I must have been fucking insane, but my fingers took on a life of their own.

To: Lydia Marsh
Subject: Re: re: re: re: Professionalism.

You heard me. Get up here, now.
NOW, Lydia.

James
James Clarke
CTO, Trial Run Software Group.

She didn't dally around, at my door within the minute, leaving me just enough time to close the window blinds. She rapped, faster than usual, slipping inside before I'd even had time to react. She closed the door behind her, then stared at me, keeping her distance.

"James, look, about what I said…"

"What happens to bad girls, Lydia?" I asked, and she raised her eyebrows, floundering for words as I raised myself from my seat, grabbing my dick through my trousers. "Look what you've done to me, Miss Marsh. I think this requires a disciplinary."

I threw her the key to my door, and she caught it in nimble fingers.

"Lock it," I said, and she did as instructed.

I caught her hands shaking. It sent a shiver down my spine.

"Come here," I hissed. "I want you over my desk."

She approached without hesitation, placing herself between me and the desk. I pushed her down by her shoulders, slamming her flat, chest down against the desk top. My pens went skidding away, order scattered.

"The noise," she wheezed. "This is a mistake."

I pressed into her ass. "It's certainly a mistake, Lydia, certainly."

She sucked in her breath as I hitched her skirt, yanking it roughly around her waist. She was wearing white panties, cute little things with a lacy trim. I slid them down around her thighs, groaning as I saw the results of the weekend. Big, dark circles of bruising, one on each ass cheek. The middles were still a beautiful park purple, rimmed with black and green.

"I bruised well this time, didn't I?" she whispered.

"You should have done. I hit you hard enough." She rocked back against my fingers as I prodded her. Her flesh still felt ridged, the bruises hard to the touch.

"That feels good," she breathed.

"You will stay fucking silent. Do you understand me?" I growled. She nodded, reaching forward to grip at the edge of the desk as I raised my metal ruler, trailing the cold edge down the crack of her ass. "This will hurt."

I slapped the ruler hard against her thighs and she lurched forward. Still she was silent, only the raspy sound of her agitated breathing loud in the room. I kept an ear out for noise in the corridor. Frank was out golfing, I knew that much, and Vanessa downstairs for the support team meeting with any luck. Just us on the floor. I didn't share my knowledge with Lydia.

The next blow was harder, in exactly the same position. She was still jiggling around on her toes when I hit her again. I landed short, sharp thwacks over the purple heart of her bruises, and her hand came up behind her, instinct breaking through her discipline. I pressed the swell of my cock against her bare ass.

"Hands on the desk. You move again and I swear you'll regret it."

"Sorry, sir," she rasped.

Three more blows and I paused, soaking in her ragged breathing. "You deserve this, Miss Marsh, for trying my patience."

"Yes, sir."

I landed another five without hesitation, and her body pressed flat to the desk, white knuckles gripping tight. "Cry for me, Cat, show me how sorry you are."

She didn't even whimper, and frustration flared in my nostrils. I'd been pushing her as hard as I dared, weeks of testing her limits, but still she wouldn't fucking cry for me. She'd go quiet, shaky, pale as a sheet with chattering teeth, high on adrenaline and right on the edge, but she wouldn't fucking cry. It vexed her as much as it did me, I knew that, but still the beast raged on. "Cry for me, Cat, let me taste your beautiful fucking tears."

I gave her three in one spot, so hard she lifted her feet from the floor. "Thank you, sir," she whimpered.

Her ass was bright red, the tiniest fleck of blood where one corner had caught her particularly viciously. I gave her another for good measure and watched the blood pool darker. "Why won't you cry for me, Cat? Why won't you fucking cry for me?"

Five more and she was shaking, her forehead tight to the table.

I could hardly hear her answer. "I can't, sir. I'm sorry, I don't know how."

My dick strained for release. I pressed down onto her, my mouth in her ear. "You have to break to cry, Cat, and you won't break. What are you holding onto?"

"I don't know, sir, I promise."

"So much pain, Cat, and still you won't break for me."

"I'm trying, sir."

"Not hard enough." I raised myself back to standing. "On your back, spread your legs."

She did as I asked, shimmying out of her panties and laying her whole weight on my desk. She looked so beautiful there, presented so pretty for my viewing. I changed position, retreating to the opposite side of my desk where I yanked her forwards until her head lolled over the edge. I unbuckled my belt, sliding down my zipper. "Look what you've done to my cock." I rubbed the swollen head over her mouth, and she opened wide to let me in, gagging as I pushed all the way into her throat. She kept it down like a good girl, cheeks straining. This time I didn't even attempt to fuck her face, I kept still, enjoying the tension of her gag reflex. "Hold your knees, legs spread wide."

She pulled her thighs up to her chest. She'd taken to shaving her pussy, but our encounter today was completely unplanned. I rubbed my fingers over her sweet flesh, catching the tiniest graze of stubble. Delicious.

"It pains me to do this to such a pretty cunt, Lydia, but your insubordination leaves me no choice." She registered my intention and began to shake. Perfect. "I'm sure I don't need to point out that my cock is in your mouth. Please mind your teeth."

God, how I smacked her cunt. She jerked like a fish, coughing against the meat in her throat. Her thighs clamped tight shut, her hands flailing in the air. I pulled her knees back open, and for a moment she fought me. "Give me your fucking pussy," I hissed.

She spread again for me, but this time she was nervous, legs trembling. I landed another and she rocked to the side, trying to choke me out of her throat. I didn't let her, simply pulled her straight back into position. "Close your legs again and I'll double the strokes."

This time she gripped her knees like her life depended on it. I gave her a moment while I circled her swollen clit. "Good girl, I want you nice and wet."

She squeaked as I hit her again, and her knees slammed shut

but only for a moment. Her chest was heaving with frantic gulps as I landed another, and she shook like a leaf at the one after that. Her cunt was blooming nicely, lips swelling with blood and pain. I gave her another two, then slid rough fingers inside her. She bucked against my touch like a good little pain slut, sucking at my cock without prompting. "That's my perfect girl, you're so fucking beautiful. I love your cunt like this."

My dick was starting to twitch, way too soon. I pulled out of her throat with a squelch, trailing her spit across her face. She gulped in breath.

"One more, Lydia, just one more."

"Thank you, sir," she rasped.

"Only this time I want to hit your sweet little clit."

I saw her eyes widen, and she clasped her legs tight around my fingers as I kept on talking.

"It's going to hurt, Cat, I'm not going to lie. It's going to really fucking hurt." I gave her a moment, working my fingers harder inside her until her thighs eased up. "Tell me you want it."

She hesitated just a moment, covering her eyes with her hand. Nervous.

"Do you want it, Cat?" I pushed. "You want to be punished for your rudeness, don't you?"

She nodded, biting her lip. "Not too hard, please sir," she breathed.

"Bad girl. *I* decide how hard I will punish you."

"Sorry, sir."

"You will spread your pussy for me. Now. Show me that sweet little clit."

Her fingers were trembling, but still she slid them down between her legs. She pulled her lips apart, presenting the swollen little nub right up for her punishment. My cock tensed and jerked, desperate to shoot my load all over her.

"Deep breaths, Cat, it's going to hurt so fucking bad."

She sucked in air, closed her eyes. I rain the cold metal over the little red bullet, loving the way she flinched. "Tell me when you're ready."

She kept breathing awhile, then stretched her pussy even wider, screwing her eyes tight shut. "Please, sir, I'm ready."

It was a perfect hit. A clean blow on the most sensitive part of her. She rolled onto her side, hands between her legs and I thought I'd done it, really broken her. She didn't even breathe for long seconds, just lay there trembling under my gaze. I ran my fingers through her hair, angling her face back towards mine with the promise of tears, but there were none. I forced down the disappointment, covering her mouth with mine as she took her first long gulp of air. She breathed into me, sucked in my breath. It surprised me to find her smiling, even with her legs still clamped shut.

"Ow," she said. "That really, really hurt. *Really* hurt, James, my clit's on fire."

I smiled. "I would imagine so. You took quite a thwack."

She reached out a hand for my cock, gripping me tight in her dainty little fingers. "Fuck me, please," she hissed. "Please fuck me over your desk."

"I'm not prepared," I said. "I don't have anything with me."

She frowned. "Shit."

"This isn't the horniest topic," I said. "But I'm clean. I don't fuck without protection. I haven't, not since Rachel."

She smiled. "I didn't expect you would, Mr In-Control."

"I mean, we could, if you're on the pill."

She kept working my cock. "I am, but I'm shit with it, I've been skipping," she sighed. "I'm sorry. I'll tighten up on it."

I smiled. "Well, we are in a bit of a quandary then, aren't we? Unless..."

She raised her eyebrows. "Unless?"

"I could fuck your sweet ass instead."

I watched her swallow. "But the other night, with your fingers... it was so tight."

"I just landed a metal fucking ruler on your clit. Are you telling me you can't take my cock in your ass?"

She grinned. "I could give it a go, I guess. It can't hurt that bad, right?"

Wrong, but I kept my mouth shut. She rolled onto her front and I angled my cock at her face. "Spit for me."

She was well-practised, coating my shaft in a thick load of saliva without a second's hesitation. I rubbed it all over me then took up position behind her. I slid my thumb in first, and she winced but didn't protest. I moved it around in wide circles, loosening her up.

"One day I'm going to stretch this little hole nice and wide, Lydia, taking a cock will be the last of your worries. You should count yourself lucky it's not my fist you're accommodating."

"Maybe one day," she smiled, shooting me dirty eyes over her shoulder. "I like your thumb, it feels nice, kind of dreamy."

"We're running out of time. You'll have to take it fast and hard if you want to do this."

She bit her lip, eyes glazed. "Better get on with it, then." She resumed her grip on the edge of the desk as I pushed my cock against her puckered little ring. This wouldn't take long, I was already close to the edge.

"Fast and hard, Cat, fast and hard. Don't scream."

She gasped as I pushed myself in. She tensed every muscle, wheezing out expletives. Her ass was so fucking tight, I had to help my cock in with my hand. She clenched around me, tight and dry and so fucking hot.

"Shit, Lydia, shit," I growled. "Fucking hell, you feel so good."

"It hurts," she breathed. "It really hurts." Her eyes were on mine again, big and glazed with dilated pupils, but she was horny. Sweet fucking Jesus, she was horny. "Fuck me," she hissed. "Fuck me, James, I want it rough."

She sent me insane, and in a heartbeat I was pounding her tight little asshole, my fingers yanking at her hair as I slammed her over my desk. I lost all sense of reason, all sense of anything, lost to everything but the soft little whimpers coming from her throat and her tight, hot hole sucking me dry.

"I'm going to shoot in your ass, Lydia," I growled. "I'm going to shoot my load in your filthy little asshole."

"Yes," she grunted. "I want it, fucking fuck me, James, fucking fuck me."

I slammed in all the way, emptying my balls inside her. She let out a shrill little squeak at the final intrusion, wriggling under my weight. It was a major explosion, shaky legs almost giving way under me. I jerked inside her, watching her tight little ring clenching around me, sucking at me like a hungry little mouth. I pulled out as I finished, loving the way my seed bubbled out with me. I kissed the filthy brown lips that had milked me and slipped my tongue inside, loving the way she squirmed.

"You're dirty bad wrong, James Clarke, you know that?" she hissed, spreading her ass cheeks for more. "So fucking dirty bad wrong."

"Yes, I am," I laughed. "And you love me for it."

She didn't laugh back.

Lydia

You love me for it. You love me for it. You love me for it.

Of course I didn't love him for it. I definitely didn't. That's what I *wanted* to say. That's what I wanted to *feel*. A rough anal pounding over a desk at work does not equal romance. White knights don't show up with red roses and metal rulers all ready to slap you on the clitoris. Ow, it still fucking hurt.

I took the stairs to the flat two at a time, happy to find the door unlocked.

"Bex!" I squealed. "Oh my God, Rebecca, you're never going to believe what the lovely James Clarke did to me today! He fucked me in the ass, at WORK, over his desk while our boss was out golfing. Can you even believe this shit?" I put the kettle on, trying to peer out onto the balcony. "It's crazy, right?" I laughed. "I'm still in shock."

"James Clarke got his cock out at the office? Well, that is a turn up." I jumped a mile at the strange voice. Its owner stepped in through the sliding doors. A leggy Amazonian with purple hair, her rich ochre skin like something from a beauty magazine. She was stunning. I choked for words, and she smiled at me. "I'm Jaz, Rebecca's ex. I own the building."

"Oh, hi, I'm um..."

"Embarrassed probably." She shared Rebecca's cackle. "I know James well, although I must say I'm surprised by the work stunt. Not really his style."

I could have died on the spot. "It was just a crazy moment, no big deal," I said, failing miserably to play it down.

"I'll have a coffee if you're making one."

I took out another mug and she joined me in the kitchen, leaning back against the fridge like she owned the place, which I suppose she did. I felt strangely uncomfortable in my own space. "You must be Lydia. I've heard so much about you."

"Yeah, I've heard a lot about you too." I smiled as broadly as I could.

"I didn't realise things were so serious between you and James," she said. "Rebecca said it was Explicit-only."

"It is," I said. "Today was a one-off. It won't happen again." I offered her milk and sugar but she waved them away.

"Tell me, then. Do you like him?"

I raised my eyebrows, handing her a mug. "Yes, I like him, we work together. He's very professional."

"Don't be coy," she said. "Do you *like* him?"

I tried to relax, assure myself that she was Rebecca's ex-girlfriend and a thoroughly nice person, but there was something off about her. The hair on the back of my neck stood on end. "It's casual," I told her. "Nothing serious."

"So, you don't have feelings for him?"

"No." I didn't realise how much of a lie that was until it was out of my mouth, but once I'd told it I knew I'd rather pull my own toenails out than tell her any different.

She flashed me a smile, but it didn't meet her eyes. "Well, that's sensible," she said. "He's a hard one to love. Very hard."

I fake-smiled back at her. "How so?"

"You could say I have some insider knowledge," she said. "I'm friends with his wife."

"Ex-wife," I said. "You mean Rachel?"

"She's still his wife," Jaz said. "They are still married."

"On paper." I took a sip of coffee and it tasted like liquid vomit.

"She still loves him. And he still loves her."

"I wouldn't know. It's only casual, we don't talk about our exes."

She slurped back coffee, eyes twinkling. "Word of advice, woman to woman. Whatever Rebecca told you about their split, she didn't do the right thing. I know she thinks she helped out by playing the *honest friend* role, but she didn't. They were getting better. *Rachel* was getting better. A few months and she'd have been through the worst of it, she and James would have made it through."

My blood ran cold, instinct chilling me to the bone. "I'm not sure what you're talking about."

"She told you, right?" Jaz asked. "She told you how she split them up?"

"Rebecca split them up?"

Jaz feigned embarrassment, pretending to slap her own forehead. "Shit, I'm such a clutz. You probably don't even know. Rebecca split James and Rachel up, told him about Rachel's little indiscretion, only she was getting better. She'd stopped fucking around, it was her final blow out, her last little moment of weakness. Rachel loved James, she never wanted to hurt him."

I couldn't subdue the rage. It bubbled behind my retinas. I saw Stu in the hallway begging forgiveness like a spineless little worm. "Funny way of showing it."

"People make mistakes," she said. "Rachel made a few. She regrets them."

"I guess she'll have to take that up with James, then, won't she?" I snapped, meeting her eye to eye.

"Oh, she will." Jaz grinned. "And he'll listen, when he's ready. He'll have his fun, and then he'll realise how much he misses her.

He does miss her you know, he was crazy about her, you should have seen them together. Gorgeous. He was besotted. Not hard to see why, of course, she's beautiful."

"I'm sure," I said, tipping my coffee down the sink. "If you don't mind I need to grab a shower. Shall I tell Rebecca you called?"

She put down her mug. "Don't worry, I'll let myself out, and don't worry about Rebecca, I'll catch her at work tomorrow. I came to see you, actually." She grinned again. "I thought it was about time we met. It's been so enlightening, we'll have to do it again sometime."

Not on her fucking life. I stayed in the bathroom until I heard the door slam behind her.

"Jaz was here?" Bex snapped. "On her own?"

"Yep, bold as brass," I said, pouring a wine. "She seems quite a character."

"She's a character, alright. She shouldn't be in our fucking flat, I want that key back off her."

"She is the landlady, I guess."

"Even so, she's taking the fucking piss." Rebecca kicked off her boots and sprawled on the sofa, wine in hand. "So, what did she have to say?"

"More important is what I said to her," I said. "I thought it was you on the balcony. I told her, *you*, that James fucked my ass over his desk at work."

"Fuck," she said, eyes darkening. "And what did she say to that?"

"She said a lot." I sat down opposite. "You didn't tell me about Rachel, that you split them up."

"I did *not* split them up, that's fucking bullshit."

"That's not what Jaz said."

"That bitch needs to stop with the shit-stirring." Rebecca sighed, leaning forward. "Rachel was on her final warning. She'd already fucked James over with a whole host of fucking men. He'd been more than fair, I mean seriously, she had way more than enough chances. I told her I'd tell him the truth if she kept on, but she didn't listen. One night she was at Explicit, and she didn't know I was in the next cubicle. I heard every fucking word she said."

The hairs on my arms bristled. "What did she say?"

"She was planning another fling, talking it up with one of the regulars, Davey, one of their mutual friends. It wasn't the first time they were getting it on, and it sure as shit wasn't going to be the last. Jaz can say whatever the hell she wants about Rachel mending her ways, but the bitch was a slut. She tramped her way around the whole pissing club, and would have gone round for a second circuit if I hadn't blown her cover."

"So, you told him?"

Her eyes were heavy, boring into mine. "Yes, I told him, and he was grateful for it. Jaz and Rachel not so much."

"Jaz didn't agree with you, then?"

"Jaz and Rachel were thick as thieves. No, Jaz didn't agree with me, said I should mind my own and let Rachel get on with it. It was the beginning of the end for us, that whole affair, but James was my friend and he would have done the same for me. I didn't want her making more of a fool out of him than she had already."

"Must have been tough."

"Wasn't much fun, no." She drank her wine. "Look, this whole thing was going on for about six months before I blabbed my mouth off. He knew about her flings, she promised she'd stop, that she'd get some therapy, sort her shit out. Only she didn't, she didn't stop at all."

"Why do you think she was fucking around that much?"

"Rachel lives for attention. She's lived her entire life for attention. James' attention wasn't enough, she wanted adoration from the whole male populous beside him. They came to Explicit to spice things up, figured they could open their horizons as a couple, you know? Only Rachel opened her horizons a damn sight more than he did, and opened her legs with them. She was fucking more outside of Explicit than she was in it, and James knew, he's no idiot. He gave her a lot of warnings, a lot of chances. Hell, she'd fuck them in front of him, Christ knows why she was so bothered about fucking them behind his back as well."

"And you telling him, that was the final straw?"

She sighed. "Yeah, that was the end."

"Hard being a good friend, isn't it?"

"The hardest. I'd tell him over again in a heartbeat. He's a good guy, Lyds. A fucked-up guy, a brutal guy, a strange, private weirdo kind of guy, but he's straight up honest. He wouldn't fuck people around. Fuck them *up*, for sure," she laughed. "But not around."

"Jaz said Rachel wants him back, said she still loves him and he still loves her."

"Jaz is full of shit," Rebecca said. "Rachel may still want James, but he's well done with that crap. Hell would freeze over before they got back together, regardless of how he felt about her."

My heart was dancing in my ribcage. "Do you think he does still love her?"

She sighed. "I dunno. He did. I'm not sure about now." She met my eyes. "I'm sorry, Lyds, I'm not sure how he really feels about her, that's the honest truth."

"You've got nothing to apologise to me for," I said. "I'm not his girlfriend." The words churned in my gut.

"Maybe," she smiled. "Maybe not."

"It's casual," I protested. "Really, as casual as it gets."

"Oh yeah, so what's with the sex at work shit? That really isn't his style by the way, so either he's lost his mind, or he's got a major crush going down on our cute little Lyddie Marsh."

I felt my face burn up. "Lost his mind, I think."

"I don't," she beamed. "And I know you're feeling it too. Don't think I haven't noticed it, the spring in your step. The way you look at him when you're at Explicit."

"Now *you've* lost your mind," I laughed. "We fuck at a sex club while he's wearing a mask, that's it."

"Yeah yeah, and I don't like hot, wet pussy." She poked her tongue out. "Did he hit you, over his desk?"

"Did he ever. Metal ruler."

"Fucking ow. Right on the clit, I'll bet."

I grinned. "You know him so well."

"Yes, I do." She raised her empty glass and made after the rest of the bottle. "And I'm telling you that James has many habits, but screwing at the office isn't one of them. It can only mean one thing," she said, topping up my glass.

"And what's that?" I smiled.

"The man's in love, Lydia. He's in love with you."

I found myself wishing I believed her.

CHAPTER 13

Lydia

"So, tonight's the night?" Rebecca dropped her cigarette and stubbed it out with the toe of her stiletto. "Will there be tears?"

I looked towards the wooden doors across the street. "I don't know *how* to cry, Bex."

She wrapped an arm around my shoulder. "It's easy, baby, let it all go and those tears will flow."

"So I keep hearing." I watched Cara totter on ahead, waving at some other regulars just arriving.

Rebecca pulled my attention back to her, tapping my forehead with a long, red fingernail. "Whatever's in here, Lyds, all your reservations, all your pride, all your self-control. You've got to give it all up. Let yourself break for him, and he'll love you for it." She took my hand and led me to where Cara was waiting. "Believe me, baby, cry for him and he's yours."

I took a breath as we made our way inside. Cry for him, sure, no big deal. Like I hadn't been trying for weeks.

Masque was already at the bar, the sculpted muscle of his shoulders glowing blue under the neons. I took a seat next to him, smiling as he ordered me a wine. *Cry for him and he's yours.* If only that one tiny statement didn't mean so much.

I made no time for small talk, leaning straight into the musky warmth of his neck. "Cane me, tonight. Please, Masque."

He turned to me, the line of his mouth deadly serious. "What's with the urgency, Kitty Cat?"

I sighed. "I want to cry."

His mouth curled into a smile. "The tears I want from you are an *emotional* release. The cane will hurt like a motherfucker, I promise you, but there's more to it than that."

"Yeah, I know. I have to *let go*. I'm trying," I sulked.

He brooded awhile, shadowy eyes staring me out. "If you're serious about this, you'll need a safeword."

"Doesn't that kind of defeat the object?"

"Not at all."

I sipped my wine. "I'm not going to use the safeword, Masque."

"Then there will be tears," he said simply.

"Promise me you won't stop," I said. "Not before it's done."

He pulled me in close until his breath tickled my mouth. "You don't need to worry about that, my pretty little Cat's eyes. Your safeword is Paris."

PARIS, PARIS, PARIS. I SWORE TO MYSELF I WOULDN'T NEED IT, BUT standing there, naked, under the dark gaze of the chimera in playroom one, I wasn't quite so confident. I turned my back to the faces at the window, blanking out everything but the man before me. He gestured to the flogging bench, and I took up position on all fours, my breasts mashing tight against the bench's contoured padding. Masque buckled my ankles into the cuffs, leaving me spread wide open for him.

"You've healed well," he said, stroking my ass. "A nice fresh canvas for stripes." He fastened my wrists, pulling my chin up towards him. "Last call, Cat. Do you want this?" He brandished the cane before my face, letting rip with a healthy swish. I flinched but didn't falter.

"Yes, sir. Please."

I couldn't read his expression, just took comfort in the soft caress of his thumb against my lips. He disappeared from my eyeline, taking the cane with him. "Only use the safeword if you really have to," he said. I nodded, straining to keep him in sight as he walked around me. "Look straight ahead, relax."

I did as he asked, twitching in my bonds involuntarily. They held firm. I jumped as warm breath teased my pussy lips, and I groaned like a whore as he buried his face. He bit me as he pulled away, hard enough to make me whine.

"Such a sweet juicy cunt," he growled. "I love how wet you are for pain."

I heard the familiar swish of the flogger, but kept my eyes straight ahead. The tails pinched at my back, a frenzied assault of tiny bites which ramped up with every circuit. He aimed hard for my thighs, curling around my hips to snap at tender skin. I rolled into it, sinking into the sensation, breathing evening out as the endorphins began to rise.

"Good girl," he said. "Nice and pink."

I gasped as he worked me with the tip of the cane, poking hard against my pussy. "Yes!" I groaned. "Fuck me!"

He pressed harder, skewering me in one slick motion. "Dirty bitch," he growled. "So fucking dirty."

"Please, Masque, sir, make it hurt," I wheezed, floating into the warm arms of subspace. My throat was dry, fists clenched tight, every sliver of my attention on the sharp point of the cane inside me. I pictured him flipping me over, just like on his desk, forcing my thighs wide open to receive his pain.

"I'm going to hurt you so much, Cat, so fucking much..." No sooner had the intrusion disappeared than I heard the swish in the air. The first strike took my breath, all of it. It hurt more than my very worst expectation, skin searing on contact and wrenching me forward in my restraints.

"Shit!" I wheezed. "Ow, ow, shit!"

On the second stroke my body moved without bidding, rocking back on my knees as far as movement would allow. I spluttered out expletives, one long breath of crass relief.

He landed the third across my thighs and I howled like a banshee, gripping for the edge of the bench and clenching my legs as tight as they'd go. Number four landed harder, and I slammed my forehead hard into the padding, no breath left to exhale.

I found more breath through five and six, squealing without reservation. My head flew back, eyes desperate to keep the cane in sight, animal fear thundering through my ribcage. This wasn't like I imagined. He came to my side, smoothing down my hair with his fingers.

"Cry for me, Cat, cry and it will stop."

My eyes were wide and frantic. "I can't!"

He retreated for another stroke, and this time the tip of the cane curled around my ass, savage on untouched flesh.

"OWW!" I screamed. "FUCKING HELL!"

"CRY FOR ME!" he thundered. "LET IT GO!"

I spluttered through the next few, until they became a blur of agony. My thighs were trembling, mouth bone dry, every nerve screaming for release. There was only pain. Pain and Masque, his low groan loud in the air.

"FUCKING HELL, CAT, LET IT GO!"

He landed a stripe on the tender line where my ass met my thighs, and I wailed like a wounded animal. I felt sick, teeth chattering, the adrenalin spike rushing through my limbs. My throes became less frenetic, morphing instead into a slow rhythmic sway, back and forth as far as the bench would allow. My ears began to ring.

His growl snared my senses. "Cry for me, Cat, show me your fucking tears."

He changed position and the cruel tip of the cane bit the inside of my thigh. I heard myself wheezing, but it felt so far away.

My heart was hammering, nerves on fire, muscles twitching for escape, but there *was* no escape. Only him, only Masque. I heard myself whimpering, acceptance of my bonds stealing my fight.

He pressed the cane against my ass, poking at the ridged flesh.

"More, Cat, I'm going to give you so much more."

I shook my head, resolve breaking. "No."

"No? You want to use the safeword?"

My mind cracked open, adrenaline rising to new heights. "No."

"Which is it to be?" he pushed.

My breath hitched, pooling in my throat, toes curling. I couldn't use the safeword, I just couldn't. "More."

"More what?"

"More pain, please, sir," I wheezed.

"Good girl." He didn't let up, landing three in quick succession. I spluttered incomprehensible words, choking as they forced their way out, and there underneath were tears. I could feel them welling up, feel the lump tight in my throat. I crested my tolerance, every nerve crying for release. He hit me again and I coughed out a sob, chest heaving. I heard the lust in his voice, the soft groan of need. "That's it, Cat, that's it..."

I closed my eyes, ready to give it all up, ready to cry for him, but no sooner had the tears risen than they eased away again, retreating behind the wall of self-restraint. Masque must have witnessed the change, the way my body turned tense and rigid.

"No, Cat, no, no, no. Don't close up on me now."

The cane was more savage than ever, blow after blow without pause, and I screamed and screamed and screamed.

"NO! PLEASE, NO!"

"CRY FOR ME!" he screamed back. "FOR FUCK'S SAKE, CAT, CRY FOR ME!"

But I couldn't cry. There were no tears left for me, and right there, bound and bruised, I realised I was *scared*, not of the cane, or of Masque, or of the strangers at the windows. I was scared of crying, scared of breaking. I was absolutely fucking petrified of letting it all go. I was shouting before I registered my own voice.

"PARIS! PARIS, PARIS, PARIS!"

There was instant silence, only the ringing of my ears in the stillness. Then there was him, his fingers at my ankles, my bindings undone in a heartbeat. He freed my wrists and then I was off the bench, in warm arms, cradled between his thighs as he rocked me on the floor.

"Jesus, Lydia, I'm so fucking sorry." I caught my breath, feeling his heartbeat almost as fast as my own. "It was too much," he said. "Much too much."

But it wasn't. That wasn't it.

"No," I said. "It wasn't you." I raised my eyes to his and started in shock. "Your mask!"

"Shh," he said, stroking my cheek. "It doesn't matter."

"But they can see you!" I turned to the window, finding everyone else as shocked as I was.

"Just tell me you're ok."

I managed a smile. "I'm ok. I'm fine, now. I'm fine."

He kissed my eyes and I wished beyond wished there were tears for him. "We'll stop now, let me get your clothes."

He made to move but I held him tight, snaking my arms around his neck. "No," I said. "Please, don't go."

"Only for a second," he appeased.

"No," I hissed. "Please. I want *you*."

He raised his eyebrows. "*Me*? Here? Now? Right now?"

I pulled his fingers down between my legs. "Now. Right now."

"Shit, Lydia, you're still wet."

I lay back as he pulled his mask on, gasping at the cold press of the floor against my bruises. He followed me, covering my body with his, but I didn't want that. I wriggled out from under him, rolling until he was pressed hard into my back. My eyes fixed on the faces at the window, at their gaping expressions. I was no longer scared of them, no longer embarrassed. I met their gaze with my own, rocking my hips back to coax Masque into me. He pulled my leg back over his, spreading me wide for their viewing. I groaned my approval.

"You like this now, hey, you dirty little bitch? Like their hungry eyes on your pussy? Look at them, hard for you, Lydia. They're all hard for you."

I turned my head to face him, pressing my mouth into his. "That's not it," I wheezed, bucking back against the thrust of his hips. His cock spread me open, forced its way right inside. "I don't want them to see *me*, Masque, I don't care if they're hard for me." I pulled his hand around to my breast, moaning as he twisted my nipple.

"Tell me," he hissed. "What do you want them to see?" His hips slammed into my bruises and it felt so fucking good. "Tell me, Lydia. Look at them and tell me what makes you wet."

He changed his angle, and his cock strained inside me, pressing on all the right places.

"I want them to see *this*," I moaned. "I want them to see *you* inside *me*. Show them how I belong to you..."

He wrapped his hand around my throat, pressing his mouth into my ear as he slammed me harder and harder. "I'll show them, don't worry. I'll show them who owns this tight little cunt." His fingers were on my clit, working me for just a second before he hooked two fingers inside, forcing them in alongside his cock. I whimpered, my pussy on fire. "Take it, Lydia, fucking take it."

He wriggled his way in further, pushing a third finger in alongside, and it hurt, it really fucking hurt. "Shit, Masque, shit..."

"Tell me to stop," he murmured. "Tell me to stop."

"No," I breathed. "Stretch me, Masque, please God, fucking stretch me! I want it!"

He was lost to me, grunting and thrusting and pounding his way inside. I arched my back and hissed for more, clenching my teeth until the brutal pulse of orgasm ripped through my senses. We were animals, beasts, and I clawed at his arms as he savaged my insides, loving the bellow of his eruption. He came inside me, a juddering rack of muscle and sin, breathing hot in my ear and pulling me tight.

"Fucking hell..." he groaned. "Jesus fucking Christ, that was good."

"Ow," I laughed, flinching as he pulled himself out of me. I kissed him hard, sucking his tongue into my mouth like I'd never get enough of him. "What are you doing to me?" I giggled, high on endorphins. "This is crazy."

But he didn't laugh back, didn't even hear me. His attention was on the window, and the woman staring back at him.

CHAPTER 14
Lydia

Masque pulled on his jeans in silence, and I didn't dare speak a word. The woman through the window flashed a smile, blowing him a kiss, and I watched his expression darken, lips nothing more than a tight slash of rage. I got dressed, suddenly self-conscious and awkward, trying not to meet our observer's eyes. She was pretty, *really* fucking pretty, with a gentle cascade of perfect blonde waves bouncing around her shoulders. She had a tiny nose, gorgeous full lips, and eyes of sky blue, and her figure... well, she could have stepped straight off the cover of *Vogue*. Inadequacy slapped me around the face, and then, I knew the woman was Rachel.

He took my hand without a word and led me away like she meant nothing, despite his expression screaming otherwise. Cara was standing at the bar with her arms folded, tapping at a stool with her shoe. She smiled as she saw me, but it was such a nervous little effort. I spotted Rebecca a few metres behind, a mass of angry arms and jerky gestures, getting right in the face of some other woman. She moved enough for me to see beyond and I recognised Jaz's purple hair. I clenched Masque's hand tighter, but he didn't grip back.

"Wait here for me, Cat." He dropped me with Cara and barely pecked my cheek before he turned away. I could only watch him leave, pacing straight for the corridor and the perfect blonde waiting there.

"Sorry," Cara said. "Raven wanted to warn you, but that crazy cow started mouthing off."

"Just piss off!" I heard Rebecca shout. "Trouble-making bitch!"

"You're the trouble-making bitch that started this whole thing in the first place!" Jaz screeched.

"Don't confuse me with that trampy fucking whore in the corridor over there," Rebecca raged back. "Do the whole fucking place a favour and take her the fuck home, will you? She's not fucking welcome here!"

"I'm not going anywhere, and neither is Rachel, not until she's had her say."

"Knock yourself out," Raven spat, turning on her heel and flashing Jaz the finger.

She took me by the hand and Cara by another, trawling us through the main floor and into the ladies room.

"I meant to warn you, Lyds," she said. "I'm sorry. I can't believe that shit-stirring bitch pulled this stunt."

I bit my lip. "She wants him back, doesn't she? That's why she's here."

"She can want on," Bex snapped.

I looked at my reflection in the mirror, the pale wash of my face under smudged make-up. "She's so pretty."

"She's alright," Cara shrugged. "If you like that kind of thing."

I smiled at her attempt to make me feel better. "So, what do I do now? Do I go home? Wait for the storm to ride out?"

Rebecca grabbed my chin, forcing my eyes right onto hers.

"You will do no such fucking thing. You will hold your ground. This is *your* place now, with Masque."

"Not really," I said. "I've got no claim on him."

"More than she fucking has," Bex spat. "She's a stupid, selfish cow."

"Who's married to him..." I mumbled.

"On *paper*, nothing else."

"I hope you're right." I twisted my hands together, nerves taking hold.

Cara squeezed my arm. "Don't let her do this, you're good together."

"Rachel's not going to *do* anything," Rebecca snarled. "This is your chance, Lyds, you have to take it."

"Take it how?" I shrugged. "What am I supposed to do?"

She pointed at the exit, at the floor beyond. "You get out there and stake your claim. This is woman to woman. You march up to them and you take him by the hand and make it clear that *you're* the one he's with now."

"But I'm not..." I sighed.

"May as well be," Cara smiled. "You're with him every week, he hasn't been with anyone else since you've been here. Hasn't even looked."

My stomach was tangled in knots. "You really think I should do this, just walk up to them, bold as brass?"

"Yep," Rebecca said. "For *her* benefit, not his. Smile and take his hand and say you'll be at the bar waiting. Say *anything* really, Lyds, just make it clear that he's with you and you aren't some scared little puppy dog. That's what she wants, for you to scurry away."

"I'm not running," I said, resolve firming up. "I've done nothing wrong."

"Go, go, go!" Cara squeaked. "Put your flag in the ground!"

I looked back from the doorway, heart in my throat.

"Go, baby!" Raven whooped, air-punching like a cheerleader. "Show that bitch he's yours!"

MY NERVES DRIED UP HALFWAY ACROSS THE MAIN FLOOR, AND I slowed right down, pulse thumping as I peered around the corridor to where they were standing. Everyone else had vacated, making them easy targets for my snooping. I could hear Rachel's voice, husky... just the perfect edge of *bitch* to it. I pressed myself to the wall, and they talked on, oblivious.

"Why do we have to go over and over this," he hissed. "I don't want you here."

"And *I* told *you* that I'd come back."

"Why, Rach? What's the point? You hardly needed this place to get yourself laid. Go find somewhere else to amuse yourself, will you? Leave me the fuck out of it!"

"You know why I'm here," she said, running her hand down his arm. "I miss you. I miss us."

"You need to move on," he sighed. My heart swelled, *thank fuck*. "I have."

Her eyes narrowed. "So I heard. Back on the work-dating scene now, are you? You said you'd never do that again. Where will you run to next, hey? Manchester, Bristol, Birmingham? This is your home, *here*. Don't blow it for a silly little girl playing the keen submissive."

"Leave Lydia out of this," he barked. "She's nothing to do with this."

"So, she's *not* your girlfriend?" she smiled. "What is she, then?"

He turned away from her, hands on his temples. "It's none of your business."

"We're still married, James, I'm still your *wife*."

He laughed, low and bitter. "Funny, isn't it? When we were together you couldn't get enough of telling people we were estranged, and now we're estranged you can't get enough of telling people we're married. You've got it the wrong way around, sweetheart, that ship sailed a long time ago."

"So, what's going on?" she snapped. "What is she to you?"

I took a step away, unable to watch. The silence dragged on forever before I heard him sigh, only the rush of my pulse loud in my ears.

"She's a mistake, if you must know," he said, his voice dull and bitter. "A huge fucking mistake."

My stomach pained like I'd taken a bullet, right in the gut, and then there were the tears I'd been trying so hard for. They came hard, they came fast, they came without restraint, how fucking ironic.

I sloped away before I could hear another word.

James

I STARED INTO EYES I USED TO LOVE, USED TO LIVE FOR, BUT THEY meant nothing to me. Rachel shifted her weight onto one hip, waiting for an answer. Like she fucking deserved one.

"She's a mistake," I growled. "A huge fucking mistake."

Her face lit up, relief glowing on her cheeks, and I could have choked the life out of her.

"I'm glad you've still got some of your senses."

"I haven't fucking finished," I snapped. "She's a *huge* fucking mistake, a mistake I swore I'd never fucking make again, not ever. But you know what? I made it, and now I'm not sorry I did. She is *not* some silly little girl playing submissive. She's an incredible woman with incredible integrity."

"So, she *is* your girlfriend."

"I don't even know how to have a relationship anymore, so no, she's not."

"And that's my fault, I suppose?" she snapped.

"If the cap fits..."

"That's fucking cruel, James, really fucking cruel. How many times can I say I'm sorry? How many times before you'll give me another chance?"

"You're all out of chances," I said, bluntly.

"You still love me." Her face was flushed, tears pricking at her eyes. She was always so easy with the tears. "I know you do."

"I did love you, Rachel, but it's over. *We're* over."

"You really want her more than me?" A tear spilled down her cheek and she made no attempt to brush it aside.

"Don't sound so surprised, it's really not that close a competition."

"Bastard! You love her, don't you?" she cried, blubbing like a baby. Once upon a time I'd have been putty in her hands.

I walked away. "Maybe one day I'll know what love is again, Rach, but it won't be with you."

She charged after me, wrenching me back by the wrist. "This *thing* you've got isn't about Lydia, it's about Katreya!"

I shook her off. "It's not about Katreya."

"Her eyes don't mean shit, James, she'll never be her!"

"But I don't *want* Lydia to be Katreya," I said, shocking myself as much as her. "Lydia's too fucking perfect as she is."

Rebecca was waiting for me on the way to the bar, face like thunder.

"It's sorted," I said. "And now I need a fucking drink."

"You're a fucking idiot," she snapped, shoving her phone in my face.

"What the hell?!" I took the handset from her.

I'm a huge fucking mistake. Gone home, please don't follow me. x

"She's a mistake, is she? Is that really what you think? And you told her that?" Rebecca hissed.

I groaned inside. "Sweet Christ, she was listening."

"Yeah, she was listening, I sent her over. More fucking fool me, Masque."

"Give me some credit, will you? That isn't what I said, it's been taken out of context."

She covered her eyes with her hands. "This is one huge pissing nightmare, this is."

"Relationships always are, that's why I abstain."

"So she *isn't* a mistake?" she asked, folding her arms.

"We'll find out, won't we?" I abandoned my craving for scotch, cursing my luck. "Give me your keys."

"She won't want to talk to you, she's upset."

"Your keys, Rebecca," I snapped, then checked myself. "Please…"

She eyeballed me with a pouty lip, then finally relented, handing them over. "Don't fuck this up, Masque, don't you fucking dare!"

I wasn't planning on it.

I KEPT MY FEET LIGHT ON THE STAIRS, SLIPPING THE KEY QUIETLY IN the lock. I made my entrance, eyes scanning the place for signs of life. There was only the dull orange glow from a table lamp, spilling out from the corner of the living room. Lydia's voice cut out, shrill. She sounded so fucking pained.

"You didn't have to come home," she wheezed. "I should have known I was just a stupid mistake. He doesn't give a shit about me, and why would he? That woman's like a goddess."

"Goddess of adultery, maybe," I said, turning the corner.

She jumped a mile, skitting back into the arm of the sofa, eyes wide. "I really, really need to stop doing that."

I took a seat. "Doing what?"

"Assuming people are Rebecca. Although you can see why I'd assume such a thing, considering we are the only two people who actually live here."

I smiled. "Intruders are a regular occurrence here, are they?"

"Only you and Jaz. She was here the other day."

My brain whirred. "That would make some sense."

"Like I said, I thought she was Rebecca, I said some things I probably shouldn't have."

"We can all say things we probably shouldn't have."

Her eyes were so sad. "You don't ever need to apologise for telling the truth, James. What are you even doing here?"

I soaked her in. The pale beauty of her legs held tight to her chest, the soft slope of her shoulders, the dark mess of her tangled hair, thrown up into a pony. She was wearing just a tiny pair of panties and a faded old pink camisole. She'd never looked more exposed, not even with her pussy spread wide for all the world to see. Her eyes were red, puffy. Maybe I'd broken her after all, just not as I intended. I reached out a hand, brushing her ankle with my fingertips.

"Is this your regular home dress? Rebecca must be rubbing off on you."

"This is considerably more than Rebecca wears," she said. "My nudity habit hasn't scaled her heights quite yet." She bit her lip, nervous. "Really, James, why are you here?"

"You didn't hear me finish." I fixed her in the calmest stare I could muster.

"I heard enough," she sighed. "It's my own fault, anyway, I shouldn't even care."

"If you'd have stayed around even a minute longer you'd have heard the rest. You *were* a mistake, Lydia, but I'm not sorry I made it. I told Rachel as much, I told Rachel a lot of things."

The tremble of her lip stirred the beast, and I wanted her all over again. "You don't need to say that."

"I know I don't."

"Our thing is Explicit-only, casual. I know that, I was happy with that."

I pulled her feet across my lap, resting my hand on her knee. "Things change. They spiral, that was always the danger."

"I'll get over it," she said. "I can cope with casual, I know I can. I *wanted* casual."

I raised my eyebrows. "I don't want you to *cope* with casual."

Tears pricked at her eyes, but again she forced them away. "So, this is it? It's over?"

I smiled. "That would be the wisest move, I'm sure, but I don't want that. I never did, not from the moment I barged into your hotel room."

"Neither do I." She reached out her hand and I folded her dainty little fingers in mine. "So, what now?"

"I have no idea," I admitted. "This isn't a position I'm used to occupying. I can't say it's entirely comfortable."

"We could carry on..." she said. "As we were."

I shunted my way toward her, craving her body more than ever. "I don't know if I can be the man who can offer you more. I'm not sure that's me."

"So don't." Her smile was soft. "Just be the man you *are*." She leant her head into my shoulder. "I don't want to lose what we have. You make me feel so alive."

My stomach churned in rapport with her words. "I can't offer you a relationship, Cat, it would never work. I'm too private, too closed, too set in my ways. And I can't lose my career, I've worked too fucking hard. Order is my only constant, my routine is my salvation, my road through any storm."

Her eyes glittered like moondust, pale as the kiss of a ghost. "Please talk to me. What happened to you? Was it Rachel? Was it bad?"

I sighed. "It wasn't a good time."

"You came here for a reason," she whispered. "Because you care. At least try and let me in."

"I need a drink," I grunted, brushing her legs aside. She didn't follow me, just sat and watched, eyes haunting my every move. I opted for a coffee, and made Lydia one too, brooding around my own resolve as the kettle boiled. This time I positioned myself away from her, my elbows on my knees.

"Rachel was already married when I met her," I began. "We

worked together a long time before anything happened. She was married to our boss's best friend, it's how she got the job initially. Her husband worked long hours and she was bored, he figured she could do with a hobby and along she came, to join me as a junior even though she wasn't such a junior."

"Go on," she encouraged, eyes wide and so fucking compelling.

"Rachel's first husband was a lot older than her, *boring*, she called him, but I suspect he worshipped the ground she walked on. She was spoiled, but frustrated, claiming the passion had all dried up. For about six months it was all she'd talk about, how much she wanted to leave him. She told me she'd moved into a separate bedroom at first, that they weren't having sex. She'd say too much, bemoaning the fact she was a red-blooded woman without a man, and me, well I was a red-blooded man without a steady woman. She came back to work after a long Christmas holiday that year and told me they'd agreed to separate. I believed her, I mean, why wouldn't I? It'd been a long time coming. I guess it was around that time she decided she wanted me for real, and hell did I know it. She'd message me on my personal email, listing off fantasies she'd never fulfilled, and some of them made my mouth water. Some of them were so fucking filthy."

"So, you fucked her?"

I smiled, despite myself. "Many times, and she was as filthy as her fantasies. She lapped up every single crazy thing I had to give her, and back then I was stupid, I thought we could hide it, I thought it wouldn't matter. But Rachel craves attention more than she craves sex, only I didn't know her well enough to realise that. She'd photograph every mark I ever made on her, emailing me a copy so I could take pride in my work outside of office hours. I figured she'd delete them, figured she'd be careful, but Rachel isn't careful, she doesn't think through her actions."

I watched Lydia watching me, and she was biting her lip in the way that I love, the way that makes my dick twitch.

"Go on..." she prompted.

"I'd been in that company since university, Cat, it was like a home to me, my whole fucking life was there, years and years of work. I'd worked my way up to the top, and it meant the world to me."

"What did she do?"

"Rachel didn't *do* anything, it's what she *didn't* do. She didn't delete her photographs and she didn't delete her emails. Every single photograph and sordid conversation was right there for the taking, and her husband did the taking, he read the whole lot of it, copied every single picture on her phone, and then he went insane, called me a wife-beater, a psychopath, every fucking name under the sun. He even called the police, and when Rachel wouldn't press any kind of charges, he emailed the all-staff email group on our company email and attached every single photo she'd ever taken of us. My boss went berserk, reeling for his friend. Life caved in, and the rest is a lot of painful history."

"He fired you?!" Lydia asked, mouth open.

"No. It would have been easier if he had," I sighed. "He didn't fire me, but he made it clear every fucking day how disappointed he was in me. He railed me for unprofessional conduct, started micro-managing every single thing I did, claiming he couldn't trust me anymore, but worse than any of that was the way he looked at me. He looked at me like I was a monster, and the rest of the company followed suit. If you've never experienced that, Lydia, I hope you never will. People you've known for years whispering in the corridors, looking at you with suspicion and mistrust, like you're some kind of savage animal who needs locking up. Women in the office didn't want to be alone with me, women I'd known for years unwilling to meet my eyes, and some of the men, well, they made it pretty clear what they thought of me."

"Shit, James, I'm so sorry." Lydia was pale, her eyes wide in sympathy. I had to look away to continue, staring at nothing but the floor.

"I wasn't a monster, Cat, I never did anything to her she didn't ask me to, and I never would. I'm not a rapist or a wife-beater, I'm no thug."

"I know you're not," she smiled. "You're nothing like that."

I couldn't help but smile back, the absurdity tickling me. "I like hurting women, but only if they want me to. I understand why that may be difficult for some people to comprehend."

"Did you leave, then, leave your job?"

"I had to, in the end. I just couldn't take it anymore. Rachel left first, moved in with me and got a job in a beauty salon. *It'll blow over*, she said, *just give it time*. But it didn't blow over, people don't let that kind of shit go. I would have always been the monster."

"What did you do?"

"We moved, here, to London, and eventually I got the job at Trial Run. I worked hard, kept my head down, and worked my way back up to CTO. I'd lost everything last time around, my friends, my job, my respect. Rachel was all I had, and for a while it was ok, I loved her, I really did. Her divorce came through and we got married, started rebuilding a life together, but this time around I was wary. I compartmentalised my life, splitting myself into two different people. The side at home, and the side at work. Rachel didn't understand it at first, it frustrated her, but she met back up with Bex, a friend she'd known since school, and our lovely Rebecca just *got* it, she got *me*. Along came Explicit, to expand our horizons, and I found the liberation of the mask. It worked for me. In the mask I could be the beast inside, the beast who craves tears and pain and hot, wet cunt. The other James Clarke went to work, and kept himself private. I never even introduced Rachel to my new colleagues, she never came to a single work party. She hated me for it, I know, but it was the only way I knew to be safe."

Lydia moved closer, just close enough to rest her hand on my knee. "I had no idea. No idea at all."

"That's always been the plan, Cat, to keep it all separate. The chimera is my embodiment of my lifestyle choice. One body, two creatures. I was comfortable like that, it was a way to make it work."

"I get that," she said. "I get it, James."

"Anyway, the relationship didn't work out. I got busy at work, and Rachel didn't understand. She craves attention, like I said, and my attention was no longer enough for her. We had a healthy open relationship within the bounds of Explicit, so I thought, but she must have disagreed. She fucked around so much it was embarrassing. I forgave her, told myself it didn't matter, that it was part of who we were, but it's a fine line, trust, and over time we fell apart. She never kept her promises, and I stopped expecting her to. We gave it one final shot. No other partners, no more lies." I finished my coffee. "It was Rebecca who finally pulled the plug, she told me Rachel had been cheating all along."

"Jaz told me that," she whispered.

"Jaz didn't agree with Rebecca's decision, but I'm glad Rebecca told me. I walked in on Rachel with another man, a man I'd come to know quite well within Explicit. He was more mortified than she was, I felt strangely sorry for him if truth be told." I looked at

Lydia, at the soft pools of her eyes, the sloping interest in her brow line. "And you know what he said?"

She shook her head.

"He turned to Rachel, full of rage, and he said, *I thought you said you were fucking estranged?*" I laughed bitterly, just like I had at the time. "I guess I had that one coming, since I inadvertently did the same thing, no doubt, to husband number one."

"You didn't know!" she said, squeezing my knee. "It wasn't your fault."

"Maybe, maybe not. Anyway, it's all old news now, history. I was devastated after Rachel and it took me a long time to pick myself up. I figured I'd focus on work-James, keep my life stable, and keep Masque private, weekends only. It was working well, until one day I stepped into the office kitchen and found myself staring into the green eyes of heartbreak personified. You snared me right then. You were so fucking beautiful, so raw."

She smiled. "You got under my skin too, Mr Clarke. So much, before I'd even seen Masque, before I knew anything about him."

"Rebecca claims I wanted you at Explicit the whole time, maybe she's right, maybe I always wanted that."

"Well, you got it," Lydia said gently. "And I got Masque."

"I can't risk my life falling apart again, Lydia, I can't open myself up for that shit. I know what it feels like to watch everything you've built up crumble into nothing. I don't want to do that all over again."

"I don't expect you to," she sighed, resting her forehead against mine. "I'll never do that to you, I swear. I'll never leave you so exposed, and I'll never risk your job. I'd leave myself before you suffered, I promise."

I kissed her nose, breathing in the soft hint of Amber. "I don't want you to leave your job, and I don't want to leave mine, that's one of the problems."

"This is a conversation for a long time away," she sighed, yawning. "It's not for now, now is just us, Cat and Masque. James and Lydia can sort that shit out one day far away, if they ever get that far."

"And you're happy with that? Seriously? You can live without sandwiches at lunchtime and a public declaration of adoration?"

She grinned, eyes sparkling. "I can live without those things, I just can't live without Masque." She breathed deeply, her mouth just a fraction away from mine. "I would like more, though, nothing much, just a little more than Explicit. I want some real time with you, when you're not wearing a mask and we're not at the office. Like in Brighton, I love it there."

"I can't promise anything, but I'll try. I can't let go of this wall I've built up, I don't know where *it* finishes and *I* begin."

"I can relate to that," she laughed. "I'm the one who can't cry, remember?"

"I guess we'll both try our best and see what happens."

"That's good enough for me," she said. Her sweet little mouth pressed onto mine and I pulled her right the way onto my lap. "It's late, James, I'm really tired."

"Bed time for tired little girls," I said, rising from the sofa and taking her with me. I walked through to her room, laying her out on her bed.

She smiled up at me through sleepy eyes. "Goodnight," she said. "I'll see you on Monday."

"You'll see me a lot sooner than that," I said. "Scoot up, will you? Unless you want me to sleep in Rebecca's bed, she might get a shock."

Lydia scuttled along, throwing open the covers. "You're staying? Really?"

"It seems a good night for firsts, don't you think?"

I threw off my clothes, slid in beside her. Her bed smelt of Cherry Blossom and White Lily and *her*. It smelt of her. I pulled her into me, her head on my chest, and she felt so fucking good.

The beast slept, finally. He slept like a baby in Lydia Marsh's arms.

CHAPTER 15
Lydia

I woke with James beside me, my head in the crook of his shoulder as he slept. The night still felt a blur, but he was here, he was real. He rolled towards me in his sleep, wrapping me in warm arms, and slowly, ever so slowly, he opened his eyes.

"Good morning, Miss Marsh, what a pleasant surprise."

"Not that surprising," I whispered. "Considering this is *my* bed."

"That is a fair point." I felt his swollen cock against my thigh. It sent a flurry of nerves around my stomach.

"Horny, James? I didn't think sex in a bed would be your style."

"I'll make an exception," he said. "Do excuse me if I taste of stale scotch."

I opened my mouth for his tongue. "You taste like you, *and* stale scotch," I breathed. "I like it."

He pinned my arms above my head, moving to rest on top of me. "I'll take your beautiful cunt any way I can get it," he groaned. "I can't get enough."

We both jumped at the rapping on the bedroom door. Rebecca hardly left it a second before she launched her way in.

"Hey lovebirds, sorry to gatecrash, but I'm having a bit of a personal crisis out here. I've been waiting a fucking age for you two to wake the fuck up."

James didn't move his arms, just looked over this shoulder at her. "It seems quite the time for personal crises."

She perched herself on the bed without any hint of reservation, resting her head on his shoulder. "It's Cara," she said. "I fucked up."

James eased himself off me, freeing my wrists. "I think we can make room for another small one, can't we, Lydia?"

I nodded, pulling the covers back enough for Bex to join us in bed. It felt surprisingly normal, but my standards of normal had already warped considerably. Rebecca lay back on my pillow, staring at the ceiling while her arm draped across my waist.

"It's Jaz's fucking fault," she said. "All of it. We were arguing, after you'd both left. I was up in her face and she was screaming at me, and then we were in the toilet, and she pulled my hair and I'm pretty sure I gave her a decent thump around the jaw, you know how it goes."

James raised his eyebrows. "And then?"

"And then I was fucking kissing her," she sighed. "I have no idea how the pissing fucking crap it happened. I was kissing her, and pulling her hair, and telling her how much I fucking hated her, and then there was Cara in the cubicle doorway, and she looked so fucking sad."

"Did you go after her?" I asked, squeezing James' hand under the duvet.

"She'd already gone," she said. "And Cara still lives with her parents, I didn't want to be rocking up there like some deviant Casanova, howling at her window. I went home with Jaz and we argued until morning."

"And now, what? You regret it?" James quizzed. "Has our little Cara wormed her way into your cold heart, Mistress Raven?"

"You're hardly in a position to take the piss, James," she laughed. "And yeah, maybe she has."

"Call her," I said. "Put it right, say it was a one-off, and you're sorry."

"I tried," she admitted. "Straight to voicemail. We agreed this shit was casual, now we're all over the fucking place."

"Casual has a habit of rolling that way." James smiled.

"Doesn't it fucking just?" She rolled her eyes. "Weird how it can take a stupid bloody cock-up to make you realise how much you give a shit, don't you think?"

"Amen to that," James said, tickling my thigh under the duvet. "So, which of our fucked-up little threesome is putting the kettle on?"

None of us jumped to volunteer.

I SAW JAMES OUT AFTER BREAKFAST, LINGERING IN THE DOORWAY while he checked he'd picked up his phone, his keys, his wallet... I got the slightest suspicion that he was dawdling as much as I was, unsure of what to say from here.

"Thanks for staying," I said. "I enjoyed it."

"Me too. It wasn't all that bad for a foray into domesticity."

"Maybe one day we'll do it again," I smiled.

"Stranger things have happened." He leant down to kiss me, countering the romance by twisting my nipple through my cami. "I know you want more of this." He tipped his head towards the flat, towards the slice of normality we'd had together. "But please go softly on an old man set in his ways. I propose dinner, next

Saturday. I'll pick you up before Explicit. I'll give you dinner, in exchange for a little gesture." His eyes were hooded and glazed, his cock already swollen in his jeans.

I teased him with my palm. "What do you want in exchange?"

He kissed my ear, his breath loud and hot. "I'll take you out, Cat, if you'll piss in my mouth next weekend."

I pulled away in shock, blinking up at him. "Are you serious?!"

"Deadly, and don't act so surprised. I could have asked for a lot more, and I *will*. Believe me. I'll ask you for a lot more than that."

"I'm not sure I'll be able to do it," I said. "I can't imagine it."

"Dinner in exchange for *drinks*, Cat, that's my proposition."

"You actually want to drink my pee, that's what you're saying?" I was already burning up, I could feel it.

"That's *exactly* what I'm saying," he smiled. "Will you piss for me, Lydia, yes or no? The clock's ticking."

I jittered nervously from one foot to another, stomach in knots.

"I'm sorry, Miss Marsh, but I'm going to have to push you for an answer…"

"Ok, yes," I said, before I could stop myself. "But I'm not sure I'm going to return the favour and guzzle down any of yours, I'm pretty sure that's a hard limit of mine."

He smiled, and it was the smile of the beast, dark and horny and dirty as sin. He backed away, retreating onto the street.

"We'll find out," he growled. "I think you may surprise yourself."

I hoped he wouldn't hold his breath. The idea was squicky as hell, *nearly* squicky enough to stop me jilling myself crazy over it later, but only nearly.

Even with Salmons eating healthily into our work schedule the week really dragged. It dragged in a way I'd never felt before, not once since I'd been working with James. I guessed it was the contrast, the glimpse of what could be outside of that place, with its corporate mentality and its hush-hush agreement.

Work was undeniably different, regardless of how hard we tried. We kept our business-as-normal front on it, but things had definitely changed. There was something more in his eyes than the previous sheen of professional camaraderie, something deeper and darker and much more raw. Maybe he saw it in my eyes, too, I don't know.

I kept it all firmly to myself, ignoring the temptation to spill some of the emotional beans to Steph. The option presented itself mid-week when she began calling, but I forced myself to avoid and ignore. I told myself she was probably full of more junk about Stu and let it go, having no time for that crap anymore.

Rebecca was my only accomplice, and me hers. We'd talk more than we'd ever talked before, long nights over coffee, laughing about love and life, and weird, dirty sex in public. I loved her for it. My little heart stretched its wings, the tiniest sliver of hope for the happily-ever-after, for the blossoming of romance unlike any other. Maybe white knights *did* turn up to slap your clitoris, after all? Maybe that's what true love is all about?

I hoped so.

Most of all I hoped for a chance with him, my man in the mask. A *real* chance in the *real* world.

It's often the small decisions that are the catalysts for the major events, and my life that week was no different. I just didn't see any of it coming.

Rebecca had picked out my dress, all ready for my nice, posh meal and piss-gate beyond. It was a classy red number, fitted satin with a long split at the back.

"Bingo," she'd laughed. "Multi-functional. This little gem will look cracking in the dining hall, and possibly even better when you piss in the thing."

I took her word for it.

I spent the whole day getting ready, and yet I was still late. James was picking me up at seven, nice and early, in line with the time Rebecca and Cara had scheduled their kiss-and-make-up chat. Their reconciliation was inevitable. They'd hardly been off the phone since the blow up.

I scrubbed myself in Rebecca's posh oriental body wash, taking an age to shave off every scrap of body hair I possessed, then wrapped myself in a towel in time to do my hair and make-up. Rebecca obliged, layering on lashings and lashings of mascara and eye-shadow while I blow-dried my hair in a frenzy. I was just about done when Cara rang the buzzer, merely taking a final moment to adjust my waves before getting dressed.

Bex buzzed Cara on up and stood back to admire her handiwork.

"Hot to trot, baby, you'll knock him senseless," she purred, then laughed as she flicked up my towel. "Look at the state of you, Kitty Cat, you still have fucking tigger-stripes, our James Clarke will be chomping at the bit when he sees those beauties."

I laughed along with her, turning myself in the mirror to check them out for myself. "He hit me bloody hard," I said. "It hurt like an absolute bastard."

"Lydia?! Oh my God! Lyddie?!"

My eyes flicked to the doorway, instinctive horror flooding right through me. Cara stood with her hand over her mouth, eyes screwed shut in mortification, but she was the least of my concerns. At her side was Steph, wide-eyed and wide-mouthed, her jaw flapping as she struggled for words.

"Steph? Shit! What are you doing here?"

I struggled to back away from her but she was at my side, her eyes all over my bruises. "What happened to you?!" she screeched. "Who did this to you?"

Rebecca yanked Cara by the elbow, dragging her through to the balcony. Cara mouthed 'sorry' and Bex mouthed 'stupid cow', I appreciated both sentiments.

"Calm down," I said. "It's nothing."

"It doesn't look like bloody nothing!" she thundered. "Someone's beaten the shit out of you! It's that suit man, isn't it?!"

"You don't understand!" I told her. "You wouldn't understand. I'm fine, Steph, I'm really fine."

I wrenched out of her grip, retreating to my bedroom for my dress. I felt so much safer with it on, but still she wouldn't let it go. "It's sick, Lyddie, sick! What kind of man would do this to you? What kind of man, Lyds?!"

"He didn't *do* anything to me, Steph, I wanted it."

"This is all fucked up. It's so fucked up. I knew you being here was a bad thing." She pointed at the roof terrace with flailing arms, and I saw Rebecca poke her tongue out at Steph's back. I fought the urge to laugh. "These people are WEIRDOS! They are CRAZY!"

"They aren't crazy." I rolled my eyes. "I like it here. I'm *happy* here."

"You're coming home with me right now!" she yelled. "Where these people can't hurt you again!" She tried to pull me along by my wrist, but I had none of it, twisting away.

"I'm not going anywhere, Steph. This is my *home*. These are my *friends*."

"And what about me?" she snapped. "What am I? What is Stuart?"

Stuart's name thumped me in the gut. "Stuart is my *ex*-boyfriend. A nobody. He got someone else pregnant behind my back, I couldn't give a fuck about him anymore."

"That's why I'm here!" she wailed. "That's what I've been trying to tell you, if you weren't too busy with these weirdos to listen to your fucking messages!"

I folded my arms. "What are you here to tell me?"

"It's Stu," she said. "He's not the father! Carly admitted it the other night, admitted it clean out. The baby isn't his, it was all lies. I doubt he even fucked her in that alleyway, not really. She may have sucked him off, sure, but I don't think he took it all the way, he was too drunk to remember, and she took advantage. He's not going to be a dad, Lyddie, he's not, and he's so bloody sorry, all he wants is to make it right with you. It's his second chance. He knows how bad he's messed up."

"I don't want Stuart," I seethed. "Baby or no, it makes no odds. I don't love him anymore."

She turned purple, her bottom lip jutting out in rage. "You'd rather a man that beats the crap out of you, would you? You've lost the fucking plot, lady, these people have fucked with your mind."

I looked at the clock, horrified to find just ten minutes to spare. I lost my temper, needing her out and away before my twisted-as-sin chaperone crashed her little monologue.

"I'm *happy*, Steph. Just leave me alone, will you? I don't want Stuart, I'm not coming back to yours, I don't want a cutesy little life of peaches and cream and evening quiz shows. I want to be *here*."

"You don't mean that," she screeched. "You don't know what you're saying!"

"I know exactly what I'm saying!" I yelled. "It's you who doesn't understand."

She slammed her mouth shut, eyes like cinders. "Fine, I'll leave, but this won't be the end of it, not by a fucking long shot. You're my friend, and friends don't abandon each other, friends are always there!"

I marched her to the door. "I appreciate it, Steph, honest I do. We'll clear this up another day, OK? I'll call you."

I closed the door before she could object, praying she was well clear before James arrived.

JAMES WATCHED ME ACROSS THE TABLE. HE'D PICKED WELL, ITALIAN cuisine over candlelight. His eyes looked darker than ever, sucking in all the light in the room.

"So here we are, Lydia, you and I out for dinner."

I raised my glass. "So we are."

"Talk to me, Cat's eyes. Regale me with conversation, that's what *couples* do over dinner, isn't it? They talk."

"What do you want to know?" I smiled.

"Besides from how your sweet your piss tastes?" he breathed, so low I could only just hear him.

"Besides from that, yes."

"Tell me about little Lydia Marsh. What's new, pussycat?"

I took a breath. "Well, my mum's met someone," I said. "He seems ok this time."

"Really?" he smiled. "Not another loser out for money and free rent, then?"

"Doesn't seem to be, not from the bit I've heard. He's got a job. A *good* job. A warehouse manager apparently. Divorced, two adult children, likes hiking and snooker and foreign travel."

"Ideal step-daddy material."

"Steady on," I grinned. "And get this, he's teetotal. Doesn't drink a drop."

"Well, that is good news, surely?"

"I can hope. She seems really happy. He doesn't want to move in yet or anything, happy in his own place. They met at bingo, when Auntie Syl dragged Mum out a few weeks back. He was there with a neighbour, keeping her company. It went from there."

James raised his glass, leaning forward across the table until it clinked into mine. "Well, that does sound promising. Here's to Mr Bingo, and all the happiness love can bring."

"To Mr Bingo," I smiled. "And to *us*, James, to our beautiful, screwed-up *thing*."

"I note you didn't use the word relationship."

"Would you want me to?" I asked, eyes hard on his.

"I'll let you know when I know." He winked at me, and it set my stomach into a dither. "Sensible James is ironing a few things out, give him a chance to get his bearings."

"He can take his time." I reached across the table for his hand, and he didn't pull away. "*Thing* will do just fine for the moment."

"To our *thing*, Lydia," he toasted afresh.

"To our *thing*, James."

Except it wasn't just a thing to me anymore. Not at all.

IN THE SHADOWY ALLEYWAY ACROSS FROM EXPLICIT, JAMES CLARKE transformed to Masque. He'd slicked back his hair before we'd left the restaurant, transformation phase one complete, now it was just the mask. I smiled as he fixed it on, heart fluttering at the promise of what lay ahead. Unlike usual, Masque wasn't dressed in low-slung jeans. Masque was dressed to perfection in a fitted black suit, hugging his frame in all the right places. He took my hand unprompted as we crossed the road.

"I've never arrived here with anyone. Not since Rachel."

I smiled up at him. "Well, then I'm honoured."

"Your half of the bargain now," he whispered as we made our way up to the main floor.

"You really want me to do this?" I shot him an expression full of squick, and he smiled at me.

"It will surprise you, Cat, I promise. You'll enjoy it."

The lights on stage started up as we sipped our drinks, but this time Masque didn't move us. I watched the shadows play out, a woman's scream cutting loud across the music. I leant into the man at my side, breathing in the hot musk of his neck. "One day I want you to take me up there," I said. "Like you did, Violet."

"You want me to gape your cunt in front of an audience? You really are coming along. I'm impressed."

"I want you to cane me up there," I said. "I'm not sure about the gape thing."

"Last week didn't put you off all that much, then?" He grinned. "I am glad. The cane's a favourite of mine."

"You took your mask off for me," I whispered. "I won't forget that." I slid my hand along the hard ridge of his thigh.

"I won't be making a habit of it."

"Even so, thank you."

"You're welcome, Cat." He tipped my wine glass as I was drinking, forcing me to glug it all right down.

"Trying to get me drunk?"

"Trying to fill your bladder."

He called the barman for another bottle.

The scene was still raging onstage as the urge to pee reached boiling point. I held off mentioning it at first, nerves getting the best of me, but eventually Masque called me out.

"You must need a piss now. You'll be going like a racehorse at this rate."

"Sorry, maybe I should go first? Take the edge of it?"

"No fucking way," he growled. "I've worked up quite a thirst."

"I do need to go," I admitted. "I'll have to try not to piss myself the moment I get off this stool."

He smiled and took my hand. "Perfect timing, everyone's on the main floor, which can mean only one thing."

"What's that?"

"There's an empty wet room with our name on it."

The room was empty, just like he anticipated. It was stark and plain, all white tiles and fluorescent lighting. It reminded me of a public swimming pool shower room, with a load of detachable showerheads jutting from the walls at regular intervals. One large drain sat ominous in the middle of the floor. Masque hung his jacket up on a coat hook by the entrance, un-cuffing his shirt and draping it along with it. He took my bag and placed it on a bench, and held his hand out for my shoes. I handed them over.

The room was cold, every noise echoing all about us, metallic and clinical. I caught the faint whiff of pine disinfectant. It made me feel even dirtier.

"Are you going to piss in that dress, or out of it?" Masque quizzed. "Your call."

I opted to preserve the gown, despite what Rebecca had intended, and wriggled out of it, tossing it to him for safe keeping. He groaned on sight of my bruises, and I bloomed with a confidence that was still new to me.

I watched him undress. Every movement was calculated, every breath considered. His cock rose huge, allaying any doubt that the man really wanted this. He pinned me to the tiles in a heartbeat, tongue fierce in my mouth as his fingers found my clit.

"Trust me," he breathed. "You're going to feel so good, Lydia, so fucking good. Tell me when you can't fight it anymore, I'll be ready."

The pressure built up, exasperated by the throbbing of my clit, but I kept quiet, forcing it back. He moved his head lower, sucking my tits into his mouth one by one. He slurped his way between them, wet and slick, teasing my nipples to life.

"I love your tits," he hissed. "They're so fucking ripe for me."

I rested my head back against the wall, looking down on him through glazed eyes. I yelped as he bit down hard.

"Please," I gasped. "Please, Masque, make it hurt." He clamped his teeth with added force, savaging my flesh until I whimpered.

He pulled away with a smile.

"One day soon your tits will know real pain. So much beautiful pain, so much pain all for you."

He ground his thigh between mine, pressing so hard I tried to move from under him.

"Not there," I begged. "I won't be able to hold it."

"That's the fucking point," he growled. "I want to drink from you. I want to spread your sweet little cunt and lap at your slit like you're the fountain of fucking life itself."

Nerves jangled as the need to piss threatened to consume me. I focused on the ache between my thighs, on clenching every muscle as tight as it would go.

"I don't know if I can do this. It's so dirty, Masque."

"If I can do *this*," he slipped the mask up from his face, tossing it over to the bench. "Then *you* can give me what I need. No boundaries, no barriers, no mask, just you and me. I want to know every part of you, every secret of your body. *Every* secret." His face was so close to mine, so close I could taste the scotch on his breath. "Trust me, please."

I raised my hands to his face. "You said you wouldn't do that again, take off the mask."

"I'm doing a lot of things lately that I thought I'd never do. Now it's your turn. Please, Cat, please give me a taste."

His hand was hot between my thighs again, balling my clit with his thumb. "Shit," I moaned. "I can't hold it anymore. I'm going to piss, I need to go. I can't hold it!"

"Good girl," he breathed, dropping to his knees. I didn't fight him as he spread my legs, didn't make a sound as his fingers spread me open. "There it is, all ready for me. I wish you could see how beautiful your sweet little piss-slit is." He wriggled his tongue against me, digging at a hole way too small to penetrate.

"Please, James, I can't hold it," I gasped, screwing my eyes shut.

"Look at me." His tone was hard, insistent. I looked down. "I want this."

My body made my decision for me, caving under the pressure. The first rush of fluid spilled out without warning, and his mouth was on me, a primitive grunt sounding loud from the back of his throat.

"More," he groaned. "Give me more."

I moaned as the surge erupted, relief humming right through

me, and once I started I couldn't stop, not even if I'd tried. He kept his eyes on mine as he drank from me, swallowing some down, and spitting the rest back up to dribble down his chin. It felt so fucking wrong. It felt so dirty, and humiliating, and bad, and seedy, but so fucking amazing. It felt like bliss, the ultimate release, the most beautifully fucking filthy thing I'd ever done in my life.

"Oh my God," I wheezed. "Oh my fucking God." My legs trembled, knees buckling, but he held me in a vice, sliding three fingers inside me mid flow. He pumped me as I gushed for him, and it felt so right. It felt so fucking right.

He didn't stop, not even when I was spent and euphoric, pressed against the tiles like my life depended on it. He sucked on my clit, moaning and grunting and hissing out words of endearment that made no fucking sense. White heat exploded behind my eyes, the grip of orgasm ripping right through me. I bucked against him, screaming his name, *both* his names, and he didn't seem to care, burying his face in my pussy like I was salvation personified. I came down slowly, and let myself drop into his arms. His mouth tasted bitter, but I was past caring, lost in everything he had to give.

"My turn," he moaned. "Do you want me?"

I didn't register even the slightest shock, immune to any deviant thrill his mind could conceive. "In my mouth?" I asked. "Is that what you want?"

"Not today," he smiled. He got to his feet pulling me with him. "Spread your legs wide for me, that's my girl, show me your beautiful clit."

"Ok," I breathed, pulling myself open. "Whatever you want, do it. Fucking do it!"

"Watch how fucking wonderful this is."

He worked his cock in his hand, hard and ripe and so fucking big. I shuddered as he began to go, a short, sharp burst at first, before he picked up a steady flow. He aimed his dirty yellow jet straight for my clit, and I moaned like a whore as he hit the spot.

"Yes," he hissed. "Dirty girl, getting off on my filthy fucking piss."

"It feels so fucking wrong," I groaned. "So wrong." I reached for his cock, mashing him tight against me, until his hot golden river splashed all the way down my thighs. "Don't stop," I whimpered. "Please don't fucking stop."

"That's my girl," he breathed. "That's my beautiful dirty girl." He groaned as he finished, squeezing the base of his cock tight. "Get on your knees and taste me."

I dropped down onto the wet floor, heart racing, and there, soaking wet and kneeling in his filth, I let my walls come down. I opened my mouth, gagging for just a moment as he slipped his filthy wet meat between my lips.

"Fuck," he hissed. "That's right, that's fucking right. Suck me clean, Lydia. I want to come in your tight little cunt, all the way inside you."

I moaned around his cock, delirious and lost, right the way until he pulled himself out of me. He flicked on a shower without warning, and I squealed as a cold jet of spray soaked us both. He pulled me to my feet, angling my face into the jet until I was spluttering cold water, then raised me further still until my legs wrapped tight around his waist and his cock buried all the way inside me. I gripped onto his shoulders, dragging myself up and down his chest, and the friction of his skin against mine felt so fucking good.

I rode him hard until he tumbled over the edge, bucking, and groaning and jerking his hips up against me. I wrapped my arms tight around his neck, peppering his face with kisses, and all the while he cried my name. It was the sweetest sound in the world.

When he was all done he lowered us to the floor, pulling me to rest on top of him in a mess of endorphins and tangled limbs. The water turned itself off, gurgling to nothing, and I lay spent and helpless in his arms.

"James," I breathed. "I've never felt like this before."

He kissed my forehead. "I know."

"I mean it," I whispered. "I've never felt like this."

He tilted my face up to his, eyes warm. "If we say it, that's it, a whole new ballgame. You can't undo the words, they change everything. Is that what you want?"

I silenced myself with his tongue until the urge subsided.

CHAPTER 16
James

THINGS ESCALATED REALLY FUCKING QUICKLY. I FELT EDGY AT WORK, disjointed. Haunted by the memory of all that had been before. I tried to push it aside, remind myself that Lydia Marsh was nothing like Rachel, nothing at all. Her life wasn't consumed by the quest for attention, the temporary fix at the hands of strange men. Lydia was a different animal. A *nicer* animal. One I could rely on for discretion, who wouldn't sell me out down the river of sensationalism, or so I hoped. I figured she was worth the risk, she had to be worth the risk.

My nerves were appeased as she presented me with the latest Salmons update, her tone curt and professional, as always. Her eyes lingered on mine for just a moment, then calmly returned to the realm of professional colleagues. She handed me a printout of development updates with just a fleeting smile. It was me who broke protocol, reaching out to clamp her wrist in my hand, and gliding my thumb across her knuckles. She stared in shock, tense and uncertain, as though I'd gone completely barking mad.

I slumped in my chair as she took a seat opposite.

"Are you ok?" she said. "Do you need a coffee?"

"No, thank you," I smiled. "I don't need a coffee."

A flicker of a grin ghosted across her lips. "Anything else I can get you?"

"A personality transplant," I sighed. "Jesus, Lydia, there's so much I want to give you, but here, in this place it seems so untenable. I can't break out of the compartments I've placed in my own life. What does that make me?"

"Human..." she whispered. "Scared..."

"Weak," I said. "It makes me weak, and it makes this *thing* we have seem all the more intangible."

"We shouldn't talk about this," she sighed. "You're breaking your own rules. This isn't from me, it's all from you. You're the one who's putting such weight on this whole work-home divide, not me."

"Sorry," I said. "Monday blues."

"I've got a case of Monday purples myself." She grinned.

We were interrupted by a knock at the door. Frank blustered his way in, fishing for status updates. Lydia handed him the Salmons file, smiling as he thumbed his way through it. "Good stuff," he announced. "This is looking fine, very fine indeed."

"Lydia and I are heading up the accounts briefing at head office in a few weeks' time, phase one should be well in progress by then."

Frank smiled his golfing-all-weekend smile. "You're getting quite a taste for these out-of-office jollies, James." He nudged Lydia. "You couldn't get him away for love nor money at one point, didn't like the break in his routine."

"A bit of chaos never hurt anyone," she laughed.

"That's what I said, isn't it, James? Variety is as good as a rest, that's true alright."

I held my hands up. "Fine, I get it, tag-teamed on a Monday

morning. I'm not even on my second coffee yet. Give it a rest, will you?"

"Tetchy," Frank groaned. "So very tetchy. You must be a saint to put up with this all the time, Lydia." He winked and I rolled my eyes, turning my attention back to my monitor.

My extension rang, Hazel from reception. I took the call gratefully.

"Mr Clarke, is Lydia Marsh with you?"

"She is, why?" I heard shouting in the distance, Hazel's muted voice as she clamped her hand over the mouthpiece, snapping at someone. "Hazel?"

Lydia took a step closer, eyes curious. Frank hovered too, gawping at the both of us. Finally Hazel came back on the line.

"There's someone here to see her," she said. "He says it's important."

"Who says it's important?" I asked, more demanding than warranted.

"He says his name is Stuart Dobson. Says he's her boyfriend. He's pretty wound up, Mr Clarke, demanding to be let through. I think I should maybe call security," she whispered.

"I'll be right down," I said. "Don't let him up here, Hazel."

I hung up, and Lydia stared at me with big, demanding eyes. "What's going on?"

"You have a visitor in reception," I announced, keeping my tone as deadpan as possible. "Hazel said he's agitated, believes she should call security."

"Well who the flipping hell is it?" Frank pondered.

"Stuart," Lydia said, biting her lip. "It's Stuart, isn't it?"

"That's what Hazel said, yes." My eyes crashed into hers, wondering what the fuck was going on. "I said I'd go down, I don't want you down there if he's like that, Lydia."

She jumped about a foot in the air, ditching her paperwork all over my pen arrangement. "No," she said. "It's fine. I'll go, honestly. I can handle him."

"He's agitated," I snapped. "Enough that Hazel wants to call security. You don't need to go down there, I can handle it."

"No!" she hissed. Frank raised his eyebrows at me, and I blanked him completely.

"You can't go down there, Lydia, you don't know what's wrong with him."

"That's just the thing," she said, eyes full of panic. "I think I do." She was on her heels in a heartbeat, slipping out through the door. I made to follow but she raised her hand, her gesture tense. "I mean it. don't follow me."

I sat down, heart thumping in my chest. It was Frank who made the call for me.

"Well, I dunno about you, James, but I think we should get on down there, find out what the hell's going on."

I didn't need prompting twice.

A crowd was already gathering by the time we arrived on the scene. The girls from admin were pretending to use the franking machine, keeping beady eyes on the action. Hazel was rooted firmly behind her desk, staring openly at the argument in front of her.

"Not here, Stuart!" Lydia spat. "We can take this outside or you can piss off home, this is my *work*. You have no right to be here!"

Frank hung back, letting me tackle the fall-out. "Are you ok, Lydia?" I asked. "What's going on?"

She paled on sight of me, eyes wide and skittish. "It's fine," she hissed. "I'm handling it."

I took in the figure that was Stuart Dobson. He was toned, but a little lanky, with a trendy-rockerish mop of sandy blonde hair that was far too young for his age. He was angry too, really fucking angry. I felt my hackles rise.

"Stuart, right?" I said. "I'm James Clarke, Chief Technology Officer, we were in the middle of a meeting, so if you wouldn't mind…"

"You're James Clarke?" he said, and there was rage in his eyes, real fucking rage.

"Leave, James," Lydia said. "Please, I've got this."

Stuart turned towards her, eyes wild. "That's *him* is it? That's the fucking sicko that beat the shit out of you?"

"Fuck off, Stuart!" she screeched. "You have no idea what the hell you're talking about! Get out!" She lunged for him, but he was stronger, twisting her arm behind her back and knocking her off balance. She toppled into him, and he held her tight, yanking up the hem of her skirt before she could even try and fight him. I heard the intake of breath from the room, watched the letters fall from Zena's hand at the franking machine. Lydia's thighs were streaked purple, even through her flesh-tone tights. Stuart Dobson was pissed, his nostrils flaring with rage. He spun around the room, until his eyes landed back on mine.

"It was this sonofabitch!" he yelled. "This sick fucking sonofabitch hurt her. He beat the fucking shit out of her! Tell them, Lydia, fucking tell them what he did to you."

She elbowed him hard in the ribs, gasping for breath as he let her go. Her eyes were as wild as his, but wild with fear. "Leave me alone, Stuart!" she screamed. "FUCK OFF!"

"I won't fucking fuck off!" he boomed. "I'm not leaving you

with that fucking monster! You can't fucking love him, not after that!" He reached out for her again, snaring her arm and dragging her towards him.

I broke my stance, pacing out towards him. "Let her go," I seethed. "She doesn't want to go with you."

"Fuck you!" he thundered. "How fucking dare you, you piece of shit? You're not in Brighton now, you sick motherfucker. You can't hole her up in some hotel room for your sick little fantasies this time. I won't have it!"

"Let her go, Stuart." The beast flared in my veins, screaming for release. "Let Lydia go right now, or so help me God, you'll wish you had."

I breathed in relief as he dropped her arm. She scuttled over, eyes wide with horror and shame.

Stuart weighed me up for size. "You want a piece of me, hey? Want to pick on someone your own size, you sadistic piece of shit?"

"Get out," I hissed. "Clear the fuck out of here."

"Make me," he fronted. "Come on, hard man, fucking make me!"

Lydia's fingers were on my arm. I brushed her away on instinct. "Please, James," she said. "Leave it, he's not worth it."

"COME ON!" Stuart goaded. "You think you're fucking hard, do you? Lydia doesn't even know how to fight back!"

"Shut up!" she screeched. "Let's go, James!"

I shook my head. "You need to leave, Stuart, right fucking now."

"Make me."

"Call security," Frank yelled to Hazel. "Get them up here before this gets out of hand."

"It's already out of hand," Stuart growled. "I'm gonna rip his fucking spleen out."

"STUART!" Lydia tried again. "Please, will you just FUCK OFF!"

I saw his attack from a clear mile away, ducking from his path in a flash and sending him careening on past me. I caught him with his back to me, wrenched his arm up unguarded. I breathed into his ear, gripping him tight. "Move and I'll break your fucking wrist," I hissed. "You need to get out of here, before this gets fucking serious."

I shunted him through reception, while he lashed out with his feet, trying to topple me off balance. Grunting out a stream of abuse and struggling in my grip, I delivered him into the hands of oncoming security and they took him down from there. I heard him screaming all the way, screaming to anyone who'd listen that James Clarke is a fucking wife-beating monster, a sick fuck who likes to beat women, a sick fuck that beat *his* beautiful Lydia black and blue.

Lydia looked at me through broken eyes, swimming in horror and disbelief. I surveyed the scene, heart ricocheting in my ribcage as history repeated itself. Nobody would look at me, not even Frank. Not one single person would meet my eyes as the thrum of gossip danced around the crowd. I was done here.

I stalked through them with angry paces, ignoring the pleads from Lydia at my back. Ignoring everything but the soft promise of sanctuary calling from my office upstairs. She caught up with me at the top of the stairs, pulling me round to face her.

"Please, James, don't hate me!" she said. "Please don't hate me! I didn't know this would happen, I swear I didn't know! He's just an idiot, a stupid fucking idiot."

"It's not your fault," I said. "It's mine. I walked straight into it, just like I did last time. Please, Lydia, leave me alone."

I slammed the door behind me.

I FINALLY LET HER IN AFTER LUNCH, STARING BLANKLY AHEAD WHILE she wrung her hands in front of me.

"Don't do this, please," she wheezed. "Don't block me out. We can get through this, ok? I've told them he's an idiot, that he's crazy, that he's a drugged-up fucking asshole. They don't believe him, I swear! They don't believe him!"

"They saw the bruises, Lydia, they'll believe him. Frank hasn't been up here yet." I met her eyes, flinching at the animal panic I found there. "You forget, I've been here before. I know the lousy fucking drill."

She shook her head. "No fucking way, not this time. Everyone likes you, James, nobody would ever believe him! Last time was different, I'm not Rachel. I don't crave the drama. It will blow over, I swear, I'll make it blow over."

I scoffed in her face. "How can you make *this* blow over? I'll have to quit again and move on again, far fucking away from here. My life here is done."

Her lip trembled, it smacked me right in the gut. "No, James, I'll go. You don't need to go!"

"Don't be ridiculous. It's not you they'll brand the psycho. It's me."

"You aren't a psycho, and no one here will believe it. They *know* you, they know *us*."

"I never made friends with them, Cat, not one of them," I admitted. "They don't *know* me. I thought that kept me safe, but it seems not. I've been such a fucking idiot, walking straight into the same fucking mistake."

"Some mistakes are worth making," she breathed. "You know they are. *We* were worth making, James."

"It's easy to say that now, you aren't the one who has to walk away."

"You don't *have* to walk away," she insisted. "It's not that bad! This time it *will* blow over, we'll be ok. Give us a chance, please, just one little chance?"

"What's the point?" I seethed. "We'd never have worked, Lydia, never. This is what happens when I get close to people."

"That's not true!" she said. "I lived my whole life trapped behind a wall, not daring to let anyone in. All I wanted was to be the strong one, the indestructible one, the one that was so in-control nobody could ever fuck my shit up again, but these last few months I learnt something. I learnt something from *you*. I learnt it's ok to let go, it's ok to be weak, it's ok to cry... I've learnt it's ok to fucking trust someone, James! That there's something out there worth taking the risk for!"

My eyes flared with rage. "I *was* learning to trust someone. I *was* learning to love again, but it was a stupid fucking dream. *This* is the reality, right here, right now. *This* is what *love* leads to."

"So, what now?" she wheezed. "We're over, just like that?"

My heart thumped so fucking hard, begged me to run to her, begged me to fight for her, but I turned away.

"Just like that," I said. "Stuart's outburst was for the best. It's shone the light of clarity in a way I've been blind to for months. This whole thing is for the best."

"You don't mean that!"

"I wish I didn't," I sighed.

"Say you won't leave, please!" There were tears in her eyes as she spoke, and my heart lurched. "Please don't quit over this."

"It will take me a while to find another job," I said. "It won't be imminent, but I will be leaving, Lydia, I'm sorry."

She didn't stay to argue, and I hated myself from the moment she left.

Frank finally surfaced mid-afternoon. He knocked with a hearty flourish, swinging his way through the door with a shake of his head. I braced myself for it, for the tirade of abuse, but it didn't arrive.

"Bloody hell, James, what the fucking hell was that craziness about this morning, hey? That bloke was a tee short of a putt, I tell you. Lydia should count her lucky stars she got away from that one."

"He seemed a bit on-one," I said warily.

"On-one?! He was bloody cuckoo! Poor Lydia, did you see those marks on her legs? I wouldn't be surprised if they were from him, you know. We'll have to keep an eye on her from now on, make sure she doesn't go running back there. I'd hate it if anything happened to her." He scratched his neck. "I'm surprised you didn't punch him one, all that shit he was spouting about you. By God, man, what an absolute loony-tune, you should've landed one right in the jaw." He smiled, sitting himself down opposite. "I have to admit, I wondered it myself, if there's anything going on between you and our Lydia. If there is then don't be put off by some psycho-ex, it'll blow over, you wait and see."

"There's nothing going on between me and Lydia," I said numbly.

He sighed. "Oh well, I thought we might have the first Trial Run wedding. Never mind, eh?" He grinned, leaning towards me. "You'll have to go grab a coffee at some point, the whole admin team are gaggling themselves crazy. They think you're some kind of superhero now, rushing to the aid of the lovely Lydia. You got him in that arm lock real bloody quick-smart, it was quite a move."

"They're saying what?" I quizzed, mouth dry.

"They're all gaggly over you, my lad, think you're the hero of the bloody year. You'll never hear the end of it, I tell you. It'll go down in history as the day our James wrestled a psycho-intruder through reception," he chuckled.

I could barely swallow. "Where's Lydia?" I asked. "Is she ok?"

He sighed loud and long. "Ah, poor Lydia. I don't think she coped so well. She's gone home sick. Can't say I blame her either, it was quite a shock to her system. God only knows how bad it could have been if you hadn't been there. Lord knows what the crazy fool would have done to her. I put her in a taxi, don't worry, she'll have got home safe." He raised himself from his seat. "You could give her a call, check she's ok. She didn't look so good, shock I guess."

I was dialling her mobile before the door clicked shut behind him, but it was no good. My call went straight to voicemail.

CHAPTER 17

James

I paced my living room and listened to her voicemail click in for the hundredth time. "Lydia, call me, please."

She wouldn't, of course, she hadn't returned a single call all day. I fisted my hands in my hair, and finally plucked up the courage to call Rebecca. She picked up on the third ring.

"Is she ok?" I asked. "Please tell me she's ok."

"Fucking hell, James," she hissed. "What the fuck? No, she's not fucking ok! Just stay away, will you? She doesn't need you right now."

"Fine," I said. "I know she's hurt. I know that."

"You don't fucking know! You don't know anything! That girl loves you, James, she opened her poor, bruised little soul right up on a plate, and you shit on her. You shit all over her, and now she thinks it's all her fault!"

"It was Stuart," I said. "He showed up here, shouting his mouth off. He must have found out from somewhere. I freaked, Bex, do you know how big a deal this shit is to me? Do you?"

"A bigger deal to you than Lydia is, clearly," she snapped. "And that's the fucking saddest thing of all. Just leave her alone now, please. You've fucking broken her."

"I told her about Rachel, Rebecca, I told her everything that happened, and still this shit landed on my doorstep."

She laughed, but it was full of bitterness. "You think that was Lydia's fault? Do you? If you want to blame anyone you'll have to blame Cara. It was her who let that stupid bitch Steph up with no warning. *That's* how this happened, James, one stupid mistake. No trail of stupidity, or attention seeking, or game playing, just one stupid case of bad timing. Cara's sorry, if you want to know. She hasn't stopped crying. Blames herself for this whole sorry mess."

"Take care of Lydia, Bex, please. Tell her I'm sorry."

But Bex was already gone.

I PRAYED EVERY DAY THAT LYDIA WOULD BE AT MY DESK IN THE morning, a fresh cup of coffee in hand, but she never was. She called in sick before nine without fail, I saw the emails. Generic *she's unwell* shit. It ate at me through every minute, but still I couldn't break through my own fucking barriers.

What is love, anyway? What does it mean? Did I love Lydia Marsh? Was that even enough?

I drove myself insane, throwing every waking hour into the Salmons project and barely sleeping, pleading that one day soon the ache for Lydia would pass.

But it didn't. It got fucking worse.

So many times I wanted to turn up at hers, armed with a taxi full of roses and promises of happy ever after, but I couldn't promise that, couldn't promise something I was uncertain I'd be able to deliver. I'd baulked at telling Frank about us, even though he suspected already, baulked at the very first fucking hurdle. How the fuck would I ever give her the relationship she deserved? I couldn't even admit the truth of it to myself, let alone anyone else.

I wasn't expecting a knock on the door at ten am on Friday morning, and I definitely wasn't expecting it to be Emily Barron, the scatty blonde girl from Lydia's team. She took a seat across from me without invite, beaming like a big smiley dullard. I raised my eyebrows in question, not really giving a shit what she wanted.

"I'm here about Salmons," she said. "I need briefing, since I'm taking over the project management."

"Sorry? You're doing what?"

"I'm taking it over," she repeated. "Now that Lydia's gone."

My blood turned to ice. "What the hell do you mean, Lydia's gone?"

She looked at me like I was retarded, like I was the only person on the planet not in the loop.

"She's in the main meeting room with Frank," she said. "Handing in her notice. Wants to get away from an ex or something, you know the one you kapowed in reception? Seems you giving him the shoe wasn't enough, she's off. Brighton apparently, got a job with White Hastings McCarthy."

I felt the colour drain from me. "She's doing what?"

"Poached by Trevor White I think, rumour has it there's something going on there. I hope so, Lydia's a nice girl."

"Where is she now?" I hissed.

She rolled her eyes. "I told you already, she's down with Frank, signing off her leaving arrangements. She's not coming back, not even for a single day, how shit is that?"

"Excuse me, Emily." I stormed from my desk, uncaring of the way she was flapping her mouth for my attention.

"But what about me?" she said. "What about Salmons?"

I pointed to the file on my desk. "Knock yourself out. I couldn't give two fucking shits about Salmons."

My heart jumped into my throat as I caught sight of Lydia through the meeting room door. She looked pasty, sick, worse than she had done those months ago in the kitchen. All over again I watched her dither, a tiny sparrow on a branch, clawing for grip. I hovered awhile, until finally her eyes met mine through the glass panel. She looked away instantly, straight down at the paperwork in front of her. Frank carried on oblivious, chortling on about some bullshit or other, I'm sure.

I opened the door without knocking, and Frank jolted in his seat. "James!" he said. "Come to say goodbye? It's so bloody sad, isn't it? We're all so sorry to see you go, Lydia."

"I need to speak with Lydia a minute, please Frank, outside."

He looked from me to her, then turned his attention to his paperwork. "I've got some forms to fill in," he said "Carry on."

"Please, Lydia," I said. "Just a minute."

She shrugged, sliding from her seat like a ghost, trailing me to the doorway. I shut the door behind us, all so aware of the bustle all around. We were right in the heart of the admin gossip hive, right amongst the thrum of twitchy ears and twitchy mouths.

"Can we go upstairs?" I asked. "It's much more private."

She shook her head. "I don't have long. I've got to sort my things."

"You're really going to Brighton? To Trevor?"

"It was that or Warwick," she said. "And Mum's doing fine without me, she's happy with Mr Bingo."

I cast my eyes about, checking for eavesdroppers. "I'm so fucking sorry, I never meant to hurt you."

Her eyes pooled instantly, but this time she made no move to choke it back, none at all. "It's ok," she said. "It was casual, we both knew that."

"It wasn't casual," I whispered. "None of this was casual."

"It's funny," she said, with a sad smile. "I spent my whole life trying to be strong, trying not to cry, but I was wrong. Breaking isn't weak, James, it's strong. Being able to wear your heart on your sleeve and let other people see your pain, that's strong. I was hurt after Stuart, really hurt, but it never hurt like you did. Losing you was a million times worse than Stuart ever was, and that's ok, because it set me free." She smiled as she wiped tears from her eyes. "You know, I got so sad I even rang my mum. I rang her and I told her everything, because nothing could feel worse than I felt anyway, nothing she could say would be that bad."

My eyes were heavy, they burnt under the weight of her gaze. "What did she say?"

"She said a lot," Lydia smiled. "More than I expected, and it helped. You know what I figured? I spent so much of my life being strong for other people, that I had no idea how to let them be strong for me. I never gave Mum a chance to be there, I never ever let her in." She put a hand on my arm. "Thank you," she said. "Thank you for breaking me."

My hands were clammy, shaking. I could hardly swallow for the pain in my throat.

"Don't do this. Please don't go. You were right and I was wrong, we can get over this, it was nothing, a storm in a teacup. The world didn't end here, Cat, not with Stuart storming in, it ended when you walked out. Please don't leave."

"And then what? We go back to being Lydia and James, professional co-workers?"

"No... yes..." I said. "I don't know."

She smiled a smile so tender it took my breath. "It's not enough. I need someone who'll put themselves on the line for me, like I put myself on the line for you. I want someone who can love me, who can be with me for who I am. I never wanted that before, but I do now. If I'm here with you I'll never find that person, there will only ever be you."

"And what if I *am* that person?" I breathed. "What if I *can* be that man?"

"But you can't, you said it yourself. Your life is too compartmentalised, too rigid. There's no place for chaos. There's no place for *me*. I've got to go, Frank's waiting."

I fisted my hands in my hair. Palpitations ratting through my chest. I was sweaty, hot, exposed, thoroughly out of my comfort zone and hating every second of it. People were gathering at the sidelines, keeping a nosey eye on our exchange. I found I no longer gave a shit about any of it, about my stupid job, or this stupid place, or Salmons, or stupid fucking Trevor White. I no longer cared what any of them thought of me, because none of them mattered.

Only one person mattered.

Lydia.

I pulled her towards me, and she wheezed at the contact. "Let me go," she breathed. "Please don't make this any harder than it already is."

"I can be that man," I said. "Let me be that man."

Her lip trembled, eyes welling up again. "Don't," she said. "Please, James, don't break me like this."

"I'm not breaking you," I whispered. "I'm breaking me." I

searched her eyes with mine, begging for absolution. "Do you love me, Lydia?"

The tears I craved spilled freely from her. "More than you could know," she said. "More than *I* could've known."

"Then be with me, Cat, please, I can be that man."

"Stop it," she hissed. "Please, I can't take it!"

"I mean it," I said. "I want to be that man. I *am* that man."

"And you'll stand at my side in front of the whole world, will you? Declaring it to everyone who'll listen?"

I wrung my hands together, knuckles white, trying to jam my thoughts into some kind of order as she stared up at me.

"Thought not," she said. "Goodbye, James."

"Fucking hell, Lydia Marsh," I seethed. "I can't believe you're fucking doing this to me. I'm going to slap your ass so fucking hard for this little stunt." I yanked her elbow, pulling her into my arms as the whole of the fucking admin team looked on. For all their gasps and open mouths, not one of them looked so shocked as Lydia herself. She bit her lip, just like she always does, and this time I really did suck it into my mouth. I kissed her like my life depended on it, and after a moment's hesitation she kissed me right back.

I broke away to find Lydia's eyes like saucers, staring up at me as if she'd seen a ghost. Frank stood up from his chair, gawping through the window at us, and I found that I was smiling. I was smiling my fucking head off.

I paced through to the meeting room.

"Is this Lydia's letter of resignation?" I asked, stealing the paperwork from under Frank's nose.

"Um, yeah, James, it sure is."

"Not anymore." I tore the thing into tiny pieces, dumping it straight in the wastepaper basket.

On my way back to my office. I made sure my voice was loud and clear, carrying the full length of the room.

"*Yes*, I'm in love with Lydia Marsh, *yes*, it's the real fucking deal, *yes*, we have a wonderful fucking sex life, thank you very much, and *no*, she isn't going to Brighton. Any more questions?"

Nobody made a sound, including Frank who'd appeared in the meeting room doorway.

"Good," I said. "Carry on." I turned back as I reached the stairs, my eyes firmly on Lydia. "Coffee please," I yelled. "If you're making one. We've got a whole fucking week's worth of work to catch up on, best get a move on."

She didn't disappoint me.

CHAPTER 18
Lydia

I packed up the last of my things. They barely filled more than my original suitcase, nothing like packing light.

"I hate this," Bex said. "I'll miss your perky ass in the morning so fucking much."

"You'll have a new perky ass to keep you amused soon, Rebecca," I said. "When's she arriving?"

"Next week," she smiled. "I guess we might be the real deal too."

"You've done well. Cara's a lovely girl."

"She is, but I'll still miss my Cat's eyes."

"I won't be a stranger," I smiled. "You know it."

"Better not be, or I'll kick both your asses, you can't escape me now, either of you. We're friends for keeps."

I hugged her tight, no longer afraid of the lump in my throat. "Friends for keeps. Forever, Bex, I mean it. You've done so much for me."

She wiped her eyes, and I smiled to myself. I never thought I'd see her cry.

"Shit, I forgot," she said. "Your leaving present!"

"You got me a present?" I gushed. "So sweet, but honestly, I think James has everything already, you shouldn't have."

"He hasn't got one of these," she smiled. "Well, not for the wall anyway."

She handed me my gift, and I didn't even need to unwrap it. My eyes focused beyond her, to the blank space on the wall. I ripped open the wrapping to confirm my suspicion. "I can't take this," I gasped. "I really can't, it's yours."

"No," she smiled, lifting up the chimera until it sparkled in the light. "This thing is undoubtedly, undeniably, categorically yours, and it has been since the moment you clapped eyes on him."

I took it off her and wiped away a tear. "I guess it is," I laughed. "I guess it really is."

"First night back," Masque said, leading me across to the bar like a peacock. "Nervous?"

"Not anymore," I smiled. "Not now I know how to cry."

"And you really want to do this, here, tonight?"

I nodded with a grin. "Show me how it feels to be Violet, James, it's what I always wanted. My final initiation."

"I wouldn't go that far," he laughed. "But it's a good start."

The chains above rattle as I jerk in my bonds. My legs quiver, knees trembling. Adrenaline pumping.

He circles me. I feel his footfalls. Heavy, purposeful. I can smell him, too. He smells of sex, and sweat, and musk. He smells of sin.

He smells so *dirty bad wrong.*

The tap, tap, tap of the cane against my thighs, so gently. I take a breath. The cane comes to rest against my skin, and he's at my side, his mouth at my ear.

"Steady, Lydia," he breathes.

He trails his free hand up my ribs, and my body flinches. Fight or flight.

In my chains I can do neither. And I don't want to.

The heat between my legs gives testament to one simple truth.

I want *him*... the release he delivers through pain... the silky caress of the abyss beyond fear.

I want him to to break me.

I want him to hurt me.

I want him to own me.

And then I want him to love me.

"Tell me what you need, Lydia."

His savage hand on my breast. Gripping, twisting, hurting. My nipples come alive, begging for punishment, and I roll into his touch. It feels so fucking good.

I hear my own ragged breathing, the string of incoherent murmurs coming from my mouth.

He kicks my feet further apart, spreading me wide. I struggle to keep my balance, but my cuffs pull tight against the chains, taking my weight. Another tap of the cane, harder this time, and then his fingers, teasing me open, grazing my clit. *Fuck.*

Two fingers hook inside me, pressing in deep. I hear how wet I sound. He groans his approval.

My words catch in my throat, but I force them out.

"Pain... I need pain..."

He kisses my neck, and I'm lost in him, swimming in his darkness. It's all I want.

"I'm going to hurt you now, Lydia Marsh. I'm going to mark you, and break you, and own you... and then I'm going to make you cum so hard you'll scream my name. I need to see you cry, Lydia. You're so fucking beautiful when you cry."

I screw my eyes shut tight under the blindfold and take a deep breath.

I'm ready.

I'm crying before he's even hit me, tears spilling from my eyes faster than I can blink them away. Release and pain and beautiful, beautiful love.

He kisses my lips, a gentle touch, followed by little kisses up my cheek as he takes away my tears. 'I love you,' he whispers and his lips touch to mine.

THE END

ACKNOWLEDGMENTS

Massive thanks to my fantastic editor, John Hudspith, and a massive tip-of-the-hat to his soon to be released masterpiece, *Thimblerigger*. I was lucky enough to beta read this bad boy, and its beautifully dark imagery has clearly impressed itself well and truly on my subconscious. There are so many references (borrows / thefts) to *Thimblerigger's* dark, dark visuals that I'm sure I owe a debt of more than a few large beverages. Check it out, for sure, it's one crazily awesome ride.

Thanks so much to Letitia Hasser of RBA Designs for her incredible cover. I love it so much.

As for my awesome PAs, Shweta Choudhary and Tracy Smith Comerford – you ladies are incredible, thank you.
So many blogs and authors have been supportive of this novel, thank you all so, so much. It's massively appreciated! A super-duper shout out to Shani Struthers and Jo Raven, who have become such fantastic friends to me, and a mega support. You ladies make me smile so much, thank you <3
Last, but certainly not least, thank you to all the Dirty Bad Wrong real-lifers I've had the pleasure of knowing. It's been one fun ride

ABOUT THE AUTHOR

Jade is a real life submissive, and former sex chat-line operator, who is plenty used to getting people all steamed up with her dirty mouth. She has a healthy interest in pornography, men in suits and taking 100 strokes with a cane 'Mood Pictures' style.

You can find her at:

www.facebook.com/jadewestauthor

Twitter: @jadewestauthor

Email: jadewestauthor@gmail.com

Printed in Great Britain
by Amazon